THE GOLDFISH MURDERS

THE GOLDFISH MURDERS

WILL MITCHELL

COACHWHIP PUBLICATIONS

Greenville, Ohio

The Goldfish Murders, by Will Mitchell
© 2018 Coachwhip Publications

Published 1950.
No claims made on public domain material.
Cover: Goldfish © MirasWonderland

CoachwhipBooks.com

ISBN 1-61646-445-3
ISBN-13 978-1-61646-445-5

CHAPTER ONE

My Pop used to say that a good detective remembers to keep the Sabbath day holy—wholly occupied in using his eyes and ears. And Pop knew what he was talking about. Take me, for example: Christopher Lash, detective-lieutenant on Manhattan's West Side Homicide Squad. Come Sunday, my day off, there's nothing I like better than to go to a movie, where for three hours or so I can rest my eyes on some beautiful dolls. Sometimes, if there aren't too many bags of popcorn in the audience, I even hear some good dialogue.

At any rate, I was all eyes and ears that eventful Sunday of December sixth when I entered the Allison Theatre at four-thirty and parked myself in the balcony. But it wasn't until two feature pictures, an animated cartoon, and a newsreel later that I staggered out of the lobby and into the meshes of the Chadwick murder squeal.

Remember it? The sensational Chadwick affair—the "Hippogriff Homicides," the "Goldfish Murders" that forced New Yorkers to do their Christmas shopping early. Nobody wanted to be out after dark.

Maybe you've forgotten some of the names, some of the lurid details, but it's a cinch you haven't forgotten the goldfish. Remember the gorgeous blonde corpse with the goldfish between her knockers? I thought so. Well, I'm the guy who broke that squeal, the guy who wrapped it up, packed it away in the "Cases Solved" archives. In fact, the following is a blow-by-blow account of how I did, it. The story of a man blowing his own horn, you might say. . . .

Reaching the sidewalk, I stood for a minute under the Allison's marquee and drank deep of the bitter cold air. A driving rain had been pelting the city at the time I'd bought my admission ticket, but now the streets were as dry as a New York watershed. What's more, the cloudless sky overhead was so pretty that I half expected to see a calendar under it.

Suddenly a taxi pulled up to the curb, and a short, gnarled, middle-aged man reeled out of the driver's seat and onto the sidewalk. He began pawing at the air as though he were trying to catch a handful of gnats.

I knew I'd learn nothing gaping at him. Moreover, by the time my feet got the full-steam-ahead signal, a good-sized crowd had closed in on the cabbie to watch his goofy antics. So closely packed was his audience that I had all I could do to clear a passage for myself, and clearing passages is usually duck soup for me, what with my Village Blacksmith arms and Longfellow legs.

"What goes?" I demanded as I shoved the last of the gawkers aside and caught the main attraction by the scruff of the neck. "Yeah, mister, I mean you."

"A cop! I wanna cop!" he cried in a high-pitched incoherent voice. "Y'hear me? I wanna cop."

It took only a few seconds to flash my shield. The instant he saw it I thought he was going to make with a medal and kiss me on both cheeks.

"Jeez, a lieutenant!" he croaked incredulously, as though he'd pushed down the flag on his meter and won himself a jack pot. "Jeez, a real honest-to-God lieutenant!"

With a grunt of impatience I braced him against the side of the cab. Holding onto his arms—they felt as stiff as a suit of woolen underwear on a wash line in Labrador— I demanded a few whys and wherefores.

"Y'believe in miracles, Lieutenant?" he asked. "Ever see somethin' change into somethin' else, right in front of your eyes?"

I leaned closer. No, there weren't any alcoholic fumes emanating from his mouth, though I did catch something his best friends should have told him about.

"Look, it's like this," he went on. "Tonight, after the rain stops, I pulls up for chow at a little joint on 112th Street and Eighth Avenue. Fifteen minutes later when I steps out, I climbs into my cab, and I'm just about to shove off when up pops a guy in a sporty-lookin' trench coat.

"'Take me to the Allison Theatre, 181st Street and Broadway,' he says, sharplike. 'And don't spare the horses.'

"So as soon as he hops in I rolls up to 125th, crosses over to Broadway, then comes tearin' up here to the Allison. And now," he added, a tremor creeping into his voice, "and now comes the screwy part.

"The minute I pulls up to this curb I flips up the flag and waits for the guy in the trench coat to jump out. But he don't make a move, see. So I looks back at him. And so help me Harriet, he ain't nowhere in the cab at all!"

How dumb can a guy get I thought, making no attempt to conceal my disgust. "Look, sucker," I said. "That guy pulled a fast one on you, that's all. He climbed into your hack, crossed over to the opposite door, and slipped out to the street while you were starting the motor. Dammit, you cab drivers are all alike. You never look at your rear-view mirror unless there's a couple of lovebirds on the rear seat."

There was a momentary silence in which the cabbie looked at me with unveiled scorn, almost as though I'd wiped my feet on his flag.

"Jeez! Y'don't know from nuthin'," he jeered. "Here, maybe this'll put you on the right track," and with a quick movement he flung open the rear door of the taxi. "Now d'you see what I'm drivin' at?" he whimpered. "D'you see now what—"

His voice was drowned in the shouts of amazement that sprang from the lips of the onlookers. My own contribution was as loud and startled as any of them.

Believe it or not, I found myself staring at something that might have stepped from the pages of *Esquire*: a luscious, whistle-invoking blonde who had all the breathtaking beauty of Venus de Milo, plus all the cold, grim lifelessness of the old girl's statue. What I mean is, I was staring at a gorgeous stiff—a corpus delicious, as we call them at West 20th Street.

The doll lay curled on the floor of the cab in a sort of jack-knife position. Her mink coat was unfastened, and from the bodice of her bloodstained, powder-blue evening gown protruded the handle of a dagger. Unquestionably the dagger had been wielded with an upward thrust. The blade was buried directly under the babe's left breast, with the tip of the handle resting against her left thigh.

No, I didn't feel any chills of horror coursing up and down my spine, and I'm damn sure my teeth didn't chatter. After all, murder is my bread and butter. When a man spends five years on a homicide squad, as I have, he looks at sudden death in all its macabre forms as just another murder squeal to be probed and broken; just another D.O.A. that has got to be taken care of P.D.Q.

What particularly caught my attention were the fragments of frosted glass I saw sprinkled over the corpse. I couldn't figure how they got there. Then I happened to glance upward and got the answer. The dome light in the ceiling of the cab had been smashed to smithereens.

Meanwhile, my roving eyes had settled on the girl's left hand, on the third finger of which were a platinum wedding band and a square-cut diamond engagement ring—two expensive-looking baubles that precluded any supposition that robbery had motivated the crime. Yet I was much more interested in what lay near her shapely, silk-stockinged legs; namely, her gold-mesh purse.

A woman's purse, as any up-and-coming detective will tell you, is nothing but a miniature information bureau with a zipper on it. And this one was no exception. In no time at all, thanks to a driver's license, which I found tucked away in her billfold, I learned that the murder victim was Paula Chadwick; that she was one year short of entering a voting booth, and lived at the Parkview Towers, 74th Street and Riverside Drive. As for the other things in her purse—keys, handkerchief, cosmetics—I ignored them for the time being.

Slipping the purse into my overcoat pocket, I pulled my head and shoulders from the cab and closed the door—with my elbow. After all, it wouldn't do to have my prints all over the door handle when it came time for the boys at the police garage to give the taxi a dusting. A mistake like that would cost me a round of coffee and crullers and, worst of all, a lot of good-natured ribbing.

"Didn't I tell you the whole thing was screwy?" the cab driver piped up. "Jeez, I drives off from 112th with a man, and when I gets up here, he's a dame—and a murdered one, no less."

"Stop beefing," I growled at him. "Come on, help me shove some of these Peeping Toms out of the way. Give 'em the old heave-ho."

Scarcely had we begun combing the crowd out of our hair when I heard the eerie wail of a siren, which meant, thanks be, that help was coming my way. Sure enough, when I looked over the heads of the wondering herd (I was standing on somebody's feet at the time), I saw a radio prowl car zooming toward the mob.

A minute later two uniformed hulks plowed through that mass of humanity like a couple of jet-propelled snow plows. I saw taxpayers go north, east, south, and west. And if the hulks hadn't been hurriedly introduced to my shield, I think yours truly would have been scattered to the remaining twenty-eight points of the compass.

"O.K., boys, get to work on this mob," I commanded the precinct Goliaths, after giving them a peek at the corpse and just enough details to satisfy their curiosity and notebooks. Then, turning to the cabbie, I said, "Come here, Sam Willis. I want to talk with you."

Eyes and mouth agape, the cab driver edged over to me. "Say, howcha know my name?" he asked, and added plaintively, "Honest, I'm up to here with miracles. First it's the dame. Now it's you who's pullin' rabbits out of a hat."

I told him that by parking himself on the rear seat of his taxi he'd see in front of him an identification card with his name and photograph on it. I didn't have the heart, though, to tell him the photo was a dead likeness of King Kong.

Grinning, he said, "Jeez! You dicks don't miss much."

I offered him a cigarette. When he bent over to light the tip of it in the flame of my lighter, he weaved like a drunk attempting to insert a key in a lock.

"Suppose you and I have a little talk, Sam," I suggested, when he'd finally hit the bull's-eye and taken a few deep drags. "Maybe between us we can clear up some of this miracle business."

"Yeah, what d'you make of it?" he inquired. "How the heck did that dame get into my hack? She wasn't there when I drove to the lunchroom, 'cause I looked in the back when I dropped off my last fare. Always look back. People have a habit of forgettin' things."

I said, "The girl and Mr. Trench Coat must have got into your cab while you were dunking doughnuts in the lunchroom. He stabbed her, curled her up on the floor, then jumped out and waited, no doubt, in some nearby doorway for you to come out of the lunchroom."

"But why would he wanna come back to the cab?" Sam demanded. "Seems to me if a guy committed murder without anybody spottin' him, he'd be a horse's neck to come back to the scene of the crime and run the risk of stickin' his head in a noose."

"You tell me," I muttered. "I've a hunch, though, the killer wanted you to see that trench coat."

I thought, Yeah, maybe his coming back to the cab was all part of an ingenious plan to throw suspicion on someone who invariably wears a trench coat, someone who ties in with the murder victim.

Uh-huh. It made sense, sort of. At least it explained that cockeyed business of the broken dome light. If the killer had planned to return to the cab, then to safeguard that return he would have had to smash the dome light to prevent its flashing on when the time came for him to re-enter the cab and make his quick getaway. With the light out of commission there'd be no danger of the cabbie spotting the corpse on the floor; no danger of the light going on when the killer slipped out to the street. O.K., it was a crazy angle, but I'd hang onto it for a while. In this hunted-versus-hunter racket, crazy angles sometimes have an uncanny way of squaring themselves.

"Can you give me a more detailed description of the killer?" I asked the cabbie.

The expression on his face was as blank as a deposit column in my bankbook. "Jeez!" he said. "The guy came up on me so sudden-like I couldn't say for sure if he was tall or short or what. And with the collar of the trench coat pulled up around his ears, I didn't even get a squint at his face. Besides, it's kinda dark on 112th, especially on a Sunday night." Suddenly he snapped his fingers. "His hat! I remember now. A great big black fedora."

My mouth sagged open, my eyes bugged. Good Lord, it can't be! I thought. It's just a coincidence. There are dozens of Chadwicks in the city, hundreds of trench coats and big black fedoras.

"What time was it when you picked him up?" I asked.

Sam studied the smoldering end of his cigarette. "I got outa the lunchroom around seven," he replied. "So it musta been seven-two or -three."

I had other question marks to throw at the cabbie, but they could wait. I said, "You stay here, Sam. I'll be back, just as soon as I make a couple of phone calls."

It took all of five minutes to shoulder my way through the crowd. When I finally broke loose, I found myself in the lobby of the Allison, where I immediately collared the manager and demanded use of his phone.

The business of notifying the Medical Examiner's night crew that a D.O.A. awaits examination is strictly routine and takes no more than a few minutes' time. But reporting a homicide to my confrères on the third floor of the West 20th Street station house is something else again. By the time I'd covered the facts, received my instructions, and got back to Sam, it was almost eight-fifteen.

"Hop into your cab, Sam," I said. "You and I and the corpse have a date at the Bellevue morgue."

But as I prepared to step into the taxi my eye fell upon the haft of the murder weapon. Somehow I hadn't paid too much attention to the dagger. Now I was really seeing it for the first time.

The handle was a gold figure of some fierce-looking bird or beast, the like of which I'd never seen before. It had the head and claws of something that looked like an eagle, and the hoofs and tail of a horse, with two tiny rubies for eyes.

I thought, Take a good look at it, Chris. Dollars to dough-nuts you'll never see the like of it again.

But I was wrong. In the days to come I was to find two more of those hideous-looking creatures. And when I found them, each had a nice grisly corpse for company.

CHAPTER TWO

When Sam brought his taxi to a halt in front of the City Mortuary at the foot of East 29th Street, a swarm of officials and "bird dogs" was waiting for us at the curb—a sure sign that our lifeless passenger, Paula Chadwick, rated top-drawer attention. Even dapper, gray-spatted District Attorney Carl Strenz was present, not to mention the Chief Inspector, two of his deputies, and Chief of Detectives Gilbride.

As for the bird dogs (photographers, detectives, reporters), the only one who really mattered, as far as I was concerned, was Detective-Sergeant Regan, a redheaded, two-fisted sleuth from the D.A.'s office, behind whose freckled, yokel-looking face lay a brain that fairly crawled with intuitional know-how.

For the past five years Regan and I had made no bones about our intense dislike for each other, a deep-rooted animosity induced, no doubt, by the keen rivalry that exists between Homicide and the D.A.'s detective staff. Gradually, however, after locking horns a number of times on some extra-knotty murder squeals, we'd begun to develop a mutual respect for each other. Nothing sticky, mind you; just a sort of halfhearted acknowledgment that each really had something on the ball. If nothing else, it made us doubly eager to outsmart each other for the further glorification of our respective alma maters.

Regan was thirty-four, topping me by three years. We were both single, both products of the streets of New York, both totally unaware of what the inside of a college looked like. Yet our rise in the ranks had been phenomenally fast. That I outranked the Sergeant could be attributed to the fact that my father had been a detective. Indeed, Pop had begun cramming police methods into my head from the time I was six years old.

"It's never too early to learn to be a copper, Chris," he used to say. "Don't forget, son, the criminals you'll run up against someday are already out there in the streets learning their trade."

But Pop lived only long enough to see me go from harness to third-grade detective. He stopped a gangster's bullet one night, and three months later my mother joined him.

Climbing out of the cab, I walked over to the assemblage of brass, while tubby, one-eyed Deputy Chief Medical Examiner "Doc" Berlinger, armed with a flashlight and his usual supply of profanity, squeezed into the taxi and began a "cursory" examination of the corpse. Meanwhile, police and newspaper photographers were priming their cameras and flash bulbs for action.

Much to my surprise, my immediate superior, Acting Captain Dan Neely, head of the Homicide Squad, West Side Division, was a member of the group. Top brass had evidently rousted the little hellion out of his favorite easy chair and away from his television set, a deed of derring-do that under ordinary circumstances was tantamount to twisting a lion's tail.

"A full report, Chris," he said in his abrupt manner when I'd made my obeisance to his high-ranking companions. "This squeal, I don't mind telling you, is strictly dynamite."

I ordered Sam Willis out of the cab and told him to repeat his summary of the events leading up to his discovery of the corpse. Then, when he'd recited his piece to the officials and answered a flock of their routine questions, I followed through with my own detailed account, conscious that Sergeant Regan, who had edged closer to us at the beginning of Sam's recital, was taking it all in with a nasty smirk on his pan.

Curiously, when I aired my theory that the killer had returned to the cab for the express purpose of throwing suspicion on someone else, someone in the habit of wearing a trench coat and black fedora, the bigwigs took to it like a vacationing patrolman takes to an all-leaves-canceled order. All I got for my effort was a raucous razzberry from Regan.

"Why don't you give yourself up, Lash?" his rusty voice boomed out. "There ain't a dick in town who don't know who that guy in the trench coat was."

Accustomed to the Sergeant's perverted sense of humor, I ignored the remark. However, when I caught Neely's curt nod of confirmation, I knew then that the Police Department hadn't let any grass grow under its feet. Apparently my phone call to the West 20th Street station house had pried loose a lot of fat buttocks from their moorings.

"O.K., I'll bite," I said to Neely. "Who was it?" But I knew what he was going to say. Regan's remark, plus all this turnout of the big wheels, could mean only one thing: The trench coat and the big black fedora hadn't been a coincidence, after all.

Neely's seamed, leathery face took on a grim expression. He said, "Her husband, Martin Chadwick—*the* Martin Chadwick."

That was it, all right. I'd thought of Martin Chadwick the minute the cabbie had mentioned the big black fedora. But I'd shelved the idea as being too fantastic. Frankly, I still refused to believe it.

Martin Chadwick was definitely upper case, as front page as an explosion in Wall Street or a tidal wave in the Gowanus Canal; one of the most prominent criminal lawyers this side of the solar system. Yet rumor had it that he was crooked, so crooked he could cling to the belly of a wriggling snake without so much as showing a hip. In my opinion, though, it was just scuttlebutt,

malicious lies that the envious always use in their efforts to un-
dermine pedestals.

For my money, Chadwick was a right guy. I didn't know him
well enough to call him by his first name, but I'd seen him in
action plenty of times. Come to think of it, less than a month
ago he'd made a monkey of me on the witness stand. He tied me
up so neatly that in the eyes of the jury I must have had all the
earmarks of a congenital liar. Yet that night when I got home,
if a three-room, womanless apartment can be called a home, a
short note of apology and a case of rye were waiting for me in
the janitor's quarters. I could be wrong, but it seemed to me that
a guy who'd do a thing like that, apologize to a nobody like me,
had a helluva lot of good stuff in him. What's more, a guy with
a heart that big wouldn't kill a fly, let alone a delectable doll like
Paula Chadwick. True, his trench coat and black fedora were as
familiar to the public as Benny's toupee or Gypsy's G-string. But
cripes! Trench coats and black fedoras weren't exactly uncommon
in the city.

"Doesn't add up, Dan," I protested. "If Chadwick wanted to
ditch his wife, he could either buy himself a quick, painless di-
vorce or get some of his gangster clients to bump her off."

"Maybe, maybe not," Neely muttered. "But Chadwick's taken
a powder, and in my book that's plenty incriminating."

In response to my request for details, he said that a couple of
dicks from the 20th squad had been sent to the Parkview Towers
to pick up Chadwick. They'd drawn a blank. According to the
hall attendant up there, Martin Chadwick had gone off in his car
at five-thirty that afternoon and hadn't returned.

"Did anyone try looking for him in his office?" I asked. Neely
threw me a blistering look, and Regan emitted one of his needling horse laughs.

"Any resemblance to a real detective," I heard the Sergeant
stage-whisper to Strenz, "is purely coincidental."

Neely said, "We've alerted the prowl cars, stationed men at all transportation points, checked the hospitals, double-checked the hotels—yes, and even sent out an eight-state alarm. And *you* want to know if anyone tried looking for him in his office. H'm. You're not kidding, Lash. This *is* your day off."

I was used to Neely's tongue-lashings. With slow deliberation I glanced at my wrist watch and said, "It isn't nine-thirty yet, Dan. For all we know, Chadwick may be parked somewhere in a movie. Maybe he's sitting there without the slightest inkling his wife has been murdered."

"Look. Chadwick's an important man," he countered. "He's good copy, Chris. People like to read about him in the newspapers. Right?"

"Check."

"Doesn't it stand to reason, then, that the reporters would really know something about Chadwick's haunts and habits?"

"So what?"

"So this," he rasped. "A few of the reporters around here told us that Chadwick for the last year or so has been spending his Sunday nights at the Sabre Club. Never misses. Arrives at eight sharp and leaves at eleven. Yet, according to the dicks who went up to the Sabre Club a little while ago to make the pinch, Chadwick didn't show. Convinced?"

I shook my head. "Nope. I still think Chadwick's innocent. If he's guilty, then give me one good reason why he returned to the cab and pulled that disappearing act."

"That's for you to find out, you pigheaded so-and-so," he retorted, grinning. "In the meantime, God help us, we're putting you officially in charge of the squeal. Use as many men as you like, but for Pete's sake, Chris, work fast. And as a starter you'd better hop up for a look-see at the Chadwicks' apartment. Maybe, by going through his papers and things, you'll latch onto something."

"How about the papers in his office?"

"Lynch and Patterson are handling that end of it."

"Do any of the reporters know Paula Chadwick's maiden name?" I asked. "If I could get in touch with some of her relatives—"

"They've already been notified," Neely snapped. "We called her brother on the phone, a man by the name of Philip Brocton; and damned if he didn't faint away. Then some guy by the name of Frank Webster got on the wire. He's Paula Chadwick's brother-in-law or something. Anyway, the whole damn family's coming down here."

"That's for me, then."

"The hell it is!"

With that Neely turned to the tall, nattily dressed Carl Strenz, who all this time had been eying me as though he were saying to himself, "This fellow Lash can't hold a candle to Sergeant Regan."

"Give him that search and seizure, Carl," Neely muttered. Then, facing me again, he said, "Now fork over that purse you told us about."

I gave it to him. In a flash Paula's leather key case was dropped into my hand.

"Now get the hell out of here," Neely said. "And when you get up there, keep your mitts off Chadwick's liquor cabinet."

Pocketing the warrant and the key case, I made Neely promise that as soon as the corpse was taken inside to the morgue he'd send the cab to the police garage for a thorough print examination. I also exacted a promise from him that he'd put a little pressure on Doc Berlinger. If Berlinger would shake that fat fanny of his, there was no reason why I shouldn't have a complete autopsy report first thing in the morning.

"There's just one more thing, Chris," Neely remarked, his face darkening, his brow furrowing with tiny lines of worry. "The

D.A. here"—he jerked his gray-thatched head toward Strenz—
"wants Sergeant Regan to work on this squeal with you. In fact,
the Sergeant's waiting to take you uptown in his car."

I thought, Yeah. He's waiting right now to run the front
wheels over me. But aloud I said, "O.K., Dan. This'll be a fine
opportunity for Sergeant Regan to learn something about detective work."

"Is that so?" Regan growled behind me, and I felt his eyes
burning a hole in the back of my head. "Well, get this straight,
Lieutenant," he added cockily. "Me and my boys'll have Chadwick in the bag in less than forty-eight hours."

With my eyes still fastened on Neely's face I said, "Pretty
warm for December, Dan. If this hot air keeps up, I'll have to
shed my benny."

If the bigwigs hadn't been present, I think Regan would have
told me to put up my dukes. Instead, silent and sullen, he led me
to his somewhat battered sedan and opened the rear door.

"Get in the back, punk," he said under his breath. "If you was
to ride up front with me, I might get kinda mixed up and throw
you out instead of the clutch."

"Don't ever try it, egghead," I warned, parking myself on the
rear seat. "I'm liable to knock off that red head of yours and use
it for a tail light. Come on, get this coffee grinder moving before
the street cleaners come along and grab it."

As we were about to shove off, I spotted Doc Berlinger's
ample posterior emerging from Willis' taxi.

"Wait a minute, Regan," I commanded. "Let's hear what Berlinger has to say." I called to the M.E. to join us. "What's the
story, Doc?" I asked as he rested one of his ponderous feet upon
the running board and thrust his big head through the open window on my right. "Anything special?"

"Sweetest pair of knockers I've seen in a dog's age," he gloated
with all the fervor of a connoisseur. "Milky white and as shapely

as a couple of butter-dish covers. Positively beautiful, I tell you. Ah! And the rosebuds—sheer poetry, gentlemen."

I hated to interrupt his sermon on the mound, but Regan and I had to go places and do things. So I told Berlinger to snap out of it and give us the result of his examination.

"Tsk! Tsk! You've no appreciation of the beautiful, Lash," he said mournfully. "Here." He stuck his thumb and index finger under his black eye patch and gouged out his "eye," an eye-shaped magnifying glass that he always kept handy in his empty left eye socket. "Here, you take it, my boy. By God, I've seen everything now."

"Put that damn marble back in your head, Doc," Regan pleaded. "It gives me the creeps. Holy Canarsie, why don'tcha just keep your loose change in that empty socket?"

Berlinger's fat shoulders went up like a "No Sale" sign in a cash register. He'd obviously given us up as hopeless. In a voice tinged with boredom he informed us that Paula Chadwick had been killed about three hours ago. Probably sometime between six-thirty and seven.

"But don't you bastards quote me," he warned sulkily. "Whole thing's pure guesswork. It's goddamn cold tonight, and cold weather speeds up cadaveric rigidity like nobody's business. Furthermore, I doubt whether she died instantaneously. In all probability, death occurred anywhere from five to fifteen minutes after the dagger pierced her heart."

"Any chance of it being suicide?"

"Hell, no," he answered, removing his foot from the running board and thereby permitting the two left wheels of the jalopy to touch the ground again. "Too much force behind the blow. Besides, there weren't any 'hesitation marks' on her body. Anyone set on slashing himself with a razor, or stabbing himself with a knife or an icepick, usually makes a few halfhearted attempts before he finally has guts enough to make the final plunge. Hence

the little scratches or hesitation marks. Incidentally, here's something that might interest you boys. I found it lying nice and cozy-
like between those beautiful knockers," and he placed something
limp and slimy in my hand.

"What the hell is it?" Regan demanded, leaning over the front
seat.

I could scarcely believe my eyes. Skyrockets and Roman can-
dles were going off in my head. "A dead goldfish!" I exclaimed,
my voice tense with wonder. "So help me God, Sergeant, a dead
goldfish!"

CHAPTER THREE

I placed the goldfish in an envelope and tucked it away in the inside pocket of my suit coat. A few minutes later Regan had his cement mixer streaking toward the West Side Highway. I'd heard Regan was a Jehu at a wheel, but I'd no idea until now that he drove with his eyes closed.

"How'd that goldfish get between her lung worts, Lash?" the Sergeant inquired. "I've heard of dames using Chanel Number Five," he added, "but a gal would be crazy to expect the same effect from a dead goldfish."

I didn't answer him. You can't talk when your heart's in your mouth.

"So you won't talk, eh?" Regan's rusty voice had the sting of a rubber hose. "O.K., wise guy, if that's the way you want it, it's jake with me," and he lapsed into a sulky silence.

The Parkview Towers was a swanky, streamlined apartment house on the southeast corner of 74th Street and Riverside Drive. The place had class, all right, sixteen stories of it, and almost instantly a young hall attendant in a Marshal Goering uniform ran out to the sidewalk to make with the salaams.

"Take us to the Chadwicks' apartment," I commanded the flunky, giving him a squint at my shield.

There was an immediate change in his attitude. From a towering gold-braided icicle he melted into a mere drip.

"Right this way, gentlemen," he purred as Regan and I piled out of the car and followed him into a spacious main hall that was a cross between the Taj Mahal and the Roxy Theatre.

"Where are the two dicks who were sent up here?" I asked, surprised that their commanding officer hadn't ordered them to keep an all-night watch on the house.

The flunky said, "Across the street in a squad car. Said they'd wait there just in case Mr. Chadwick showed up. Ah, here we are. Apartment One-B," and he brought our little safari to a halt in front of what I took to be a full-length mirror until I saw it had a couple of locks and a doorknob.

I pulled the leather key case out of my overcoat pocket and one by one began fitting the keys to the locks. On the third try I hit the jackpot, but when I attempted to push open the door the flunky placed a timid yet restraining hand on my arm.

"Mr. Chadwick's not going to like this," he said nervously. "You fellows got a search warrant?"

I produced the warrant and shoved it under his nose. "And now that that's settled," I said, "suppose you brief us a bit. For instance, when did you first see Martin Chadwick today?"

"Shortly after five o'clock," he explained. "I came on duty at five, and a few minutes later Mr. Chadwick drove up in his car. I think he was sore about something, because when I opened the door for him, he slammed past me without saying a word."

"How was he dressed?" Regan asked.

"Same as usual—trench coat and black fedora."

The Sergeant threw me a triumphant look. "O.K., Commodore," he said to the flunky. "What happened next?"

"Mr. Chadwick rang the doorbell, and when Mrs. Chadwick opened the door, he brushed her aside and stepped into the apartment. Didn't say a word."

"How come Mrs. Chadwick opened the door?" I inquired. "Haven't they got a maid?"

The flunky shook his head. Chadwick, he told us, was a nut on collecting priceless antiques and things. Wouldn't have a servant for love or money. Wouldn't even trust a cleaning woman to come in and help Mrs. Chadwick with the housework. Not, he added, that Mrs. Chadwick was the kind of dame who would ever strain herself with a dust rag.

When I asked him if the Chadwicks had been a happily married couple, he looked at me as though I'd asked him whether a chorus girl would be safe on a home-coming troop transport.

"Their marriage was just one pitched battle after another," he said. "Scarcely a night went by that I didn't hear them wrangling."

Regan had a question. He wanted to know whether Paula had been two-timing her husband. But the flunky turned thumbs down on the idea. Their nightly battles, he informed us, were always on the same subject: Chadwick's in-laws. He wasn't positive, of course, but from all he'd heard he sort of got the impression that Paula and her family were milking the lawyer for everything he had.

One of those May-December setups, I thought. Young and beautiful doll marries fifty-year-old sugar daddy and gives the old folks at home a glucose feeding. Aloud I said to the flunky, "After Chadwick entered his apartment, when did you see him again?"

"At five-thirty. I was talking to one of the tenants when all of a sudden he came tearing out like a madman. The next thing I knew, he was in his car and heading uptown."

"And what about Mrs. Chadwick?"

"She barged out about fifteen minutes later. She was on the sidewalk before I got halfway to the front door to open it for her."

"Did she hail a cab?"

The flunky studied his brass buttons. "Couldn't say. The elevator buzzed just then, so I went upstairs. Rain or shine, Mrs. Shapiro in Nine-J always buzzes me around five-forty-five to take her dog out for an airing."

I asked him the name of the garage where Chadwick kept his car.

"We're 'way ahead of you, Lash," Regan said with a throaty growl. "Got all the dope at eight-forty. The car's a dark-green Lincoln sedan, and Chadwick keeps it in the Riverside Garage on Seventy-second Street. Took the car out at two-thirty this afternoon; and, up till eight-forty—I'll repeat that—up till eight-forty hadn't returned." Chuckling, he nudged me in the ribs. "Try *that* for size, Lieutenant."

I turned to the flunky and told him to go peddle his papers. "Look, egghead," I said to Regan when our threesome was a twosome, "hasn't it occurred to you that Martin Chadwick might also have been bumped off tonight?"

"Yeah? Well, the way I see it," he replied, "I'm more convinced than ever that Chadwick's our pigeon. The minute I saw that dagger in the corpse I figured it was a collector's item. And when the Commodore said that Chadwick was a nut on collecting things—well, what more do you want? And another thing, Lash," he continued. "You're miles off the beam if you think the killer came back to the cab just to let the cab driver get an eyeful of that trench coat and black fedora. Wanna know the real reason?"

"Shoot."

He said, "Chadwick killed Paula in the cab, then skipped out lickety-split, scared stiff he'd get caught. A little while later, though, he got thinking about his precious dagger, and it hurt him like hell to think that somebody might come along, peek into the cab, and walk off with the murder weapon. So he came back to the scene of the crime. But unluckily for him, the cab driver beat him to it. "That's why Chadwick had to pull that gimmick about the Allison Theatre. He wanted to get in the cab, grab hold of the dagger, and jump out. But the blade, I guess, was stuck too tight in her chest. And since he had to jump out before the hack really got moving, he didn't have any time to fool with the dagger."

"Not bad, Regan," I muttered. His theory had jarred me more than I cared to admit. "Not half bad. It doesn't explain, though, the broken dome light."

"Just an accident, chum. When Chadwick raised his arm to do the stabbing, the top of the dagger haft hit the dome light and smashed it."

"You're slipping, Sergeant," I said. "The killer didn't use a downward thrust. He let her have it straight up from his hip."

I pushed open the door and stepped into the Chadwicks' dark apartment. Regan's groping hand located a wall switch. Every room in the joint, including the kitchen and the two bathrooms—perhaps even the broom closet, if I'd taken the trouble to look—was crammed with dust-coated paintings, books, coins—everything, so help me, except a stuffed brontosaurus. Obviously they represented years of haphazard collecting, woefully unsystematic so far as the gentle art of collecting *objets d'art* went, yet entailing, no doubt, great cost and extensive travel.

"Holy Canarsie!" Regan exclaimed as our junket through the junk came to an end in the living room. "This ain't the Chadwicks' apartment. This is where Homer and Langley used to live."

I could well believe it. Worst of all, a stifling mustiness hung over the apartment as though the windows hadn't been opened since Admiral Dewey made his triumphal march up the Drive. The heat was unbearable. Rivulets of sweat ran down my face and legs. Nevertheless, we refrained from opening the windows for fear of choking to death in a dust storm. We did have sense enough, though, to shut off the radiator and remove our hats and coats.

By now, needless to say, my throat was parched. Remembering Neely's admonition about the Chadwicks' liquor cabinet, I began to cast a surreptitious eye around the room.

Suddenly the dead silence was broken by a mysterious tapping. The tapping, I discovered, came from one of the windows, which on closer inspection revealed a pair of faces gawking in at us.

"Bet it's those dicks from the Twentieth Squad," Regan remarked. "They musta seen the lights go on and figured Chadwick had sneaked in."

Climbing over an Egyptian mummy, two sundials, and an Eskimo kayak, I reached the window, placed my shield against the pane, and motioned the men to return to their car across the street. Then, turning about, I began the long dusty trek back to the Sergeant.

"Wow! Take a look at this, Regan," I said, pointing to a gold medallion about the size of a saucer. It lay on top of a rickety teakwood table. "Unless I'm very much mistaken, this is a genuine Benvenuto Cellini." I was just showing off for Regan's benefit. Frankly, I couldn't tell a Cellini from a cello.

With the Sergeant at my heels I led the way into the adjoining room, which, if a desk and a lot of books meant anything, was unquestionably the lawyer's den. Like the other rooms in the apartment, the den also had its quota of museum pieces.

By dint of some neat twisting, we wormed our way across the room until we reached the antiquated roll-top desk. Regan started emptying the drawers and the pigeonholes of all papers and letters.

"Ain'tcha gonna help me jot down names and addresses?" he asked peevishly, parking himself on the desk seat.

"Not me, brother," I answered. "I've got something important to attend to."

Regan gave me a toothsome grin. "O.K.," he said. "Just don't forget to call me when you open the bottle."

For a solid ten minutes Regan and I were as busy as two ter-
mites at the running of the Wood Memorial: Regan poring over
papers, yours truly searching for something I could pour. Along
toward eleven o'clock, however, the Sergeant gave a grunt of disgust and threw down his stub of a pencil.

"I give up," he said, flexing his cramped fingers and standing
up. "All I'm getting is a list of foreign and domestic art dealers."
The really pertinent stuff, he went on to say, was probably in the
filing cabinets in Chadwick's office. "Come on," he grunted. "I'll
help you look for the liquor."

At that instant the phone in the living room cried for attention.

"This is Neely, Chris," the little hellion barked into my ear
in his incisive way. "Nothing in yet on Chadwick. Strenz and I
had a long talk, though, with Paula's family. Paula's sister Helen
seems to be nice enough, and so does Helen's husband, Lew Partridge. But Paula's sister-in-law Jessica is a bitch if ever I saw one.
The two that really take the cake are Frank Webster and Philip
Brocton. Webster all but spit in my eye for not collaring Chadwick right after the murder. And Brocton, the cheap bastard, had
the nerve to ask if he could bill the City of New York for the expenses he incurred in driving down to the morgue tonight. Said
he had to stop for gas along the way."

"I'd like to meet them," I said. "All five."

"Don't worry, you will. I'm sending them up right away.
They've got plenty to tell you, Chris. Maybe if you keep your
nose clean, they'll even help you look for the hippopotamuses."
With that cryptic remark he hung up.

Regan, of course, wanted to know what was what. When I
came to the part about the hippopotamuses, he came over to me
and put his bulbous nose close to my mouth.

"You're a louse, Lieutenant," he said in an aggrieved tone.
"Why didn'tcha tell me you found the cabinet?"

"I'm not drunk, you lummox," I fired back. "I'm telling you exactly what Neely said. They're coming up here to tell us something and to help us look for the hippopotamuses."

Scratching his head, the Sergeant glanced about the room. "Well, they're certainly not in here," he said. Then, tilting his nose, he gave a series of short sniffs. "Nope—and that's definite."

"This squeal gets screwier every minute," I ranted, sitting down on a divan that Napoleon must have used for some of his lesser campaigns. "First, Berlinger finds a goldfish between a pair of chest cushions. Now Neely's sending up a gang of Frank Bucks to help us bag a herd of hippos."

It was then that I noticed the debonair air with which Regan was straightening his tie.

"Going somewhere, Sergeant?" I inquired, fishing for my lighter and cigarettes.

"Taking no chances, that's all," he replied, and his face was so crimson that it was difficult to tell where his hairline began. "This sister of Paula's. You think maybe she's as cute a dish—"

"Take it easy, lover," I cut in sternly, offering him a cigarette. "I've got enough trouble worrying about goldfish and hippos without taking on a wolf."

He grinned sheepishly. "Aw, shut up and give me a light."

I pressed the button on my lighter and held its tiny flame beneath the tip of Regan's cigarette. *Phfft!* The flame went out as though an invisible fire-eater had swallowed it.

"That's odd," I mused. Then irritably, "If you must open windows, Sergeant, at least let me know about it."

"I didn't open no windows," he protested. "If you ask me, your lighter's run out of fluid." He caught the alert look on my face. "Holy Canarsie!" he added in a hushed voice. "You don't think—?"

I didn't hang around to draw any pictures for him. Crushing my cigarette in an ash tray, I sprang from the divan and tiptoed stealthily across the floor toward Chadwick's den. As I approached I could feel a steady current of wind issuing from the room, followed almost instantly by the faint yet unmistakable sound of someone moving about.

It's Chadwick, I thought, tensing. Unconsciously my right hand began tunneling toward the bulge under my left armpit.

CHAPTER FOUR

Scarcely breathing, nerves churning my insides, finger flirting with the trigger of my roscoe, I edged along the far wall of the living room, poked my head a few inches past the doorframe, and peeked into the den.

A nifty little number, young and uncommonly pretty, was rummaging through the drawers of the roll-top desk as though she were Mata Hari herself. Her smartly tailored suit and silver-fox cape were definitely Park Avenue, yet she wore them with a certain hoydenish air that smacked of either Broadway or Hollywood. Shoulder-length brown hair, petite figure, artistically stacked nylons. Our window-climbing intruder was certainly worth looking at, especially her saucy, upturned nose, which had so pronounced an upward sweep that I knew instinctively its owner had spent a lifetime thumbing her nose at the proprieties.

"Hi, sister," I said quietly as Regan and I drooled into the den. "Looking for something?"

The girl emitted an involuntary gasp. For a split second her stricken brown eyes protruded from their sockets like balloons of bubble gum emerging from the mouths of a pair of moppets.

"Who—who are you?" she demanded in a throaty, sultry voice. "And what are you doing here?"

Holstering the gun and advancing toward her, I said, "Keep your wings on, angel. All we want you to do is answer a few questions."

A look, half anger, half petulance, clouded her pert face. She said sharply, "I've a good mind to report this to the Racing Commission. Don't you realize it's against the law for a radio quiz program to break into a person's home?" And she backed away from the desk until finally her little caboose came in contact with the window sill.

I'm six feet tall, yet I can move at times with supersonic speed. In any case, the caboose had already coupled with the sill when I shot forward, stretched out a rapierlike arm, and closed the window. And none too soon. The slick chick had already hoisted one of her gorgeous gams as a prelude to flight.

"What—just when we're getting acquainted?" I inquired, grinning at her.

She didn't seem the least bit offended. "You're not going to believe a word of this," she said demurely, looking up at me through her long lashes, "but honest, mister, I dropped in to see if I could interest you gentlemen in some lovely Christmas cards."

Her attempt at humor left me cold, although I must admit I did hear a few appreciative chuckles from the Sergeant.

I said, "Suppose you cut the comedy, sister, and make with some answers. For example, what's your name, where do you live, and why?"

There was a long, uncomfortable silence. At last the girl said, "I'd love to help you, but—oh, damn!—it so happens I'm a victim of amnesia. Uh-huh. Don't even know my nephew's first name. For that matter, I'm not even sure I have a nephew."

I was losing my patience fast. "O.K., Sergeant," I growled. "Take her to the nearest station house and book her on a charge of unlawful entry."

"Detectives?" she asked in a small meek voice.

I introduced myself, giving name, rank, and telephone number. What the hell, I like to go out with a pretty girl as much as the next guy.

"And this is Sergeant Regan," I said grudgingly, on account of the way she was eying Regan's flaming thatch. "He looks like a detective but he's really an advertisement for Fire Prevention Week."

"Don't listen to him, sugar," the Sergeant cooed. "Can I help it if I got more red corpuscles than I know what to do with?"

Without so much as cracking a smile the babe held out her arms to Regan. She said, "Shall we dance, Sergeant?"

Flabbergasted, Regan and I looked at each other. I thought, How much can a guy take? Was she trying to be cute? Or was she, as I was beginning to suspect, a fugitive from a strait jacket?

I studied her for a minute, hoping to see some glimmer of sanity. "If you're trying to be evasive, it's no go," I warned. "It's either answer our questions—or else."

She shrugged her shoulders. "You win, Lieutenant. It's only fair to warn you, though, that I shall take this matter up with the Racing Commission. Furthermore, I shall insist on a saliva test."

"All we want to know," I said to her cautiously, expecting any minute to see two white-coated attendants climb in the window, "is who you are, where you live, and what you're doing here."

Undisguised relief flooded her face. "Well, for gosh sake, why didn't you say so?"

Opening her alligator handbag, she pulled out a calling card and handed it to me. Engraved on the card was the following: "In case of accident notify the nearest hospital."

"H'm. Very interesting," I said, passing the card to Regan and pausing long enough to watch his eyes pop out. "I'm afraid, though, you'll have to do better than that. Let's see your Social Security."

Aghast, she drew her fur cape tightly across her high firm breasts, lush pouter pigeons that would have delighted Doc Berlinger. "How dare you!" she blasted, stamping her tiny foot. "Why, I've never been so insulted in— Goodness me, a girl isn't safe anywhere these days."

I blew my top. In no uncertain terms I read her the riot act.

"Take my advice and talk, sugar," Regan told her. "I know this guy Lash. He's tough. "If it wasn't for the tax deduction, he'd put his own grandmother in jail."

"O.K., you old meanie," she said to me, smiling. "My name's Jane Willoughby, I live in Greenwich Village, and I'm a sob sister for the New York *Courier-Post*. Does that satisfy you? Or do you twist my arm now to get my phone number?"

"You reporters give me a pain in the neck," I beefed, glowering at her, yet contriving for the sake of my scrapbook to give a semblance of a grin. "Incidentally," I added, "would you mind telling me how you managed to climb in? This window is a good five feet above the sidewalk."

"Elementary, my dear Lieutenant," was her flippant reply. "I simply waylaid the first male who came along and asked him to give me a boost into my apartment. Told him I'd forgotten my keys. Really, it was no trouble at all. And judging from the way the gentleman whistled, I think he was amply repaid."

I didn't doubt it; I'd seen one of her gams.

"What were you looking for in the desk?" I asked.

She made a vague gesture. "The usual thing. Letters, photographs—anything, in fact, that might tickle the fancy of my city editor."

Turning to Regan, I said musingly, "Funny those dicks didn't spot her."

"How could they?" he countered. "They're on Riverside Drive. The windows in this room face Seventy-fourth Street."

At this point the babe said, "Look. Why don't you boys be a couple of darlings and give me ten minutes at that desk? Whiz gee, fellers, a girl's got to eat, you know."

Instead of complying with her request, I took her by the arm and led her into the living room. The nearness of her, the softness of her arm, the heady fragrance of her perfume were insidiously knocking the props from under me. But when she plopped down on the divan, thus releasing me somewhat from her glamorous clutches, I was again on the payroll of the Homicide Squad.

"We've enjoyed your performance, young lady," I said with severity. "Suppose now you let your hair down. To put it bluntly," I went on, shaking my finger in her face—but not too close because I figured she was just nuts enough to bite off the tip of it—"you can dispense with the malarkey and try telling us the truth for a change."

"Hey, take it easy, Lash," Regan blazed, his jaw jutting belligerently. "If you think I'm gonna stand by and let you browbeat this babe, you've got another think coming. What the hell do you want—blood? She's told you what's what, hasn't she?"

"Go on, get lost, you dumb cluck," I said harshly. "If she's a reporter, I'll eat the *Courier-Post* down to the last splinter. Take a look at that tailored suit, that cape, that dinky hat. Can you imagine her buying an outfit like that on a sob sister's salary? And look at her king-size fingernails. Do you find scratchers like that on a dame who punches a typewriter for a living?"

"Yes, and look at her shoes, Sergeant," the girl chimed in. "Did you ever see a sob sister with shoes on her feet?"

"Shut up!" I roared at her. There was a brief pause. Facing Regan again, I said, "All right, so you're not convinced. Suppose then you look at her handbag. Isn't it odd that a Jane Willoughby should have the initials 'P. F.' on her handbag?"

Regan studied the initials with hurt, incredulous eyes. "What's the 'P. F.' stand for, sugar?" he asked the girl in a pained tone.

"President Fillmore," she answered without batting an eye.

"O.K., smarty," I said. "Quick! Give me the phone number of the *Courier-Post*. If you work there, you know the number."

Stalling for time, no doubt, she removed her cape and draped it carefully over the arm of the divan. Meanwhile, I could almost feel the thrumming of her brain as it groped frantically for the answer. Suddenly her shoulders drooped, and I saw abject surrender in her face.

"Did you say Lieutenant Lash or Inspector Lash?" she murmured, a mixture of admiration and suppressed rage in her voice. Then, patting the cushion on her right, she added seductively, "But do sit down beside me, darling. Honor bright, cross my heart, and two bucks on Firecracker in the fourth, from now on it's the truth and nothing but the truth, so help me."

I sat down. Not too close, of course. Anyone could easily have wedged a razor blade between her thigh and mine. Lies, I told her, would get her nowhere fast. I said every statement she'd make would be checked and double-checked.

She stared off into space for a while as though weighing my words. Finally she said, "My name is Phoebe Foster. I'm an actress. Not a Katharine Cornell or a Helen Hayes, of course. But I do manage to eat regularly. At present I'm hounding the casting offices, and in my spare time I'm doing soap operas on the radio."

"And where do you live?" Regan asked with suspicious eagerness.

She said, "At the Hotel Stockwood with my dog, Cuspidor."

The Sergeant was floored for a minute. "Cuspidor?" he echoed.

"Yes, darling. He's a Spitz."

"You're getting off the subject, sister," I said irritably. "Whether you know it or not, and I think you do, a murder has been committed. And unless you give me a good reason why you sneaked in here, I'm holding you as a material witness."

At first hesitantly, then with a quiet forcefulness that gave her words a ring of sincerity, the girl at last broke out with some autobiography.

About a year ago, while playing on Broadway in *Son of the Sultan,* a turkey in more ways than one, she'd been introduced to the celebrated Martin Chadwick. Well, from that moment on, a real and lasting friendship had gradually developed between them—strictly platonic, of course. Unfortunately, some of her affection for the old boy had been expressed on scented writing paper, and now that every radio in the country was blaring out the news of Paula Chadwick's brutal death—well, you couldn't blame a girl for not wanting to have her name bruited about in a murder case, particularly if the girl had aspirations for a movie career.

"And that's the whole thing in a nutshell, gentlemen," she said with disarming simplicity. "I didn't hear about—about Mrs. Chadwick until around ten o'clock, when I happened to turn on the radio. So right then and there I decided I'd come here and search for those letters of mine. Incidentally, if either of you doubt my word," she added grimly, "then name the day and hour and we'll fight it out behind Glintz's livery stable."

"Swords or pistols, sugar?" Regan inquired.

"It doesn't make a particle of difference," she snapped. "I've got a dual personality."

I thought, You ain't kidding, sister. Aloud I asked her if she knew where Chadwick was hiding.

The blank look on her face was either the real thing or a swell bit of acting.

"Hiding?" she echoed; and even as she said it I could tell by her sudden intake of breath that she'd guessed the score. "Jeepers! You don't mean—?" Her small white teeth clamped down on her lower lip like tiny marshmallows thrust deep into glowing embers.

I said, "Uh-huh. He's wanted for murder. So if you've any idea of his whereabouts, I advise you to come clean."

She shook her head. "No can do. Haven't seen him since early November. But I'll tell you this much: If Martin Chadwick's your number one boy, I'm the seventh son of a Chinese mandarin." With that she stood up and held out her arms invitingly. "Shall we dance, Lieutenant?"

"Angel, you took the words right out of my mouth," I said, tickled pink that here at long last was somebody who believed in Martin Chadwick's innocence. "Music, Professor," I called to Regan. And springing to my feet, I grabbed hold of the babe and began waltzing her around the divan. As for Maestro Regan's music—a hummed rendition of "The Merry Widow"—it sounded like something out of the *Queen Mary's* foghorn.

"Is there a law against opening the windows in here?" the girl demanded when the waltz had come to an end.

"Let's open them," I suggested to the Sergeant. "Even a mouthful of dust is better than this infernal heat."

"Suits me," Regan grunted.

We climbed over the mummy, the sundials, and the kayak, tugged for a while at the windows, and finally succeeded in opening them. A moment later the cold December wind and the dust were having a waltz of their own.

"Hey, what are you doing over there?" I cried as I wheeled about and discovered the screwball monkeying with our overcoats.

She made an impatient gesture. "Jeepers! You would turn around at the wrong moment," she fumed. "And I wanted so terribly to surprise you boys. Please don't," she pleaded as Regan and I made a beeline for our coats. "You've been so nice, so patient with me— Oh, damn! It's just a little token of my gratitude, that's all."

It's some more of her crazy shenanigans, I thought. Probably a mousetrap or something.

"We won't peek," I promised her. "But if it turns out to be a time bomb, I'll never forgive you." I walked over to the divan, picked up the fur cape, and held it open for her. "Better run along now; it's getting late. Besides, the Sergeant and I are expecting company."

Her brown eyes opened wide. "Aren't you going to check up on me? Aren't you going to call the Hotel Stockwood?"

"Sweetheart, I know the truth when I hear it," I said, slipping the cape over her shoulders and finding it difficult to tear my hands away. "All I ask is that you make no attempt to leave town."

"And don't worry about those letters," Regan put in. "If they turn up, we'll deliver them to you on an asbestos platter."

I said, "Take her out to the main hall, Regan, and tell the Commodore to put her in a cab."

Out went the screwball's hand. "Good night, Lieutenant Lash," she murmured, and there was something in that sultry voice of hers that sent little thingumajigs racing up and down my spine. "Do come up, darling," she added, "and seize me sometime."

The next instant she and the Sergeant were on their way to the foyer.

No sooner had the door closed behind them than I sprang toward the open windows and made the long dusty trek across the Egyptian mummy, the sundials, and the kayak. Cripes, it was getting to be a habit.

Reaching one of the windows, I leaned out, thrust my fingers into my mouth, and emitted a shrill whistle. Almost instantly a squad car was alongside the curb, and two familiar faces peered up at me.

"There's a dame coming out of the house in a fur cape and a dinky hat," I called to the dicks. "Do me a favor, boys. Tail her cab. Let me know if she beds down in the Hotel Stockwood. If there's any trouble, square with your C.O."

They waved assent.

Well, here I go again, I thought. Mummy, dials, kayak—and dust.

When Regan lumbered back to the living room, there was a grin a mile wide on his freckled face. But no lipstick, thank goodness. I asked him what he was grinning about.

"It's the Commodore," he chuckled. "You shoulda seen the expression on his mug when me and that dame walked out to the main hall. No kidding, Lash, he walked right up to the dame and said to her, 'Honest to God, Lieutenant, I've seen some great disguises in the movies, but this female get-up of yours beats anything I ever laid eyes on.'"

"Speaking of that babe," I said, moving over to our coats and hats, "let's see what a token of gratitude looks like."

Hurriedly we picked up our coats; cautiously we explored the pockets. A bite by a poisonous snake, I remembered, is indicated by two puncture marks, sometimes one.

"Well, I'll be damned!" Regan exclaimed, amazement in his eyes. "I'll be double damned!"

I was about to ask him what he'd found in his overcoat pocket, but the words died on my lips. For it was then that I touched *my* token of gratitude.

"It can't be! It's impossible!" I exploded, and something like cold steel twisted in my stomach. "I tell you, Regan, it's all a bad dream."

But it was grim reality that stared us in the face when we pulled out our hands and compared tokens—grim reality in the form of two dead goldfish.

CHAPTER FIVE

Strange as it may seem, now that the first jolting shock was over, I began to feel a certain elation at seeing the goldfish. Maybe my doubts as to Martin Chadwick's guilt weren't so unfounded, after all. A goldfish had been found on the corpse. Therefore, it wasn't too unreasonable to assume that Phoebe Foster might have committed the murder. Perhaps—I was grasping at the slightest straw—perhaps she'd been insanely jealous of Paula. Maybe Chadwick had professed his love for Phoebe, then, fickle-like, had given her the brush-off and swung his affections back to his ever loving wife. Uh-huh. Could be. The woman spurned, and all that sort of thing. Garbed in trench coat and black fedora, any passably good actress could impersonate a man for a few minutes. And from what I'd seen of Phoebe Foster's histrionic ability, it was more than just passable.

Something of what was passing through my mind must have been picked up by Regan's mental radar equipment.

He said, "Don't get any queer ideas about that babe, Lash. If she's the one who put that goldfish between Paula's pyramids, you can be damn sure she wouldn't be so dumb as to leave a coupla goldfish in our pockets."

"The fish might have fallen out of Phoebe's handbag and dropped onto the corpse without the screwball knowing a thing about it," I countered as I took from my inside pocket the envelope containing Doc Berlinger's catch and added it to Regan's and mine.

The Sergeant cocked an incredulous eyebrow at me. "G'wan," he scoffed. "Phoebe's no killer. Look. Why don'tcha admit you're wrong about Chadwick? You're no dope, Lash. If you'd stop kidding yourself and face facts, you'd see that everything points to his guilt."

"Regan, I don't have to tell you that my old man was a pretty smart copper," I said evenly. "He could run circles around the best of them, you and me included. Anyway, the thing he tried hardest to drum into my thick head was that the finger of suspicion is merely one finger pointing in one direction. The other three fingers of the hand, he said, always point in the opposite direction."

At this point the doorbell rang. I left the subdued Sergeant, strode into the foyer, and opened the apartment door.

I found the flunky standing outside with three solemn-looking men and two teary-eyed women behind him. One of the dames, the shorter and younger of the two, was almost a dead ringer for Paula Chadwick—same face, same eyes, same radiantly blonde hair—except that she was about thirty-seven and sort of on the plumpish side. Oddly enough, there was something drab about her appearance. She was plenty attractive, but her cheap cloth coat, scuffed shoes, and ringless fingers were a far cry from her dead sister's mink and moolah job.

"Here they are, Sergeant," the flunky began. Then realizing whom he was speaking to, he ceased talking and gawked at me in a manner that said plainly he preferred seeing me in silver fox and high heels.

"It's O.K., Commodore," I said, and added under my breath, "Go on, scram."

Fog-eyed, he lurched away as though he'd seen one apparition too many.

I turned to the funereal five and said, "Will you step in, please?"

One by one, eyes downcast, lips sealed, they filed past me, like five first offenders stepping onto the line-up platform at headquarters.

I thought, H'm. Paula's death has sure knocked them for a loop. Unless I don't know vengeance when I see it, these tight-lipped, grim-faced zombies would give anything to lay hands on Martin Chadwick.

I followed them into the living room. For a painful minute all seven of us stood simpering at each other in that speechless, asinine manner that is always the trademark of stranger meeting stranger. As we stood there a peculiar odor struck my nostrils. It wasn't perfume or highly scented face powder—just something sickeningly sweet, like ether or alcohol, and it seemed to emanate principally from two of the three males present. There was something vaguely familiar about the odor, yet damned if I could label it.

"I'm Lieutenant Lash, and this"—indicating Regan—"is Sergeant Regan of the District Attorney's staff," I said, breaking the tension. "Is it true that you've come up here to help us look for—" I'd have felt foolish saying "hippototamuses," so I shut my mouth and let the question shift for itself.

A tall, gaunt, somewhat emaciated-looking man in his late thirties, with a pronounced stoop in his shoulders and a weasel-like expression on his lean pasty face, said in a whining voice:

"It was Captain Neely's suggestion. But first, Lieutenant Lash, I think a few introductions are in order. I'm Philip Brocton,

Paula Chadwick's brother." His beady black eyes swung to the middle-aged woman standing beside him. "This is my wife, Jessica."

I looked at Jessica and nodded politely. She was almost as tall as her husband, and almost as skinny, with long, dangling arms that at one time must have been dumbwaiter ropes. Worst of all, she had one of those snooty, Look-I'm-somebody-important faces, with a perpetually crinkled nose that gave me the impression that possibly there was a piece of limburger cheese on her upper lip. Frankly, I didn't like her a bit. And judging from the way she ignored my nod, the feeling was mutual.

"And this is my older sister, Mrs. Helen Partridge," Philip Brocton continued, indicating the plumpish carbon copy of Paula Chadwick.

Helen acknowledged my stiff little bow by proffering her hand and permitting a feeble smile to crease her tear-streaked face.

As we shook hands she murmured, "Don't mind Jessica, Lieutenant. Her bark, I assure you, isn't half so terrible as her bite."

Cold fury flickered in Jessica's heavy-lidded eyes. If looks could kill, Helen Partridge was already dead and waiting for *rigor mortis* to set in.

With admirable control Old Vinegar Face said, "I suppose I should resent that remark, Helen dear. But I shan't—really. After all, I believe it's customary to be lenient with the condemned."

Almost out of nowhere, a knotty, capable-looking hand shot out, the palm of which landed smartly on Jessica's snooty face. It was a neat clip, except for one thing: there wasn't enough moxie behind it to suit me.

"Another bright remark like that, Jessica," drawled a soft yet cynical voice, "and I'll knock out your dear little bicuspids." With that the knotty hand fell upon Helen's quivering shoulder, and the cynical voice said to her, "Stop sniffling, you idiot. If you had any gumption, you'd spit in her eye."

Meanwhile Jessica—the red marks of the man's fingers stood out lividly on her face—was glaring at her husband with naked loathing. "Well?" she demanded, and I could see from the way she clenched her gloved hands that she was trembling with rage. "Aren't you going to do something?" She stamped her foot. "Don't just stand there, Philip."

"Do be quiet, Jessica," Philip pleaded in that cringing, whining voice of his. "I'm sure Lieutenant Lash and Sergeant Regan aren't at all interested in our family squabbles."

No, but I was sure interested in the guy who had dished out that Cagney slap. He was a medium-sized fellow, strong, wiry, and not overly hard to look at, with a pair of smoke-gray eyes that seemingly slumbered behind a pair of tortoise-rimmed glasses. Misfortune or something, hard knocks or hard living, had not only etched deep lines in his face, but also powdered his temples with gray. Consequently it was difficult to determine his age. Twenty-eight, thirty, maybe forty; it was anybody's guess. But there was no mistaking his disposition. That twisted, sneering upper lip of his told me all too clearly that here was a sarcastic bastard if ever there was one.

Conscious of my appraisement, he suddenly focused his smoky eyes upon me and said, "You can stop wondering now, Lieutenant. The name's Frank Webster. By marriage I'm related to the Brocton clan. Neither side, though, has ever been known to boast of the relationship. You see, Lieutenant, at heart we're really a pack of stinkers."

I anticipated a roar of protest, and I wasn't disappointed. It was Jessica's voice, however, that had the most venom in it.

"You ungrateful cur," she stormed, her gloved talon-like fingers wriggling as though she were limbering them up for an eye-gouging attack on Frank. "But for us, you fool, you'd be starving to death."

Oh-oh. Here's where she loses those bicuspids, I thought. But I was wrong. Frank, with an eloquent shrug, simply turned his back on her and sauntered over to the teakwood table, where he began toying with the medallion.

Suddenly a pudgy hand touched my elbow.

"Seems nobody around here wants to introduce me, Lieutenant," a pleasant voice piped up on my left. "And I'm really not a bad sort when you get to know me."

I looked at the speaker and liked what I saw. He was a short, squat, roly-poly man in the neighborhood of forty, slightly bald and somewhat flashily dressed (if you could overlook his run-down heels and shabby fedora). What intrigued me most, though, was his moonlike face. There was something open and friendly about it, and its entire surface was seamed with telltale lines of laughter. Here's a man, I thought, who has drunk deep from the cup of life, but whose preference, I bet, runs more toward steins and jiggers.

The regret was real in Helen's voice when she wiped away the last of her tears and said, "I'm so sorry." She slipped her hand affectionately under the fat man's stubby arm. "It *was* thoughtless of me, dear." She shifted her glance. "Lieutenant," she said, and there was that peculiar note of defiance in her voice which a loving frau invariably resorts to when she introduces a none too successful mate, "my husband—Lew Partridge."

"Yes, shake hands with him, Lieutenant," Frank Webster called over his shoulder, and added, "You'll like the guy; most people do. They say Lew's the only one of us who isn't altogether abnormal."

I shook Lew's fleshy hand and was surprised at the amount of pressure behind it.

"Let's get down to business," I suggested, when our five visitors had removed their wraps and parked themselves: Helen, Philip, and Jessica on the divan; Frank on a tufted hassock; and Lew on a chair that, if its squeaks of protest meant anything, gave every indication of collapsing. "It's almost midnight," I continued, consulting my wrist watch. "So whatever it is you want to tell us, please be as brief as possible."

It was Philip Brocton who fired the opening gun: a veritable broadside, sudden, nerve-racking.

"Lieutenant Lash," he said, nibbling nervously at his right forefinger, "my sister Helen and I have every reason to believe that Martin will attempt to murder us."

I hadn't anticipated anything so startling as this, and it sort of knocked the wind out of me. It left me wide-eyed and speechless.

"In other words, Mr. Brocton," Regan put in with an eagerness that bristled all over him, "you're absolutely convinced that Chadwick murdered your sister Paula."

"Is there any doubt?" Philip asked, raising his bushy eyebrows. "As a matter of fact, Sergeant, all of us have been expecting this calamity for quite some time. And now that Martin has done away with Paula, you may rest assured he'll not leave a stone unturned until he deals similarly with Helen and me."

The smug look on Regan's face spoke volumes. "You take it from there, Lash," he said. "It's all yours."

I asked Philip to clarify his statement, to tell me whether it was based on a hunch or something concrete.

He leaned forward, elbows on knees, and for a few seconds stared vacuously at his mutilated forefinger. At last, wetting his dry lips, he replied, "I'll let you be the judge of that, Lieutenant Lash. Last July Martin gave a birthday party for Paula on board the *Spindrift*, a yacht belonging to his friend Jonathan Barrett, the multimillionaire. The amazing thing was that all of us were invited. I say amazing because at that particular time none of us was on speaking terms with Martin."

"At first we were going to refuse the invitation," Jessica threw in haughtily. "But Paula, poor child, was so eager for us to attend that we finally consented."

Frank, teetering on the hassock, gave a derisive laugh. "The hell we did, Lieutenant. All the king's horses couldn't have kept us from accepting that invitation. We figured the golden goose, meaning Martin, was about to start laying us some eggs again. And God knows we needed them. Still do, as a matter of fact."

I thought Jessica would burst a blood vessel. If Philip hadn't placed a detaining paw on her shoulder, I think she would have leaped clear across the room at Frank.

"Nobody asked you to put your two cents in," she shrilled at the smoky-eyed man on the hassock. Then, conscious of Philip's hand on her shoulder, she turned wrathfully on her husband and cried, "I told you not to bring him with us, you fool! Why didn't you leave him home with his stupid toy trains?"

Embarrassment seeped into Philip's pasty face. He lifted his narrow shoulders and let them drop again. Hastily, as though he were afraid Jessica would open her mouth again, he said to me:

"If I remember correctly, we boarded the *Spindrift* about eight o'clock that night. In any event, we'd scarcely set foot on deck when Martin took us aft to one of the cabins, where we found Paula on the verge of tears. I regret to say it was a familiar sight, Lieutenant. It meant Paula and Martin had been having another terrible row."

"Any idea what these squabbles were about?"

"Yes. Martin, for all his openhanded generosity, was positively miserly where Paula was concerned. There wasn't anything he wouldn't buy for her, but he obstinately refused to let her have any funds in her own name. Her weekly allowance, believe it or not, was a paltry ten dollars."

Again a derisive laugh came from the direction of the hassock. "A weekly allowance, of course," Frank drawled, "which didn't go very far toward satisfying Paula's five money-hungry leeches."

"What happened in the cabin, Mr. Brocton?" I asked hurriedly, hoping to avert a free-for-all. "You said you found Paula on
the verge of tears. Then what?"

Philip's beady eyes had locked with Frank's, the way a cobra
stares at a tense and waiting mongoose. Without shifting his gaze,
he said, "Tell Lieutenant Lash and the Sergeant the rest of it, Lew."

Puzzled at the unexpected request, yet sensing, I think, the
silent combat that was going on between Philip and Frank, Lew
Partridge heaved himself to his feet.

"Sure. Why not?" he said. He waddled over to the divan,
stepped behind it, and placed his hands clumsily upon Helen's
shoulders as though he believed the physical contact might give
her the courage to withstand whatever unpleasant details he intended to dish out. Then, with a hesitant, sidelong glance at the
heckler on the hassock, who was still battling it out eye to eye
with Philip, he faced me and said, "When we asked Paula what
was wrong, she said Martin had made absolutely no prepara-
tion for her birthday party; that he'd invited us there on a fool's
errand. But Martin denied this and told us to sit down and keep
quiet. A little while later he opened a locker in the cabin and
brought out an old wooden box with a couple of silver hasps on
it. Laughing as if he'd had a few drinks too many, he opened the
box and showed us what was inside."

At this point Lew paused and peered down at his wife. Immediately she reached up and patted one of his hands.

"It's quite all right, dear," she murmured. "I—I can take it."

Lew's thick fingers tightened hard on her shoulders. He muttered, "Good girl. Whole thing's a lot of damn nonsense, if you
ask me. By this time Martin's probably—"

"The box, Mr. Partridge," I reminded him. "What was in it?"

It seemed an age before he decided to answer. "Three sinister-
looking daggers, Lieutenant," he replied quietly. "And one of
them, I'm sure, you've already seen."

"The murder weapon?"

He shifted his hands a trifle, and I noticed that on each shoulder of his wife's dress was a large stain of sweat.

"That's right," he said. "The other two are exactly the same, except that each hippogriff has for its eyes a different set of precious stones. The murder weapon, as you call it, has rubies; the others, amethysts and sapphires."

"I heard you say hippogriff. Is that what that animal is?" I inquired.

"Damned if I remember ever seeing one in the zoo, Mr. Partridge," Regan put in.

Lew gave a faint smile. "I don't think you ever will, Sergeant. It's a fabled beast of some kind. Has the head and claws of a griffin and the hoofs and tail of a horse."

If it wasn't for showing my ignorance, I'd have asked him what the hell was a griffin.

"Say, that explains the hippopotamuses!" Regan exclaimed, slapping his thigh and laughing uproariously. "Old Man Neely musta figured a hippogriff was a baby hippo." He shook his head. "Homicide men—phooey! Just dumb clucks."

It took a sharp jab in the ribs to silence the Sergeant. When everything was quiet again, I told Lew Partridge to get on with his story.

Somewhat reluctantly he complied. He said that Martin didn't remove the daggers from the box, just gave everyone present a long look at them. Then he put the box back in the locker and spent the next fifteen minutes berating Paula and his in-laws. Called them everything under the sun.

"But it was his last remark," Lew concluded, "that really made us sit up and take notice. Martin informed us that he'd bought the daggers for a very special purpose; namely, that they would help him destroy the three Broctons who made his life a hell on earth: Paula, Helen, and Philip. 'I haven't the foggiest idea when I'll get around to distributing the daggers,' Martin told us. 'But I give you my word of honor that when Paula gets hers, I'll see to it that Helen and Philip get a taste of the same medicine.'"

I didn't say anything; I was too stunned. Maybe Regan was right. Maybe I was just kidding myself about Chadwick.

"What's your opinion, Mrs. Partridge?" I asked, when the knots in my vocal cords had loosened somewhat. "You honestly believe that Chadwick will try to make his threat good?"

There was a controlled terror in her eyes. In a voice that was anything but steady she said, "Yes, I do, Lieutenant—emphatically. If you knew Martin as I do, you'd know that he never goes back on his word. It's almost a religion with him. That night on the yacht I admit I didn't take anything he said very seriously. But now that Paula has been—" Her voice broke completely, and she buried her face in her hands.

As for Lew, he stood behind her, helpless and miserable, his pudgy face twitching in an effort to fight back the tears that were welling in his eyes.

I turned my attention to Philip. He was nibbling his finger again, lost in thought. "And you, Mr. Brocton? You, too, believe you're in danger?" I'd stepped closer to the man. All of a sudden I caught again that sickeningly sweet odor, that familiar yet un-namable fragrance. This time, however, something clicked in my brain. I knew the answer. Formaldehyde.

Poker-faced, he replied, "So much so, Lieutenant, that if Martin isn't apprehended within the next few hours, I shall in-sist that my sister and I receive a maximum of police protection. Frankly, I'd demand that protection right now if the officials at headquarters hadn't assured us that Martin will be under arrest before daybreak."

I made a mental note that, come daylight and no Chadwick, I'd put a three-shift guard on Helen and Philip.

"Where do you live, Mr. Brocton?" I inquired, taking out my notebook and pencil. "If it should prove necessary," I added, "I'll see to it that you and your sister have nothing to worry about in the way of protection."

Everybody in the room seemed to relax. I could sense it. It was almost as though some palpable menace had departed. Even Helen lifted her head; and for the first time that night I saw a spot of color suffuse her white face.

It was Jessica, though, who answered my question. She said, "Fortunately, Lieutenant—perhaps I should say unfortunately" —and her eyes shot a quick, scornful look at Frank Webster—"it so happens that all of us live in the same house. We call it Highrock, an old three-story mansion on Park Terrace East in the Inwood section of Manhattan."

"Just one big happy family, Lieutenant," Frank remarked with an impish grin.

"Park Terrace East." I jotted it down in my notebook. "Isn't that near Isham Park?"

Lew put in an oar. "Yes," he said. "In fact, Highrock actually borders on the park."

Suddenly I remembered that odor of formaldehyde. Formaldehyde, I recalled, is used extensively as an embalming fluid.

I looked at Philip. "Mr. Brocton, do you happen to be an undertaker?" I asked.

His gaunt frame straightened in rigid surprise; his beady eyes popped. "Good Lord! How did you know?"

I told him. When he spoke again, there was a faint note of genuine respect in his voice.

"Yes, undertaker and licensed embalmer," he said. "At present I have a fairly large funeral home on Broadway, just north of 207th Street. Frank"—he jerked his head curtly toward the man on the hassock—"is my partner."

"Yet by no means a silent partner, Lieutenant," Frank drawled. "On the contrary, I believe I'm what you might call the garrulous type. At any rate, I'm much too talkative to suit my precious in-laws. Isn't that so, Jessica?"

There was no response from the woman. Judging from the way she moved her lips, though, I think she was swearing under her breath.

Again I made a few notations in my notebook. "When the body is released from the morgue, Mr. Brocton," I inquired, "do you and Mr. Webster intend to take care of the embalming and burial proceedings?"

"But of course!" Then his face blanched, and he said in his whining voice, "That is, if Martin doesn't get to me first. And speaking of Martin," he added, "I'm sure Helen and I would feel considerably more secure if we knew for certain that the other hippogriff daggers were not in his possession."

"You've got something there," I admitted. "Any idea where they might be?"

"Right here in the apartment. Heaven knows where he's hidden them. Still, I did hear Paula say she'd seen them not so long ago in the study, wooden box and all."

"Well, what are we waiting for?" Regan demanded.

With seven of us doing the searching, Chadwick's den got a thorough overhauling. I mean thorough. In five minutes the room looked like something you'd expect to fish out of a sewer. But it was all in vain: The daggers and the box with the silver hasps were conspicuous by their absence.

Then we spread out all over the apartment, singly and in pairs. Twice, however, we had to converge on the living room to extricate Lew Partridge's leg from the kayak. It was during the second of these two rescue periods that I took time out to look at the searchers. I almost split a gut trying to smother my laughter.

Dust had so blackened their hands and faces that if I had heard some music right then, I'd have sworn I was hobnobbing with a minstrel show.

Presently an exultant cry from Jessica pulled us all into Chadwick's bedroom, a large square room that resembled the interior of an overloaded moving van. Vinegar Face, it appeared, had found the wooden box buried deep in a clothes hamper. I was the last person to reach the room. Yet there was no need to look inside the box to see whether or not the hippogriff daggers were there. The gleam of terror in Philip's eyes, the ghastly expression on Helen's face told me only too plainly that the dagger chest was empty. Which meant—and I had no reason to doubt Lew's story of the threat—that Martin Chadwick, armed with two hippogriff daggers, was hiding somewhere in the city, waiting for an opportunity to give Helen and Philip a taste of the same medicine. Somehow it seemed fantastic. Unless Chadwick had gone berserk or something, the idea of his being a blood-thirsty killer just didn't ring true. Tomorrow, so help me, I'd dig in and do some fancy fact-finding. Among other things, I'd find out where these five money-hungry leeches were on Sunday night between the hours of six and seven. Above all, I'd do some extra-special checking on Phoebe Foster.

It was directly after the discovery of the box—twelve-fifty by my wrist watch—that the Broctons, the Partridges, and Frank Webster decided to call it a night. Silent and glum they'd entered the apartment. Now, in departing, they were even more so.

"And don't lose any sleep over Chadwick," I advised them after they'd slipped into their wraps and filed into the foyer. "Don't forget, there'll be men stationed outside your house first thing in the morning. In fact, if it makes you feel any safer, I'll have the Thirty-fourth Precinct post a couple of patrolmen right now."

Philip said it wasn't necessary; that so long as they remained a group of five there was no danger of Martin making an attack.

The real danger, he insisted, would materialize only when either he or Helen had occasion to leave Highrock alone.

"In that case," I said, "you and Mrs. Partridge had better stick close to Highrock for a few days, at least until we locate Chadwick. If you have to leave the house, one of the men on guard will escort you to wherever you want to go."

Philip said, "These guards you speak of, Lieutenant—" He paused, cleared his throat. "Am I expected to provide their meals?"

"Certainly not," I snapped. Cripes, I thought, the boys had better take along canteens or this guy's liable to charge them for a glass of water.

Regan opened the apartment door and said, "Come on, folks, I'll see you out to your car." The wily Sergeant probably had a few questions he didn't want me to hear.

As I was about to close the door behind them I heard Frank Webster give a half-smothered chuckle. "Philip, I don't want to scare the daylights out of you, old man," I heard him whisper, "but wouldn't it be a hell of a note if Martin had sneaked into Highrock while we were down here? Who knows? He may be up there now sharpening those daggers."

Nice cheerful feller, I thought, closing the door. The kind of bastard you'd like to take on a hunting trip—and shoot. But right then and there my thoughts were rudely interrupted by the wail of a siren. I dashed back to the living room, clambered over the mummy, the sundials, and the kayak, and arrived at one of the windows in time to see a squad car stop at the curb. Apparently the screwball's two shadows had returned.

"Your girl friend didn't go to no Hotel Stockwood, Lieutenant," one of the dicks called up to me as I leaned out. "Her name's Penny Forbes and she's got an apartment in the Sheldon Arms on Ninety-seventh Street and West End Avenue. Some dish, Lieutenant."

There was a muffled laugh, then the car shot forward, cir-
cled to the left, and came to a standstill on the other side of the
Drive. A minute later I saw the five vultures and Regan barge out
of the front entrance. Chuckling, I pulled in my head. If Sergeant Regan contemplated a visit to the Hotel Stockwood sometime during the day, he was sure in for a helluva surprise.

But when Regan came back to the living room, it was Lieutenant Lash who'd got the surprise of his life.

"Hey! Snap out of it," Regan barked, waving his hand in front
of my face. "What ails you, Lash? Holy Canarsie, you act like
you'd seen a ghost."

"Look," I cried, pointing to the rickety teakwood table. "The
Cellini medallion! It's gone!"

CHAPTER SIX

It was the phone at my bedside, not the alarm clock, that woke me up at eight-thirty that Monday morning of December seventh. Exhausted, I'd flopped into my nest at three A.M. But instead of falling asleep right away, I'd lain on my back, smoking in the dark, racking my brains in an effort to come up with the answers to some seemingly unanswerable questions. And I'd got nowhere. What's more, when sleep had finally caught up with me, I dreamed that I was cleaning goldfish with a hippogriff dagger and serving them to Sam Willis on a Cellini medallion.

Knuckling the cobwebs out of my eyes, I fumbled for the phone and yawned a bleak hello into the receiver. It was Old Man Neely.

A little under thirty minutes ago, he informed me, two prowl-car cops from the 34th Precinct had found Martin Chadwick's Lincoln sedan parked on Broadway at 213th Street, right next to Isham Park.

"Know what that means?" Neely fired at me.

Hell, yes. Looking at it from Neely's and the D.A.'s side of the fence, it meant that Chadwick was prowling around Highrock with two daggers in his pocket and murder in his heart. Then I remembered Frank Webster's whispered conversation with Philip

Brocton, particularly that part about Chadwick sneaking into Highrock during their absence. A cold sweat broke out on my brow.

"Dan"—I was almost afraid to ask the question—"Dan, everything's all right up there, isn't it?"

"Nobody's been bumped off, if that's what you mean."

"Did Dorsey and Ackema get their instructions?"

"Yeah. Went on guard at seven sharp; called in the minute they got there. By the way, Chris, when you go to Highrock, don't be surprised if you see half the police force hiding behind bushes. Strenz is going nuts since he heard about those cops finding Chadwick's car."

In a way I couldn't blame Carl Strenz for putting on pressure. Time and time again Chadwick had made the prosecutor for the people a laughingstock in the courts; had walked off with too many "not guilty" decisions under his belt. Strenz would stop at nothing to get his hooks in Chadwick. He'd bear down on this squeal with everything he had. And if I persisted in sticking my neck out, if I kept on shooting off my mouth that Chadwick was innocent, I'd find myself back in harness, pounding a beat somewhere in Staten Island. Not that I had any intention of backing down. My pop used to say, "If you're sure you're right about something, stick to it, no matter what happens. They can take away your rank, but by God, you won't smell that way." Smart guy, my pop.

"Come on, Dan, give out with some dope," I said. "How's about that autopsy report?"

"Got it here in front of me. Nothing that you don't already know, except that Paula was pregnant—six weeks."

"That damn well proves that Chadwick didn't kill her," I said. "Big shots like Chadwick are extra-keen about having a son. A son is a sure way to keep a famous name alive. Maybe Chadwick didn't care two pins about Paula; but you can bet your boots he wouldn't have stooped to murder. Murder would have rubbed out that potential son of his."

I heard a contemptuous snort at the other end of the line. "Some day, Chris," Neely said, "I'm going to take you up on my knee and explain the facts of life. Didn't you ever hear of a wife two-timing her husband? Well, that's probably what happened. Paula was playing around; Chadwick got wise; then—wham!— seven inches of steel."

"You're nuts," I snapped. "If there's any truth in it, then Paula's brother Philip or her sister Helen must be the father of the child. Don't forget, Dan, they're also on Chadwick's list. Say, what about that dagger chest? The fingerprint men get anything?"

"Plenty. Said it was crawling with Chadwick's prints—and *only* Chadwick's. Was that Jessica Brocton dame wearing gloves when she found it?"

"Yeah. And what about the murder weapon?"

"Same thing—all Chadwick's. And don't tell me they aren't, Chris. They have a set of his prints on file at headquarters. Got 'em during the war at the time of that air-raid precaution business."

Still harping on the subject of fingerprints, I asked him about Sam's taxi.

"Forget it," he advised. "If we ran down all the prints picked up on that cab, we'd never get done with this squeal. If it makes you any happier, though, they didn't find any of Chadwick's on the taxi. That cab driver, by the way, was released early this morning. Strenz said the guy was absolutely in the clear; no tie-in with Chadwick."

"Dan, I want you to—"

"I know," he interrupted wearily. "The Lincoln sedan. Don't worry, they'll give it a treatment as soon as it reaches the garage."

I said, "That and something else. I want a complete history on that actress, Penny Forbes."

"The goldfish dame you told me about?"

"Uh-huh. And if you hit a snag, try her other names: Jane Willoughby and Phoebe Foster. Anything you can get, Dan. In the meantime I'll pay the young lady a visit. If anything special turns up, call me at her apartment in the Sheldon Arms."

Neely was silent for a while. "Hope you know what you're doing," he said at last. "Personally, I think you ought to go to Highrock and join in that man hunt. Bet Regan and his boys are up there tearing the park to pieces."

I laughed. "Not Regan. At this minute he's tearing his hair out in the Hotel Stockwood. Say, Dan, if the Sergeant should phone, don't let on you know anything about the goldfish dame. Tell him I'm on my way to Highrock."

"O.K. But you'd better produce, Chris. Something tells me you're on your way to Staten Island." And he hung up.

The thought of meeting the diminutive screwball again made me extra-particular that morning. I showered, shaved, and spent at least five minutes at my tie rack before I decided that a maroon-colored tie would go nice with my new gray tweeds. I even decided to use the hair tonic my druggist had foisted on me last week. When I picked up the bottle, however, my eyes fell upon a framed photograph that stood on the dresser. Somehow I didn't like the smirk on Pop's face at that moment. Anyway, back went the hair tonic, unopened.

It was nine-forty when I squeezed into a Seventh Avenue downtown express and opened my morning paper.

No question about it, the newspapers had really spotlighted the crime. Even the front page of my paper, famous for its lack of sensationalism and cheesecake, had broken out with some extra-large headlines and pictures. The tabloids—I could see them all around me—had devoted their front pages exclusively to photos of Sam Willis' taxi and its beautiful corpse, with special emphasis, of course, on Paula's anything but gruesome twosome.

I began reading. From the very start it was evident that Strenz had gone all out to convince the newspapermen of Chadwick's guilt. Blast him, he'd even made a statement to the effect that if Chadwick wasn't apprehended within forty-eight hours, he'd put his top-flight sleuth, Sergeant Regan, in charge of the case. On the same page, however, was a statement from Chief of Detectives Gilbride. Gilbride was fully confident that the capable Detective-Lieutenant Christopher Lash and his West Side Homicide men would have Chadwick in custody before nightfall. I made a mental addition to my Christmas list: one box of Corona Coronas for Chief of Detectives Gilbride.

For my part the most interesting thing in the paper was a lengthy story of Chadwick's life, with pictures depicting the high spots of his career. One picture in particular caught my attention. It showed Chadwick as guest of honor at some lawyers' shindig, and sitting beside him, with a fat cigar in her mouth, was the Willoughby-Foster-Forbes dame. According to the caption, she was Miss Penny Forbes, one of the scintillating beauties in *The Goldfish Gaieties*.

Goldfish! A devastating thought began kicking the stuffings out of my Penny-is-the-killer theory. Quickly I turned to the theatrical section in the paper and ran my finger down the alphabetical list of stage attractions. Sure enough, there it was. *The Goldfish Gaieties;* John Drew Theatre, West Forty-fifth Street; matinees Wednesdays and Saturdays. Again that devastating thought: Could it be possible that the members of the cast were handing out goldfish as a sort of advertisement? Musical comedies have large casts. Cripes, it would take an eternity to check up on every performer in that show. Incidentally, I noticed there was no mention of Penny Forbes in the ad. Penny, no doubt, was one of the leg-kickers in the first line. H'm. I must get me a seat in the first row.

Flipping back to the story of Chadwick's life, I took another look at that guest-of-honor caption. The shindig had been held at the Waldorf-Astoria on the afternoon of December first. December first—only six days ago! Yet Penny told me last night that she hadn't seen Chadwick since early November.

At the 96th Street station I shouldered my way out of the train, shot upstairs, and strode north on Broadway to 97th. Turning left, I walked to West End Avenue. The Sheldon Arms, an attractive twelve-story apartment building, stood on the northwest corner. A Negro hall attendant opened the door for me.

"Where can I find Miss Penny Forbes?" I asked, showing him my shield.

The Negro's eyes widened; he clapped a hand across his gaping mouth. "Mr. Detective, I've been expecting something like this," he finally blurted out. "But she don't mean no harm, boss. That crazy fool trick Miss Penny play Friday was just her way of making fun."

I asked him what devilment she'd been up to.

He raised his eyebrows and looked at me, rather puzzled. "How come you don't know?" he inquired. "Ain't you here on complaint of one of the tenants?"

I assured him that such was not the case. I insisted, though, on hearing about Friday.

A deep chuckle rumbled in his throat. "Miss Penny, she put a goldfish in everybody's letter box. Yeah, man. And the folks here didn't like it nohow. Mr. Thompson, the gentleman on the fifth floor, said he'd get her pinched, sure enough."

Somehow my sympathy was all on the side of the tenants. With Penny Forbes on the premises, the Sheldon Arms was probably the only apartment building in town that wasn't 100 per cent rented.

Unfolding my newspaper, I pointed to Chadwick's picture on the front page. It was an excellent likeness of the distinguished lawyer, except that the photograph emphasized his belligerent

jaw and broad expanse of brow rather than his soft, compassion-
ate eyes.

"How often does he come here?" I asked.

Surprise flooded the Negro's face. "Man, you're crazy. That
wife-killer ain't never set foot in this here house." His eyes swung
nervously toward the main door. "But if I see him, boss, I ain't
gonna hang around for no second look."

For a moment I was stunned. I'd expected an altogether different answer. Frankly, I'd sort of sold myself on the idea that
Penny's relations with Chadwick weren't exactly on the up and
up. To put it bluntly, I'd figured there were two keys to Penny's
apartment, and that one of them dangled on Chadwick's key ring.

"How do you know he's never been here?" I inquired. "You're
not on a twenty-four-hour shift. Maybe the night attendant—"

Instantly came an indignant denial. He and the night boy had
discussed the murder that morning; had poured over the newspapers together. If the night boy had recognized Chadwick as a
frequent visitor to the Sheldon Arms, he would have mentioned
it—bragged about it.

Again I unfolded my paper. This time I pointed to Paula's
picture. "And what about Mrs. Chadwick?"

"No dice, boss. Take my word for it, that gal was never in the
Sheldon Arms."

I dealt myself a new hand. "While you were on duty yesterday, did Miss Forbes leave her apartment?" I asked.

"No, sir. I didn't see Miss Penny at all. Saw her this morning,
though. She came down in the elevator and asked me to run out
and buy her a flock of newspapers."

"She have any visitors yesterday?"

"No, sir. That is, up till six o'clock. That's when the night
boy takes over."

I asked him for Penny's apartment number.

"Apartment Three-twenty-two—third floor. Here boss, use the elevator."

He took me to the rear of the main hall and ushered me into a self-service elevator. He even reached in and pressed the button for me. Then I was gliding upward, a bull in a gilded cage.

When I located 322—strangely, there weren't any goldfish painted on the door—I placed an ear where it would do the most good. But all I could hear was silence. So I pressed the doorbell. Two things happened inside: A dog began barking, and muted chimes began playing "Call to the Post"—the *da-da-dee-da* they always bugle at racetracks.

After a brief interval the door swung open, and there was Penny, a vision in pink pajamas and diaphanous negligee.

"Well, of all people!" she exclaimed, and despite the fetching smile on her face, I could see she was a bit shocked. "Come in, bloodhound," she added graciously. "You're just in time for toast and coffee."

I didn't say anything. I didn't even move, just stood there dumblike in the doorway, drinking in the silken beauty of her; too transfixed even to shake off her confounded dog, which was chewing one of the cuffs of my trousers.

Finally, realizing that I wasn't in the front row of the John Drew Theatre, I said, "Good morning, Miss Jane-Phoebe-Penny. How's everything at the Hotel Stockwood?"

A crimson flush suffused her cheeks. "All right, smarty pants," she murmured. "So you're a great detective. Behave yourself, Cuspidor." She bent over, swooped the black Spitz into her arms, and took a piece of my cuff out of his mouth. "Oh, I'm terribly sorry," she giggled, handing me the strip of cloth. "But you'll just have to forgive the naughty little rascal, Lieutenant. He used to belong to a ham actor and—well, I guess Cuspidor just never got over living on the cuff."

With that she turned around and walked into her living room. So I stuffed the strip of tweed into my pocket, stepped into the foyer, and closed the door behind me.

When I joined her, she said, "Make yourself comfortable, darling. I'll have toast and coffee ready in a jiffy." And ignoring my vehement protests (I had visions of her uncorking a bottle of arsenic), she sailed into a spotlessly white kitchen.

Removing my overcoat, I sat down in an easy chair and began studying my surroundings. The living room was large, tastefully furnished, and splashed with sunlight. Yet a sort of helter-skelter, hit-or-miss untidiness predominated. Newspapers lay scattered on the floor, bowls of goldfish rested on practically every flat surface of furniture, and stacked in one corner of the room was a pile of sporting paraphernalia, including a jockey's cap and blouse and a prize fighter's aluminum cup.

The real eye-catcher, as far as I was concerned, was the large leather-bound book that rested on one of the end tables. Since the table was only a short distance from me, I could easily discern the title of the book: My Diary.

I thought, Wow! If I can get to that book before Penny pops in from the kitchen, maybe I'll find something written down for the sixth of December.

Soundlessly I eased out of my chair and tiptoed to the end table. Swiftly, with eyes riveted on the kitchen, I reached down, grasped the book, and opened it with deft, inquisitive fingers.

Wham! Something green and horrible sprang at my throat, and I unleashed a roar that all but peeled the paint off the walls. Arms flailing, I beat my fists against this green horror. Panic-stricken, I punched and pounded until the thing slithered downward and dropped silently to the floor. I looked down. An imitation garter snake of green cloth lay at my feet—one of those novelty-store serpents that pop out at you from almost anything.

Red-faced, I kicked the snake under the sofa, conscious that muffled laughter was seeping from the kitchen. I couldn't see Penny, but something told me she was leaning limply against the refrigerator with a dish towel stuffed in her mouth.

Presently the screwball's sultry voice oozed into the living room. She said, "O.K., Peeping Tom, come and get it."

Grinning, I walked into the kitchen and found her sitting at a table in a cozy little breakfast nook. There were two steaming cups of coffee on the table and a stack of buttered toast that looked like the leaning tower of Pisa.

"See what happens to nosy little boys?" she said as I sat down and reached for the sugar. "Let this be a lesson to you, Lieutenant. Remember, darling, a girl's diary is something sacred; she doesn't put it in the parlor with the family Bible."

I admitted my stupidity. I thought, Pop wouldn't have made that mistake. He used to say, "Chris, a woman may reveal her dairy a bit, but she'll go to any extreme to hide her diary."

For a minute or two we sat there, sipping coffee, nibbling toast. Even Cuspidor was nibbling. But, what the hell, it was worth a cuff just to sit there and feast my eyes on Penny. Suddenly I discovered that the toast was buttered on both sides.

"Aren't you a bit extravagant?" I asked her.

She gave me her big brown eyes. "Gosh, no. I just happen to like my lower lip as well as I do my upper. Don't you?"

That did it. I pushed away my coffee, pushed back my chair, and, standing up, pushed out my chest. "Look, Miss Forbes," I blasted. "I didn't come here for a *kaffeeklatsch*. Murder is serious business. It might interest you to—"

But the ringing of Penny's chimes interrupted me.

"Gracious! Who can that be?" she said, standing up and throwing me a quizzical look. "Some of your boys, Lieutenant? Tsk! Tsk! You should have told me; I'd have baked a cake."

With Cuspidor barking at her heels, Penny flounced into the living room. I was right behind them. Then, when Penny got to the foyer and opened the door, I almost jumped out of my shoes. Sergeant Regan stood framed in the doorway.

"Why, you dirty so-and-so!" he exploded, storming into the living room and eying me as though I were Paula Chadwick's ghost. "Holy Canarsie, Lash, howja know? Howja know this babe was here in the Sheldon Arms and not in the Stockwood?"

I told him. "And how did you know?" I asked.

He peeled off his overcoat and tossed it onto a chair. "Remember last night when I took Gorgeous here out to the hall?" I nodded. "Well, I told the Commodore to put the babe in a cab and get me the hack driver's number. The rest was simple. This morning the hack bureau put me in touch with the cabbie, and the cabbie put me wise to the switch. But I didn't know that Phoebe Foster was Penny Forbes till I had a little confab with that hall boy downstairs."

"Well, now that you've discovered who I am and where I live, just what do you two geniuses want with me?" Penny asked as she sat down on the sofa.

"I don't know about Lash, sugar," Regan said, plopping down beside her, "but my visit is strictly unofficial. I'll tell you what it is as soon as Lash clears out."

Penny studied his freckled face. Whatever she saw there, it prompted her to rise and walk over to the pile of sporting paraphernalia. Picking up a football, she sauntered back to the sofa, handed Regan the pigskin, and sat down.

"What's the idea, beautiful?" he questioned, gaping at the football.

She said, "Just in case you get any ideas, Sergeant, of making a pass."

Regan could take it, all right. He reddened but laughed every bit as loud as I did.

"Penny," I said, moving over to the sofa and standing directly in front of her, "Regan and I were a little surprised last night to find those goldfish in our pockets. Is it some sort of stunt that you and the cast are doing to advertise *The Goldfish Gaieties?* Or is it something you thought up by yourself?"

The Sergeant's ears had pricked up. "Say, sugar, are you in that show?" he asked excitedly.

She nodded.

"Shut up, Regan," I said. "You and your Annie Oakleys can wait. . . . Answer my question, Penny."

Two furrows creased her brow. "I'm afraid it's my own idea. In a way, handing them out does advertise the show. But mostly I do it because—well, because I get an awful lot of fun out of it."

"Sure nobody else in the show hands them out?"

"Nobody in the show is as crazy as I am—about goldfish, I mean."

"Then how do you account for the fact, Penny, that a goldfish was found last night tucked away in the bosom of the corpse?"

Penny blanched, and I saw the pulse in her throat increase its beat. "You—you wouldn't fool a girl, mister?" she asked shakily.

I told her it was gospel truth; that unless she came through with a plausible explanation, I'd be forced to slap a warrant on her and hold her as a murder suspect.

"But I haven't any explanation," she said, and for the first time since I'd known her there was a glint of real terror in her eyes. "Honest, Lieutenant, I haven't the slightest idea how that goldfish got there."

"Did you ever meet Paula Chadwick?" I asked.

"No, never. I admit I've heard a great deal about her from Martin, but I've never laid eyes on her. And that's the truth."

I asked her whether she'd ever met Chadwick's in-laws. "No," she answered. "But Martin told me plenty about them. Said they were a pack of chiselers."

"Where does Frank Webster fit into the picture?"

"He was married to Barbara, the next to youngest of the Broc-ton girls. Barbara and her parents were killed in a plane crash while Frank was overseas in the Army. It was a terrible blow to Frank, but he didn't kick up half the fuss that Philip and Helen and Paula did. Philip and Helen actually blamed Martin for the tragedy."

"How come?"

"When Martin and Paula got back from their honeymoon, Martin thought it would be nice if Paula's parents and sister had a little vacation. He knew Barbara was worrying her heart out about Frank's being in the war. So he pulled strings to get them passage on a plane, and sent them off to California for a two-weeks holiday. Then the plane cracked up in the Rockies, and Martin's troubles began."

My next question concerned Philip. I asked her whether she knew anything special about him.

Penny said, "For one thing, he's only Paula's half-brother. Philip's mother was the first Mrs. Brocton. She died giving birth to Philip; and about a year later Philip's father married again. The old man, I believe, was an undertaker."

"And Philip fell heir to his funeral parlor, eh?"

"No. Old Mr. Brocton had a little hole in the wall somewhere in the Bronx. As I understand it, he spent more time embalming himself in the gin mills than he did embalming his customers in the funeral parlor. If it hadn't been for his family—Philip, the second Mrs. Brocton, and the three girls—the business would have gone to the dogs. They did everything from embalming to pall-bearing. Egged on by Philip, Helen and Barbara even got their boy friends to lend a hand—for free, of course. In fact, that's how Lew and Frank learned the business. Later, Philip even put Jessica to work."

I said, "They must have made a mint of money to be able to buy that old mansion they're living in."

"Are you kidding?" Penny demanded. "It's Martin who owns Highrock—lock, stock, and barrel. He lived there before he married Paula. When he and his bride moved to the apartment on Riverside Drive, Martin let his in-laws park themselves in Highrock, rent free. He felt so terrible about the plane crash that he was willing to do almost anything for them."

"H'm. I bet they just about squeezed him dry," I muttered.

"Not Frank; he was overseas at the time. But he made up for it later. In fact, he and Philip didn't give Martin a moment's peace until he financed a big funeral home for them in upper Manhattan. Then the others went to work on him. Why, if Martin hadn't put a stop to their crazy whims, they'd have wiped him out financially. When he finally put the screws down, that was the beginning of his trouble with Paula. In all fairness, though, I think Paula was just a cat's-paw for her precious family. They made the snowballs, and it was up to little Paula to throw them."

"How about the Partridges, Penny?" I inquired. "They seem pretty decent."

"That's what you think. And as for Jessica, she's got a chemical laboratory up in Highrock that set Martin back a cool four thousand. Before her marriage, Jessica used to be a teacher of chemistry in some whistle-stop high school. Now she spends all her time in her lab trying to find a substitute for human blood. After draining Martin of his blood, I guess it was the only thing left for her to do."

There was a brief silence. At last I said, "You lied to us last night, Penny. Why did you say you hadn't seen Chadwick since early November? You were with him at the Waldorf-Astoria last Monday afternoon."

She snapped her fingers. "Jeepers, that's right, Lieutenant. Say, you do get around. But don't get the wrong slant. Martin didn't take me to that affair. I was there with the chorus of

The Goldfish Gaieties, one of the entertainers, that's all. I hardly spoke to Martin. Didn't see him until a newspaper photographer sat me down at Martin's table and snapped a picture."

I pointed to the newspapers on the floor. "I see you've read the morning papers. Do you still think Chadwick is innocent?"

"I don't believe everything I read," she retorted. "And neither do you; you wouldn't be hounding me like this if you did. But if you think I had anything to do with Paula's murder, you're barking up the wrong tree. If I were you, Lieutenant, I'd concentrate a bit on those jackals at Highrock."

I said, "Don't worry, angel, I intend to."

I wasn't kidding. One of those jackals had swiped the medallion; and since theft and murder have a certain affinity for each other, it was quite possible that the thief and the killer were one and the same person. If only Penny could explain that damn goldfish.

"Aw, you're both having daydreams," Regan scoffed. "Go ahead, Lash, tell her what happened this morning."

The babe looked at me expectantly. So I told her about the Lincoln sedan and how it sort of put an extra coat of guilt on Chadwick.

Penny sat quiet, biting her lower lip. Seconds later, she said, "I know all about that silly threat. Martin told me he didn't mean a word of it. The idea behind the whole thing was to frighten that bunch so they'd steer clear of him, leave him alone."

"Apparently Chadwick thinks a great deal of you. Penny," I said. "At any rate, he certainly doesn't mind letting you in on his personal affairs."

"When a man has troubles, Lieutenant," she countered, "he's liable to pour them out to anyone who'll listen. I just happen to come from a long line of good listeners."

"Did he tell you that Paula was expecting?"

"Yes. And he was very happy about it."

"When did he tell you?"

"Last Monday at the Waldorf."

"One more thing, Penny. I'd like you to give me an account of what you did yesterday. Where you went, the people you met, and so on."

"Give me something difficult," she said airily. "I spent the entire day in this apartment. No visitors, no phone calls, no nothing. Didn't go out until after I'd heard that ten-o'clock radio flash about Paula. And you know the rest."

I thought, Yeah. I also know it's easy to avoid being seen by a hall attendant. All you have to do is run a self-service elevator down to the basement and skip out to the street by way of the delivery entrance. But for the time being, Penny, I'll give you the benefit of the doubt.

From the bedroom came the loud peal of a telephone.

"Bet that's my bookie," Penny said, bouncing to her feet and dashing into the adjoining room.

I was two steps ahead of her. If Martin Chadwick was on the wire, Lieutenant Lash wanted an ear right smack on the receiver. I picked up the phone and signaled Penny to say hello into it. As she leaned over and spoke into the transmitter, her soft brown hair felt like a caress on my cheek.

A sharp voice crackled in my ear. Oh-oh! Neely. "Yes, Dan. What is it?" I asked.

An endless stream of words began pouring out of the receiver. For fully sixty seconds he didn't so much as draw a breath. Then came silence, swift and startling. He'd hung up.

"Get into your coat, Regan!" I cried, cradling the phone and sprinting into the living room. "Quick, Regan! Let's get down to that jalopy of yours."

"What's wrong, Lash?" he demanded as he watched me wrestle with my overcoat. "Christ, man, speak up!"

"Chadwick!" I shouted, snatching the Sergeant's coat and throwing it at him. "Chadwick sneaked into the Webster-Brocton Funeral Home about twenty minutes ago and stabbed Philip Brocton!"

CHAPTER SEVEN

Grant's Tomb was a tiny dot in the rear-vision mirror before my pounding heart and frantic lungs had the decency to lie down and keep quiet.

"Looks like I've been all wet about Chadwick," I muttered to Regan as we bulleted north on the West Side Highway. "Guess I owe you an apology, Regan."

"Forget it," he said. "Hell, everybody can't be a D.A. detective. The thing that gets me is how Chadwick managed to stab Philip without tangling with the Homicide tail."

"That's got me hanging on the ropes, too," I admitted. "Neely, damn it, didn't bust out with too much information. All I know is that Philip was attacked somewhere in the funeral parlor, and that Chadwick made a clean getaway."

"You said Chadwick got him in the back, right above the shoulder blade."

I said, "Yeah. Just a flesh wound. But that won't stop Strenz; he'll act as if Philip got it straight in the heart."

After that I lapsed into silence. I didn't feel too good. Carl Strenz would probably override Gilbride's protests and put Regan in charge. He'd insist that the negligence of a Homicide man (Dorsey, one of our most dependable boys) had made it possible for Chadwick to attack a man who was under guaranteed police protection. Strenz's real gripe, though, would be that Chadwick had been able to make a getaway. There was only one comforting thought in my mind: This latest development was proof positive that Penny wasn't going around playfully sticking daggers into people. And believe you me, I was glad. The little goldfish gal had made a deeper dent in my heart than I cared to admit.

Not until the jalopy had veered off the highway and onto Dyckman Street and Broadway did I open my mouth again.

"Go straight up Broadway," I directed Regan. "Neely said the funeral parlor's on the right-hand side, just north of 207th Street."

One block . . . two blocks . . . then we spotted it: a long, huge, vertical electric sign with "Funeral Home" in large white letters. The sign was attached to a trim, two-story red-brick building across the face of which was another sign: "Webster-Brocton Funeral Home." Obviously, the entire building housed Frank and Philip's undertaking establishment, for I could see the same type of cream-colored Venetian blinds in the upper windows that I saw behind the expanse of plate glass on the lower level.

On the south side of the building was a long ramp that led down to what was apparently a one-story brick garage. Big sliding doors shielded its wide entrance, yet I hadn't the slightest doubt that behind them stood a hearse, a mortuary truck, and possibly two or three limousines.

We pulled up behind a radio patrol car, leaped out, pushed through the usual knot of gawkers, and strode into the sepulchral quietness of the funeral home. Instantly we were stopped in our tracks by a cop who stood on the main floor midway between a broad, bronze-railed stairway and a door with a neat glass "Office" sign hanging above it. Politely, the cop stated that no visits to the reposing rooms would be permitted until one o'clock in the afternoon. Then my shield sent his white-gloved hand to his cap.

"Go right in, Lieutenant," he said, pointing to the office door on his left. "They're waiting for you."

I pushed open the door, beckoned Regan to follow me, and stepped into a small room that contained a flat-topped desk, a couple of steel filing cabinets, a leather couch, and a few leather chairs. Venetian blinds and velvet drapes hung at the windows; a gray carpet covered the floor.

There were three people in the office: Philip, Jessica, and Lew Partridge. Philip, his lean face drawn and deathly pale, sat propped up on the couch with a flock of cushions behind him. His suit coat was draped over his stooped shoulders, but I could tell by the bulge at the back that his wound had been copiously padded and bandaged. To look at him, you'd think he'd taken Iwo Jima singlehanded.

Jessica, attired in deep mourning, sat on the edge of the couch with her husband's hand clasped tightly between her own. She was pale, teary-eyed, frightened-looking. Yet the moment she saw us her eyes gave out with a look that was unmistakably hostile.

As for Lew, he was slumped in a swivel chair behind the desk, his fat face as ashen-gray as the carpet on the floor, his eyes dimmed with worry and bewilderment. On seeing Regan and me, however, he lurched to his feet, beamed a welcoming smile, and held out his pudgy right hand. Regan and I took turns pumping it.

"Helluva close shave," Lew said with a forced laugh. "Philip must have had a rabbit's foot in his pocket."

"How fortunate for the Lieutenant," Jessica sneered. "Perhaps"—and she glanced at me as though I belonged in one of her husband's boxes—"perhaps Philip and Helen would have better protection if the district attorney called off the police and handed out rabbits' feet."

I ignored her. I slipped out of my coat and hat, pulled up one of the chairs, and sat down near the couch. Regan, loosening his overcoat and tilting his hat back, parked himself on the edge of the desk.

"How do you feel, Mr. Brocton?" I asked. "Seems to me they should have sent you to a hospital."

"Frank and Lew suggested it, but I wouldn't permit it," he replied with a wan smile. "Dr. Mullen said the wound wasn't anything serious. All I have to do is take it easy for a while. As soon as I feel stronger Jessica will take me home in the car." Pausing, he fixed a shrewd eye upon me. Then in his whining voice he said, "All this has been expensive, Lieutenant. Doctors cost money. Do you think if I sent the bill to the district attorney's office—"

"I wouldn't know, Mr. Brocton," I interrupted tartly. "In the meantime," I added, "do you feel strong enough to give me all the details of the stabbing?"

He nodded and said, "At ten-thirty this morning I went downstairs to the embalming room to embalm a body that Frank and one of the helpers had brought in shortly after ten. Lew was working here in the office at the time, and Frank was upstairs in one of the reposing rooms. The corpse upstairs had purged a bit in the night and needed a shot of formaldehyde."

"Just a minute," I broke in. "Where was Dorsey all this time? Dorsey, I understand, was your bodyguard this morning."

"That's right. Lew, Frank, and I usually walk here from Highrock; but Dorsey insisted that we drive to work in our car. He even came along with us. As a matter of fact, he also went down to the embalming room with me at ten-thirty. However, he didn't stay very long. When I took my scissors and cut open the carotid in the neck of the corpse, your man Dorsey became so terribly pale that I thought for a moment he was going to be sick. He said he'd never seen an embalming; didn't think he could take it. So

I assured him that I'd be perfectly safe and sent him upstairs to catch a breath of air."

He'll catch more than air when I lay hands on him, I thought. Aloud I said, "Where is he now?"

Lew cut in; he was back in the swivel chair. He said, "Downstairs in the casket room. He's down there with two detectives from the Thirty-fourth Precinct. I'll take you there whenever you and the Sergeant are ready."

I thanked him and turned my attention to Philip again.

"Dorsey had been gone about five minutes," he explained, "when suddenly I became conscious that the swinging door between the embalming room and the casket room was slowly creaking open. At first, thinking it was Dorsey, I continued working on the corpse. But the noise behind me sounded so stealthy that I whirled around, just in time to see Martin Chadwick poke his head out from behind the swinging door and glare in at me. The instant he saw me he pulled his head back.

"Then—then I did a very foolish thing, Lieutenant. Thinking that Martin had dashed up the flight of stairs in the casket room, I ran after him in the hopes that if I reached the head of the stairs in time, I could shout to Dorsey or Lew to nab Martin at the front entrance. Unfortunately, Martin did nothing of the kind."

Eagerly I leaned closer. "Go on, Mr. Brocton. What happened?"

Philip's face was inscrutable; his beady eyes, though, showed a trace of embarrassment. He said, "Evidently Martin expected me to run after him. In any event he must have stationed himself directly to the side of the swinging door, for as I dashed into the casket room his leg shot out, and I went sprawling face down on the floor. The next thing I knew I felt a terrible burning sensation in my right shoulder."

"But if you were lying face down," I mused, "I can't understand how Chadwick missed the vital spot in your back. You were sprawled out, unquestionably helpless at the moment; yet Chadwick inflicted only a flesh wound. Were the lights out?"

Philip leaned back on the cushions, heaving a long, broken sigh. "No. The small light at the head of the stairs was on, and also the fire-exit light over the door that leads to the alleyway between this building and our garage. Still, there wasn't much light in the room. Personally, I think Martin was too eager. I'd scarcely hit the floor when he stabbed me. Furthermore, I'm almost positive he realized the harmlessness of the blow, for he instantly yanked the dagger out. I also believe that if Dorsey hadn't opened the upstairs door at that moment and frightened Martin away, he would have stabbed me again."

"Did Chadwick take the dagger with him?"

Again he gave me a wan smile. "Yes," he answered quietly. "But the next time, if there is a next time, I doubt whether I'll be as lucky as I was today."

"There'll be no next time, Mr. Brocton," I promised him. "We know definitely now that Chadwick's in this neighborhood. In fact, Captain Neely informed me over the phone that over a hundred police are searching every basement and roof within three blocks of this funeral parlor. Tell me, did Dorsey see Chadwick?"

Philip shook his head. "No. By the time he started down the stairs Martin had escaped."

I asked him whether he was sure it was Chadwick who had poked his head into the embalming room.

"Positive, Lieutenant. I'd know his face in a million. What's more, he was wearing his black fedora."

I looked at Regan. "Any questions, Sergeant?"

Regan appeared wholly at peace with the world. "Nope," he replied, grinning. "But if they don't land Chadwick pretty soon, I'll have plenty of questions," which was just the redheaded bastard's way of telling me that Carl Strenz would arrive at any minute and put his favorite sleuth at the helm.

I stood up. "Let's have a look at those rooms downstairs," I said to Lew. "Incidentally, where's Frank Webster?"

Heaving himself out of the swivel chair, Lew said, "Frank went down to the embalming room a little while ago to finish that job that Philip was working on. You'll see him when we get down there."

"By the way, Lieutenant," Philip inquired, "will it be possible to remove Paula from the morgue sometime this afternoon? If we can get the removal permit, we'd like to go ahead with the funeral arrangements." Paula, he went on to say, would be embalmed downstairs by a Mr. O'Reilly, who owned a funeral parlor a few blocks south of theirs. She would be laid out at Highrock, however, as there was no available reposing room for her in the funeral home. In fact, there'd be none available until Wednesday morning.

I told him that as soon as the bigwigs arrived I'd see to it he got a removal permit. I advised him, though, to let Frank and Lew or some of the helpers handle the business of picking up Paula at the morgue.

"Meanwhile, you'd better let Mrs. Brocton take you home," I concluded. "But don't move until I send Dorsey up to go along with you." With that I nodded to Lew and Regan, and the three of us walked out of the office.

As we followed Lew to the rear of the main floor I couldn't help but notice the elaborate furnishings in the place: intricately carved chairs, expensive statuary, thick Oriental rugs. Halfway to the rear we passed the entrances to two reposing rooms, one on each side of the main floor. Although I didn't have time to give more than a quick glance at what lay behind the entrances, I could see that here, too, an interior decorator had extended his talents and Chadwick's pocketbook to the limit. In each of these reposing rooms was a casketed corpse. Both rooms, however, were devoid of any mourners. The dead, I remembered, would have to be patient until one o'clock in the afternoon.

At the rear of the main floor we came to a pair of wide doors through the amber glass panels of which was revealed a tiny but pretentious chapel. Lew swung right, opened a door marked "Fire Exit," and led us down a long flight of carpeted stairs into a display room of various colored caskets. The room was ablaze with lights, and standing in the center, grouped around a large dark stain on the green carpet, were three men: Dorsey and the two precinct detectives.

"Johnny Masick and Ed Jacobsen, Lieutenant," Dorsey said as Lew led us over to the trio. But Dorsey, I noticed, didn't dare look me in the eye.

There were more introductions, a round of handshaking. Then, glancing around the room, I asked Lew if this was what they called the casket room. Lew nodded his head.

Dorsey, tall, thin, scholarly-looking, pointed to the stain on the carpet and said, "And here's where I found Mr. Brocton. When I got to him, he was mumbling something about Chadwick. Finally when I got the drift of it, it was too late to do anything but run upstairs to the office and tell Mr. Partridge to call a doctor."

I looked at the two bulky, impassive precinct detectives. "Any idea how Chadwick got out?" I asked them.

Masick said, "Yeah. He ran into the next room and skipped out of a door in there that opens out on the rear alley." He pointed to a trail of tiny stains leading to the swinging door of the embalming room. "You can see here where the blood dripped off the dagger as he ran out."

"As extra proof, we found that rear door in the embalming room wide open," Jacobsen put in. "Mr. Brocton said it was closed at the time he was working in there."

I walked over to the fire-exit door, opened it, and examined the outside surface. There were definite signs of its having been tampered with: deep gouges in the wood, as though someone had forced a chisel between the lock and the jamb of the door.

Closing the door, I sauntered back to Lew and the group of detectives. I said, "It's easily seen how Chadwick got in. Furthermore, it's quite possible he broke in last night and hid himself in one of these coffins. Nobody would think of looking for him here."

Dorsey dragged Lew, Regan, and me over to a gray casket that rested on a sort of dais under the stairway. The white silk lining in the casket was rumpled and soiled.

"I bet this was the coffin he used," Dorsey said. "We examined them all—thought maybe we'd find the dagger in one of them. But the best we could get was this soiled lining."

"What's this, Mr. Partridge?" I inquired, discovering a pair of sliding doors and a push-button panel in the wall near the dais.

Separating the doors, Lew revealed a dumb-waiter about seven feet long and three feet high.

"It's an electric lift," he informed me. "We use it for sending embalmed bodies up to the reposing rooms on the north side of the building. There's also one in the embalming room for the south side. Very handy gadgets."

Something was bothering me; I got it off my chest. "I know Frank and Philip are the big wheels in this mortuary, Mr. Partridge," I remarked, "but would you mind telling me what your connection is?"

His face reddened; his roly-poly body squirmed uncomfortably. After clearing his throat a few times he said, "I've been helping them out ever since"—he hesitated—"ever since I lost my job with Universal Insurance. Guess I'm what you might call their office man."

I looked at his flashy but threadbare suit, the same light-brown suit I'd seen on him last night. I thought, Judging from your shabby appearance, Lew, I'd say Frank and Philip are paying you peanuts.

Another thought began gnawing at my brain. Definitely one of the five vultures had stolen Chadwick's medallion. I had suspected Frank, because I'd seen him last night toying with the thing at the teakwood table. Now I was beginning to think otherwise. The real culprit, I told myself, was Lew Partridge. The poor devil looked as if he could use a pot of money; and a gold medallion, turned over to a smart fence, could easily supply it.

I turned to Dorsey. "Go upstairs and help Mrs. Brocton get that mealy-mouthed miser of hers home," I whispered in his ear. "And stick with him," I added.

As Dorsey cleared out of the casket room I said to Lew, "Now let's have a look at that embalming room."

Lew lumbered off between two rows of caskets, wobbled his way to the swinging door, and pushed it open. As we filed past him and entered the embalming room—the precinct detectives had tagged along with us—I saw Frank Webster standing at a long, slightly inclined porcelain table on which lay the stark-naked corpse of a white-haired old man. Frank's back was toward us; nevertheless, I could see he had a threaded needle in his hand. As I stepped closer I saw that he was sewing a small opening on the right side of the corpse's neck:

The embalming room was large, square, brilliantly lighted, and meticulously clean. White cabinets lined the four walls, their glass doors glistening as though a conscientious porter had applied considerable elbow grease. Even the tiled floor was spotless, except for that area near the foot of the embalming table where several splotches of blood had dribbled down the side of what looked to be a blood-receiving pail. Near the head of the table was a portable electric pump attached to a five-gallon tank of formaldehyde. That is, I assumed it was formaldehyde. The place fairly reeked with the damn stuff.

In the rear wall was a door that opened onto an alley, and adjacent to this door was a steel locker. The four windows in the room were of frosted glass.

Frank looked diffidently over his shoulder at us. "Hello there, Lieutenant. Hi, Sergeant," he drawled with no particular enthusiasm in his voice. "Seems to me you boys would be ashamed to show your faces around here."

I let it slide. Pointing to the rear door, I said to Jacobsen, "Is that the door you said you found wide open?"

He answered, "That's right, Lieutenant. Mr. Webster asked us to close it because it was getting cold in here."

"It's none of my business, of course," Frank drawled again over his shoulder, "but wouldn't it be more to the point, Lash, if you and your rum pots got out and hunted for Martin?"

I could take just so much. I strode over to the opposite side of the table and faced him. "Look, mister, stop needling me," I warned him quietly. "You stick to sewing up necks, and I'll stick to sewing up this squeal."

Behind the tortoise-rimmed glasses his smoke-gray eyes peered at me intently. He said, "Make damn sure you do, Lieutenant. I'm not overly fond of coppers. Coppers, in my opinion, don't try extra-hard when a big shot's involved." A grin broke the severity of his mouth. Snapping the thread, he patted the corpse on the cheek. "O.K., Mr. Perkins," he said to the lifeless form on the table, "you're ready now to be shaved, dressed, and laid out in your casket."

Suddenly Dorsey was back with us again. "You're all wanted upstairs, Lieutenant," he said, smiling. "And that means everybody. Carl Strenz and two carloads of top brass have arrived, plus an army of reporters."

Regan and the two precinct detectives were off like a shot. As for Dorsey, he rounded up Lew and Frank and, despite Frank's protests, shooed the two men out of the embalming room.

Alone, I began walking toward the swinging door. As I approached it my eye fell upon a tall wire trash basket that stood in the left-hand corner of the room. There was something near the bottom of the basket, something big and bulky and brown.

I investigated; plunged my arms deep into the trash; touched; pulled; shook it free of dust and scraps of refuse. Then I spread it out. A bloodstained trench coat! I looked at the manufacturer's label. An inch below it was a strip of adhesive tape with a name printed in ink. Martin Chadwick? Hell, no! Was I seeing things? Good God, there it was as plain as day: *Frank Webster*.

CHAPTER EIGHT

By one-thirty that afternoon everything was pretty much back to normal. The four reposing rooms in the funeral home were filled with mourners; Martin Chadwick was still at large; and—miracle of miracles—yours truly was still officially in charge of the Chadwick murder!

The miracle had taken place around one o'clock in the office of the Webster-Brocton mortuary. Carl Strenz, flanked by high officials, had summarily castigated Sergeant Regan for his apparent negligence of duty. I wasn't a witness to this dressing down, but later Neely had given me the gist of the thing. Strenz, it seemed, had gone to all lengths that morning in his efforts to locate the Sergeant. Via radio he'd continuously contacted the prowl cars in the neighborhood of Highrock, but nobody had known Regan's whereabouts. Regan, so Neely told me, had used the goldfish angle as an excuse. The Sergeant should have known better. Strenz was a dyed-in-the-wool Chadwick Is Guilty fan, and any information to the contrary was poison to him. The lambasting had ended with the Sergeant storming out of the office and tearing up to the vicinity of Highrock to take it out on his boys.

From one-thirty on I was busier than a detective at a pickpockets' convention. I sent Philip and Jessica home, with Dorsey as bodyguard; sent Masick, Jacobsen, and the uniformed cop back to their station house; took the officials and the newspapermen on a tour of the Webster-Brocton basement; arranged for Paula's removal from the morgue (Frank and a helper by the name of Scott drove off immediately in the mortuary truck); and last but not least, surreptitiously slipped Neely the bloodstained trench coat, admonishing him to turn it over to the police lab. If the blood on the trench coat matched with the blood on Paula's powder-blue evening gown, Frank Webster would have some tall explaining to do.

"Dan, how'd they make out with the Lincoln sedan?" I asked as the officials and the press made a general exodus, from the funeral home. "And how about that background on Penny Forbes?"

Neely eyed me as though I were bereft of my senses. "Good God!" he blustered. "Does Chadwick have to give a public demonstration before you'll admit he's the killer?" Then he must have remembered Frank's bloodstained trench coat, which he'd tossed into one of the official cars. "Dammit to hell, Chris," he added, yanking out his notebook and flipping its pages with exaggerated disgust. "One of us is crazy, and I know it isn't you."

He gave me the details: The steering wheel of the Lincoln had only Chadwick's prints on it. Nothing had been found in the car, no gloves, no keys, no blood stains.

As for Penny Forbes, Neely had contacted Actors Equity. Judging from the scrawled notes in the Old Man's notebook, Equity must have given him everything but the birth date of Penny's great-grandfather:

Penelope Forbes, born September 17, 1926, Harrisburg, Pa.; attended public schools there; won scholarship to Mary Washington College, Virginia; left college (1946) to play in touring stock company; came to New York (1948) to play in *Son of the Sultan;* radio, summer stock (1949); presently appearing in *The Goldfish Gaieties.* Excellent character references; no criminal record. Specialties: dancing, singing, and male impersonations. Parents (John and Ellen) presently residing in Scranton, Pa.

I gave Neely a sharp look. "Well? Don't tell me you missed it."

He put away the notebook, frowning a little. "If you mean that part about the male impersonations," he said, "I don't agree with you. Penny Forbes could have impersonated Chadwick on Sunday night, but she certainly didn't impersonate him this morning. Couldn't have been in her apartment and up here at the same time."

I didn't argue the point. Besides, the bigwigs were ready to shove off. So I let Neely go, watched the cars pull away, then ambled across the street to grab some lunch.

There was a sea-food restaurant near the corner that looked so inviting that I marched in and plunked myself at one of the tables. But when a waiter came over, what with Penny on my mind and everything, I came damn near ordering a mess of fried goldfish.

All during lunch I wrestled with some skull-breaking questions. Was it possible that Frank and Philip were working in cahoots? Frank's bloodstained trench coat was the hub around which my conjectures were revolving. Maybe Frank had killed Martin Chadwick prior to killing Paula, then with Philip's help had embalmed Chadwick and hidden his body somewhere in the funeral home. Days, even a week or two later, after a little hocus-pocus with a death certificate, they could get a burial permit and bury Chadwick as John Smith or something. And the attack on Philip today? H'm. Philip, I reasoned, could have easily inflicted that dagger wound on himself; could have made up that story about seeing Chadwick. Maybe the tampered fire-exit door, the soiled casket, and the wide-open rear alley door were just so many red herrings. But what about motive? I could understand Frank and Philip having a motive for killing Chadwick: The lawyer had ceased being their patsy; had probably begun to demand a lion's share of their profits as a rightful return on his investment in the funeral home. But what would be their motive for killing Paula? Frankly, I couldn't think of any at the moment. I'd soon latch onto one, though, if I could find Chadwick's body concealed somewhere in that building across the street.

I returned to the funeral home, drifted into the office, and found Lew Partridge talking on the phone. He hung up when he saw me, and though he gave me a broad smile I could see that my dropping in on him had caused a fuse to blow somewhere in his nervous system. His hand actually shook as he waved me to one of the chairs.

"That was Helen on the phone," he explained. "She says everything's O.K. at Highrock, and that Philip's resting quietly in his bedroom. Is there anything I can do for you, Lieutenant?"

"Yes. I'd like to make a phone call."

I called West Side Homicide and gave the assignments officer the guard schedule for that night: Patterson and Lynch at Highrock, outside; Daniels, inside; Moore and Eichler at the rear and side alleys of the funeral home.

With this off my chest I turned to Lew and told him I was about to make a thorough search, basement to roof, just to convince myself that Chadwick hadn't sneaked back for another go at Philip.

"So if you've any special rooms or closets that are locked," I suggested, "you'd better give me some keys to take along."

Lew opened a drawer in the desk and handed me a bunch of keys. He said, "Not a bad idea, Lieutenant. But watch your step."

Leaving him, I hastened down to the casket room. Only two lights were on: a dinky light at the head of the stairs, and the fire-exit light. Somehow they seemed to cast a weird, ghoulish glimmer on the caskets. Fortunately, my groping fingers located a light switch in the wall at the foot of the stairs before my imagination could conjure up any blood-curdling skeletons. When the room was flooded with light the keys in my hand stopped jingling.

For the next three hours I searched the funeral home, poking into every nook and corner that might possibly conceal a corpse. I examined the electric dumb-waiters and their shafts; explored every casket in the casket room, every cabinet in the embalming room, including the steel locker; and even went down to the subcellar to look at the furnace and its oil-burning equipment. Moreover, I tapped walls; rummaged through closets and supply rooms; searched the chapel; and spent a long time in the garage. In addition, I even had the gall to examine the four reposing rooms, peering behind drapes and flowers and caskets.

In the reposing room on the south side I came upon a casual acquaintance: Mr. Perkins. Shaved and dressed, he lay in a gray casket, surrounded by his bereaved family.

I was a very tired and discouraged man when I came down from the roof at five o'clock and returned the keys to Lew Partridge. This time he didn't give me his big-brother smile.

"Frank and Scott are back from the morgue," he informed me glumly. "And Mr. O'Reilly's on his way over to do the embalming."

I thought, Hell, this is no place for me. I'm so dead tired that if I happen to close my eyes for a minute, somebody's bound to drag me downstairs and embalm me. So I grabbed my hat and coat, spruced myself up a bit in the men's room, and sallied out to the street to look for an embalming place with a brass rail on the floor.

I found me one in 207th Street. The hooker of rye with beer chaser did little or nothing to alleviate my gloom. What I needed was a flock of laughs; someone to cheer me up; and if that someone happened to have a beautiful face, so much the better. I fished in my pocket for a nickel and barged into a phone booth. After being in a funeral parlor all day, I felt as though I were walking into an upturned casket.

"Hello . . . Penny?" I called into the phone. "This is Christopher."

"Why, Mr. Columbus!" came her sultry reply. "What on earth are you doing ashore?"

Already I was feeling better. "Look, Penny," I pleaded. "How about you and me having dinner together?"

Instead of answering my question, she asked one herself. It concerned Philip. She wanted to know whether she should send flowers to the hospital or to the undertaking parlor.

"Oh, he's very much alive," I told her. "Confidentially, I'm the one who's dead, Penny. But I've a hunch a good dinner and you will work miracles."

"Well, let's see, darling. I've got to be at the theatre by seven-thirty at the latest. It's five-thirty now. That means—" Suddenly she gasped. There was a pause, and seconds later I heard her say in a scarcely audible voice, as though her head were turned away from the phone, "Martin! Martin, what are you doing here? . . . No, Martin—please!" And then there came a click and a dead, nerve-shattering silence.

CHAPTER NINE

I didn't even hang up the receiver. I burst out of the phone booth, galloped to the street, and leaped into a cab that was parked at the corner. Showing the cabbie my shield, I barked at him that if he didn't get me to 97th Street and West End Avenue in fifteen minutes, I'd rip out his shoulder blades and sharpen them on the soles of his shoes.

On hitting Dyckman Street, however, I spotted a prowl car. Before the cabbie could bring his hack to a complete halt I was out of the cab and giving orders to the two cops.

With the motor wide-open, with a wailing siren to clear the road ahead of us, the prowl car made the trip in a neat twenty minutes. It took us an additional two minutes to reach the door of Apartment 322.

The door, I noticed, was slightly ajar. For a moment I had a squeamish feeling that Chadwick had done some bodily harm to Penny; had struck her down and taken it on the lam without shutting the door behind him. But—no. Chadwick was much too fond of Penny. Likely as not he'd left it open a trifle to warn him of approaching danger. And here we stood with heaving chests, panting and puffing a warning to him. Hell, by this time he was probably halfway down the fire escape.

Pulling out my gun, I signaled the cops to follow me, shoved open the door, and rushed into the living room. We thundered in at the very moment that Penny, bearing two plates of soup, came in from the kitchen.

"Sit down, Christopher," she said sweetly, placing the plates upon a card table decorously set for two, except that in the center of it was an unlighted farmer's lantern. "Dinner's ready, darling, and I'm sure you're famished." She struck a match and lighted the lantern.

"But Chadwick? What about Chadwick?" I demanded, striding to the bedroom and poking my head in. Dazedly I crossed over to her. "Penny, I distinctly heard you say—"

"Oh, that," she cut in with an airy gesture. "Jeepers, darling, I was already cooking my dinner when you phoned. And since I hate to eat alone—well, it was the quickest way I could get you here. Besides, darling, it'll be so much cozier than sitting in a restaurant. Now tell your little friends to run along before this soup gets cold."

To this day I don't know what I ate that evening in Penny's living room. All I know is that I spent the nicest ninety minutes imaginable. The food, whatever it was, was delicious; and Penny, adorable-looking in a cute little ensemble, looked extra-delectable in the soft glow of the smoking lantern. I was so bewitched, so thoroughly enchanted by the screwball that it wasn't until I'd dropped her off at the theatre and re-entered my cab that I discovered that Cuspidor had ripped another cuff to pieces.

Mentally refreshed, replete with food, alive and tingling again, I leaned back on the rear seat of the cab and directed the driver to Highrock. Tonight, come what may, I'd try to find out where the five vultures were on Sunday night between six and seven. While I was at it, I'd get Lew Partridge off in a corner and sweat him for the whereabouts of Chadwick's medallion.

As the taxi approached the Webster-Brocton Funeral Home
I saw Sergeant Regan walk out of the front entrance and climb
into his cement mixer. Commanding the taxi driver to stop, I
climbed out, paid my fare, and yelled to the Sergeant to wait for me.

Regan's mood had improved considerably. Opening the door,
he said in a much too friendly voice, "If you're on your way to
Highrock, chum, climb in." I slipped in beside him, and he added, "Whatcha do—go home for supper?"

"Yeah."

He reached out, removed my fedora, and dropped it into my
lap. A goldfish was stuck in the hatband. "And in case you don't
know it, Lash," he said, "Cuspidor's torn up your other cuff."

"What were you doing in the funeral parlor?" I inquired,
hoping to change the subject.

Regan started the motor. "Just nosing around. I see you've
got two of your boys guarding the alleys."

"Uh-huh." I tossed the goldfish away and put my hat back
where it belonged. "Lew and Frank still there?"

"No. The night man's in charge—feller named Quinn."

Regan drove the car north one block, swung left into Isham
Street, then turned on the headlights full blast. Another turn,
this time to the right. In the glare of the headlights I saw we
were ascending a narrow road that cut a serpentine path through
a myriad of desolate looking trees, the leafless branches of which
formed a bleak and gloomy canopy over our heads.

"Where the hell are we?" I demanded, inwardly marveling
that here in New York City—within the space of a couple of minutes, mind you—one could leave the dazzling lights of Broadway
and find oneself in an almost impenetrable darkness.

"It's called Park Terrace West," Regan replied with a chuckle.
"If you ask me, though, it's like being inside one of Philip Brocton's coffins with the lid nailed down."

Up the winding hill we rode until we reached 215th Street. Then Regan swung the car to the right, drove forward a hundred yards or so, and finally made another right turn, this time into Park Terrace East. A minute later he brought the car to a halt in front of a gravel driveway that curved gracefully toward a huge, rambling, three-story structure of stone. The house, scarcely discernible because of the numerous shrubs and trees surrounding it, had old-fashioned gables, quaint chimneys, and big latticed windows. Though most of these windows were lighted, the light emanating from them failed somehow to dispel the haunted appearance of the mansion.

"So this is Highrock," I muttered.

"Yeah," Regan said. "And if Chadwick decides to do any stabbing up here, he couldn't pick a nicer spot."

Regan maneuvered his crate into the driveway and parked it behind a mortuary truck, one of those corpse-in-a-wicker-basket, house-to-funeral-parlor vehicles. It had "Webster-Brocton Funeral Home" in small gold letters on the side, so I knew that somewhere behind those grim, sullen-looking walls of the mansion lay the remains of Paula Chadwick. Frank and Lew, no doubt, had brought her to Highrock immediately after the embalming. It was surprising to me, though, that the gravel driveway wasn't lined with cars. Surely by this time Paula's friends should be dropping in to pay their last respects.

We piled out of the car and crunched our way over the gravel toward a long, wide veranda that stretched across the front of the building. Suddenly a spectral figure confronted us.

"Where do you think *you're* going?" inquired a man's voice, tense yet truculent.

I emitted a chuckle. "Keep your shirt on, Lynch," I said. "It's me, Lieutenant Lash—and something I picked up at a rummage sale."

Detective Lynch, his pock-marked face half hidden by an upturned coat collar and a turned-down hat brim, heaved a sigh of relief. "Hell, I thought maybe it was Chadwick prowling around."

I asked him if everything was under control.

"Quiet as a tomb, Lieutenant," he informed me, swinging his arms in an effort to keep warm. "Patterson's on guard in the rear, and Daniels, the lucky stiff, is stationed inside."

Jerking my head toward the driveway, I questioned him about the lack of cars.

"Don't you read the papers?" he asked. "Mrs. Brocton told a bunch of reporters this afternoon that nobody but the police and the immediate family would be admitted here. If anyone wants to view the deceased, it will have to be done Wednesday at the funeral services."

"Smart gal," Regan commented. "Guess she figured if the public was admitted, Chadwick could slip into the house easy."

Satisfied that everything was O.K., I instructed Lynch to remain at his post until the relief men, Edwards and Wheeler, took over at midnight. Then Regan and I walked up on the veranda. There was an antiquated bronze knocker on the nail-studded front door, which I wasn't at all timid in using. My lusty knocks brought an immediate response in the form of the gangling, coughdrop-devouring Detective Daniels.

"Come in," he said, swinging the door wide. "Christ! It's cold enough to freeze the balls off a Christmas tree."

We stepped into a somewhat stuffy vestibule. Through a circular pane of glass in the upper half of the vestibule door I saw a long, wide, brilliantly lighted hall with a broad stairway on the right-hand side near the rear.

"Where are they all, Daniels?" I asked as Regan and I followed him into the hall and hung up our hats and coats.

He pointed to a pair of tall mahogany sliding doors in the right wall between the stairway and the vestibule. Directly opposite, in the left wall, was another stately looking pair of doors. None was open.

"Mr. Partridge is in the drawing room over there," he said, exuding his usual fragrance of menthol. "He's a bit high, Lieutenant. Been hitting the bottle pretty steady all evening; that is, until Mr. Brocton went in there and locked the liquor cabinet.

"Mr. Webster," he went on, "is downstairs in the cellar with his choo-choo trains, and Mr. Brocton and Mrs. Partridge are upstairs in their bedrooms. Mrs. Brocton"—he made a wry face as though he had an aspirin in his mouth instead of a cough drop—"is in her lab on the top floor."

"And where's the corpse?" I asked. "In the drawing room?"

"Yeah. They've got her laid out pretty nice. For the last hour I've been doing nothing but sign for floral pieces. Talk about a cheapskate! Mr. Brocton raised hell when I suggested he give me some moolah for tipping the flower luggers. Said I should lay it out of my own pocket and send the bill to Martin Chadwick."

I asked Daniels to give me the directions to Philip's room. I wanted to tackle Lew Partridge first, but politeness decreed that I go upstairs and inquire as to Philip's well-being. To talk with him, though, I'd probably have to drag him from under the bed.

Daniels said, "One flight up, first door on your right. You'll have to knock, Lieutenant. He's got his door locked; says he's taking no chances."

Regan and I marched down the hall, mounted the stairway, and paused at the first door on our right. As I crooked my knuckles to knock, a high-pitched, angry voice issued from the room. It was Helen Partridge's.

"I'm sick and tired of your pushing us around, Philip!" we heard her exclaim. "Why, you and Jessica treat Lew and me as though we were servants. Who do you think you are?"

"We didn't ask you to come here," Philip whined. "If that good-for-nothing husband of yours hadn't squandered all his money on horses and liquor, you wouldn't have been forced to accept our charity."

Helen gave vent to a shrill, scornful laugh. "Charity!" she cried. "My God, Philip, you and Jessica don't know the meaning of the word. I work my fingers to the bone around here. I do all the cooking, all the housework, all the shopping. And what do I get for it? Nothing. Nothing but a lot of abuse from that she-devil wife of yours."

Philip didn't answer right away. When he did, there was a deep-down vibration of anger in his tone. He said slowly, "Nobody's forcing you to stay, you know. If you and Lew don't like it here—"

"Yes, and poor Lew!" Helen broke in as though Philip's words had made no impression on her. "You work him like a dog at the funeral home. And for what? I'll tell you: Two skimpy meals a day and a bed to sleep in. If it wasn't for Frank, Lew wouldn't know what a dollar looks like."

"Frank's a fool," Philip lashed out. "If he wants to throw his money away, that's his business. I'm supporting you and that sluggard of yours, Helen. Therefore, the least Lew can do is earn his keep at the funeral home. Remember, nobody's forcing you to stay."

"Well, don't be surprised if we move out," she retorted.

"What do you mean? You and Lew haven't a cent you can call your own."

"Maybe I've changed all that," she said, lowering her voice. "Do you think I was just twirling my thumbs last night in Martin's apartment? Let me tell you something, Philip. While you were looking for those daggers—" She broke off, and a ripple of nervous laughter escaped from her lips. "Well, anyway, don't be surprised if any day now Lew and I clear out of this miserable hole."

So it was Helen who had stolen the medallion!

"In the meantime," she continued, "I suggest you hire a cook and a housekeeper. I'm through being your servant. Do you understand? If Jessica can play the great lady around here, so can I.

What's more, I refuse to let Lew continue at the funeral home unless you pay him a salary."

"Have you lost your senses completely?" Philip demanded. "What am I going to use for money? Hasn't Martin been hounding the life out of Frank and me? How can we possibly meet Martin's demands every month unless we scrimp on every penny we take in?"

"Don't make me laugh. Have you forgotten that Martin's in no position to demand his money?" Helen asked jeeringly. "From now on you can forget the payments— as if you didn't know. With no payments on your mind, Philip, you can afford to do a *lot* of things."

From the floor above came the slam of a door and the sound of light footsteps. Jessica had evidently come out of her lab and was heading toward the stairs.

"Quick! Let's get out of here," I whispered to Regan. "We'll come up again later."

We tiptoed away from the door and scooted down the stairs. When we got to Daniels, I asked him how to get to the cellar.

He led us to the big sliding doors in the left wall, separated them, then stepped into a well-lighted dining room that was almost as large as Madison Square Garden. At least that's the impression I got as we walked in. It had a beamed ceiling of smoke-blackened rafters, Jacobean walnut-paneled walls, and a flagstoned floor that you'd expect to find in some old English castle. A decorative frieze and a fieldstone lighted fireplace lent a certain grandeur to the room, which was offset somewhat by the plain but sturdy mission furniture. What really took my breath away was the gigantic table that stood in the center.

Daniels took us to a swinging door that was in the right wall at the other end of the dining room. He pushed open the door and led us into a butler's pantry, and thence to a large square kitchen, where George Washington must have heated his hot toddy. There was a modern gas range in the room, plus an up-to-the-minute electric refrigerator, but from there on everything was strictly 1776. Both the pantry and the kitchen, I noticed, were generously illuminated.

"Here it is," Daniels announced, halting at an opened trap door in the floor. "Just watch out you don't break your neck on those stairs."

He waited until Regan and I had safely hit bottom. Then, calling down to us a cheery "Look out for that four-eyed third rail," he hurried back to his post near the vestibule door.

The lights in this part of the cellar weren't anything to brag about. But when we passed through the furnace room with its thrumming oil burner, we stepped into a large open space in the center of which were six ping-pong tables that formed a solid square under a row of fluorescent lights. On top of the tables was a complete toy railroad—everything from trains and tracks and bridges to miniature cities and mountains. Sitting at a sort of control board, with his back toward us, was Frank Webster, his spectacled eyes focused on the four sets of trains that rattled over the labyrinth of tracks.

"Hello, Frank," I said affably. "That's a swell-looking railroad you've got."

"Oh, it's you again," he drawled, flashing us an annoyed look. "Don't you boys ever go home?"

"Not when a killer's running around loose," I answered. "And particularly when I've got a lot of questions to ask."

A red light flashed on his control board. He shut off the power, got to his feet, and tinkered with a derailed caboose.

"Save your breath, Lieutenant," he muttered. "I don't know where Martin's hiding. I couldn't even make a good guess."

"O.K., Frank," I said quietly. "Suppose then you tell me where you were last night between six and seven o'clock."

His eyes popped in amazement. "That sounds very much as though you don't think Martin's guilty, Lieutenant," he remarked with an amused expression on his face.

I said, "Maybe I'm a Doubting Thomas. Maybe it's hard for me to believe that Chadwick"—I paused, fixing him with a steely look—"owned the only trench coat in town," I finished significantly.

He didn't go pale. His eyes didn't show a flicker of fright. Either he had nerves of steel or that bloodstained, trench coat of his was a false alarm.

"Frankly, I don't think it's any of your damn business where I was last night," he said insolently, yet softening it somewhat with a sardonic smile. "But if I tell you, will you please clear out and leave me alone?"

I said, "Fair enough. Shoot."

"Let's see. Quinn—that's our night man—relieved me at four o'clock. Later—"

That's the best I could get. For at that moment Helen Partridge, dressed in black, her face pale and twitching with fear or rage, came tearing in from the furnace room. She pulled up short, however, when she spied Regan and me.

"Oh!" Her hand went to her throat. "I—I thought you were alone, Frank."

"It's quite all right, Helen." It was the first time I'd heard Frank speak in a tender tone of voice. He slid past us, crossed over to the young woman, and placed a friendly hand on her shoulder. "What's wrong, kid?" he asked, uptilting her quivering chin and looking down at her.

She looked at us, murmured a somewhat incoherent apology, and pulled Frank over to one side of the cellar. In low tones she began talking to him, and with each word she uttered the friendly look on Frank's face gradually disappeared. By the time she was done the man's face was stony and expressionless.

"Let's go upstairs, Lieutenant," he said flatly, coming back to Regan and me. "I've some unpleasant business to attend to."

Without waiting for a reply he whirled and set sail for the furnace room, determination in his fading footsteps.

"It's really all my fault, Lieutenant Lash," Helen informed me as we followed slowly in Frank's wake. "I had some words with Philip and Jessica a few minutes ago. Then foolishly I went downstairs and told Lew about it. I tried to stop him but he insisted on going upstairs and giving them a piece of his mind. When Lew's had a few drinks in him," she added fretfully, "he doesn't stop at anything." I quickened my pace. "No!" she pleaded, holding me back. "Please don't interfere, Lieutenant. Let Frank handle it. When Lew's a bit under the weather, Frank is the only one he'll listen to."

As we streamed out of the dining room and entered the hall, Daniels confronted us. There was a big grin on his face.

Popping a cough drop into his mouth, he said, "Just a family squabble, Lieutenant. I ran up there when it started, but I came right down. After all, it was none of my business." He jerked his head toward the stairway. "Yeah, it's all over now; can't hear a thing. Mr. Webster must have put the quietus on it."

A stifled sob of relief came from Helen. I looked at her. She was jittery, all right; the big blue eyes under her tear-wet lashes showed plenty of mental and emotional confusion. Now, I thought, is the time to fling that damn medallion business in her teeth. Sometimes you have to hit quick and low in this racket I'm in. You feel like a first-class heel when you do it; but if you don't strike at an opportune moment, your quarry often tightens up and laughs in your face.

"Is there someplace we can go where it's quiet, Mrs. Partridge?" I asked. "Sergeant Regan and I would like to have a few words with you."

"Yes," she answered slowly, searching our faces. "But if it's anything concerning Martin, I'm afraid I can't be of much help." I kept my mouth shut. "Very well then," she said resignedly. "We'll go to the study."

Beckoning us to follow her, she led us all the way down the hall to a door in the right wall directly under the stairway. Opening the door, she nodded us ceremoniously into a large comfortable-looking study. Like all the rooms I'd seen so far, it was ablaze with light.

From floor to ceiling the walls of the room were lined with countless sets of expensively leather-bound books. In the wall facing the doorway were two latticed windows, between which a wood fire crackled cheerfully in a small marble fireplace. A huge mahogany desk with leather-upholstered swivel chair occupied the center of the study, flanked by a terrestrial and a celestial globe. There was a tall wooden cabinet and a pedestaled bust of William Shakespeare against the wall on our left, and in the wall on our right, opposite the desk, was a connecting door that I felt certain opened into the drawing room.

"Sit down, Mrs. Partridge," I said, indicating the swivel chair.

She sat down and looked up at us expectantly. "Yes, Lieutenant?"

"Mrs. Partridge," I snarled, and for good measure I even slammed my fist on the desk, "where's the gold medallion you took last night from Martin Chadwick's apartment?"

Up went her hands to her breast; her face paled as though Frank or Philip had suddenly pumped out every drop of her blood. She swayed forward, eyes dilated, bosom heaving riotously. As I leaned over to prevent her from pitching face down on the desk, she reared and slumped back in the swivel with her head lolling on her left shoulder.

Then she sprang up, pointed a trembling finger at one of the latticed windows, and let out a piercing scream that must have resounded throughout the old mansion like a cry out of hell.

I looked where she pointed, and my hair almost stood on end. A man in a big fedora hat was looking in at us through the windowpane. There was hate in the face under the hat brim, and fear. I recognized the face instantly. The man on the other side of the windowpane was Martin Chadwick!

CHAPTER TEN

The idea that a drowning man reviews his entire life as he struggles in the water, during the final gasping and gurgling seconds of his existence, has always impressed me as being just so much poppycock. I know if I were drowning, I'd be thinking only of one thing: Where the hell are the life guards?

Yet a rush of thoughts raced through my brain when I saw Martin Chadwick's face at the window. In a split second the events of the last two days flashed into my mind. I thought, Chris, you aren't half so smart as you think you are. Since Sunday you've been yackety-yacking Chadwick's innocence to the housetops, chasing red herrings and goldfish, instead of concentrating on the incontestable evidence that's been under your nose from the very start. Well, you can shove it down the drain now. You've seen Chadwick with your own eyes. And if ever you saw hate and murder in a man's face, it's there on the other side of that windowpane.

It was Regan's rusty voice, thank goodness, that kicked the props from under my reverie.

"There he goes!" he roared as the face disappeared from the window. "Come on, let's grab him while the grabbing's good."

With a nimbleness I'd rarely seen him display, the Sergeant hurtled across the study, unlatched one of the windows, and climbed out with a speed comparable only to the hasty exit of a lover who hears a husband's key in the door.

I knew better than to follow suit. My bulk and lankiness of leg would never clear that latticed mouse hole. So I lunged to the open window, pulled it shut, and latched it. Then, turning to Helen, who had sagged frantic-eyed into the swivel chair, I cautioned her to remain where she was. I doubt whether she heard me. She was staring off into space, her fists beating hysterically on the arms of the chair, her body writhing as though subconsciously she were twisting and turning it to avoid the downward plunge of a hippogriff dagger.

Much as I hated to leave her in this condition, I had to. With a killer running around loose in the park, there was no time for patting her hand, no time for murmuring little tidbits of comfort. But at least I could minimize the chances of Chadwick's sneaking in and dealing her a death blow. I'd already locked the window; now for the doors.

I sprang to the connecting door and turned the key in the lock. Four long strides brought me to the door through which we'd entered the study, where I quickly removed a six-inch tubular key. Leaping into the hall, I locked the door from the outside. As I slipped the key into my pocket Daniels came tearing up to me.

"Who screamed, Lieutenant?" he inquired worriedly. "Christ, it gave me goose pimples."

"Chadwick's outside," I said quickly, grabbing his arm and sprinting toward the vestibule with him. "So help me, Daniels, he looked in at us."

As we reached the vestibule door and pulled it open, a voice boomed out from the head of the stairway. Turning, we saw Frank. He had a bewildered look on his face.

"What's happened?" he called down through cupped hands.

"Chadwick!" I yelled. "He looked in the study window. Warn everybody up there, Frank, to stay in his room and keep the door locked."

"O.K.," he answered. "But I'm getting in on this, Lieutenant. I know the park like I do the palm of my hand."

"Good boy!" I shouted back. "Just make sure you shut the front door behind you."

With that Daniels and I dashed through the vestibule, leaped out onto the veranda, streaked down the short flight of stone stairs, and raced off into an unlighted section of the park. From all directions I could hear raucous exclamations and smothered oaths; and when there were no voices, the air seemed filled with the swishing of fallen leaves and the cracking of dead branches. Occasionally I caught the gleam of zigzagging flashlights. Apparently Regan, Lynch, and Patterson were going through the park like a herd of wild elephants.

"Go left, Daniels," I commanded, veering to the right. "And don't go trigger-happy on us. Remember, Chadwick isn't the only one in the park."

From nine-fifteen until nine-thirty I wandered among the trees, damning to hell every root and stone I stumbled over in that infernal darkness. I poked into bushes, explored kid-dug craters, and got a whale of a kink in my back from peering up into denuded branches.

Suddenly I heard a twig snap not more than five feet away from me. Instantly every muscle in my body tightened. I held my breath, ears straining to catch the next telltale crack, eyes clawing at the darkness like two cats in a burlap bag.

If I reach for my gun, I thought, the noise of my hand sliding over rough cloth will sound like something scraping over sandpaper. If I just stand here, though, and wait for Chadwick's next move, I can jump him.

I sank to a half crouch. As my weight shifted to the balls of my feet a loud crack came from under me. Mrs. Lash's little boy Christopher had put almost 190 pounds of beef on a little twig.

Simultaneously with the crack of the twig came a juggernaut of muscle and bone against me. I went down on my back with a thud that must have shattered the seismograph at Fordham University. Swiftly I rolled over, scrambled to my knees. But it was too late. A muscular arm snaked under my armpit and across the nape of my neck, followed by a blinding, bone-crushing pressure that drove my face deep into dead stinking leaves.

"This—this is for Paula, Martin," I heard my assailant hiss through clenched teeth. "I'm going to break your neck."

He wasn't kidding. Yet there was still enough strength in me, thank goodness, to let out a strangled flow of protest.

"Frank!" I gasped, "Let up! It's me—Lash—Lieutenant Lash."

A sharp cry of astonishment ripped out above me, and almost immediately the boa constrictor slid off my neck. For a moment there was a strained silence.

"Lash!" Frank cried, his voice apologetic. "Good grief, man, I didn't know it was you. I—"

"God damn you!" I spluttered, spitting out a mouthful of dead leaves. "Why the hell did you have to work this side of the park? Regan's got a neck like the trunk of an oak-tree."

Profuse with apologies, Frank helped me get to my feet. "I'm sorry, Lash," he said, and fortunately for him there was no banter in his voice. "Really, old man, when I heard that twig snap—"

"Aw, shut up and let's get back to the house," I growled, beating the dirt out of my clothes. I thought, I *would* wear my new suit. First the cuffs get chewed up; now I don't know if I'm wearing tweeds or weeds.

"Hadn't we better keep on with the search?' Frank asked.

"Talk sense," I snapped. "By this time Chadwick's halfway to the Bronx."

At that instant two beams of light stabbed the darkness and rested flush on our faces. A few seconds later Regan, Daniels, Lynch, and Patterson popped out of the underbrush.

"Any luck?" Lynch wanted to know, playing his flashlight on the ground as though he expected to find Chadwick stretched out.

"Yeah, I'm just lousy with luck," I griped, and I shot a grim look at Frank. "After tangling with this guy I'm lucky I'm alive."

Daniels said, "Chadwick must have lammed down the hill to Broadway." He reached into his pocket. "Anybody want a cough drop?"

"No!" I snarled. "Put those damn things away; they're sleeping pills. And these two lugs"—I glared at Lynch and Patterson—"must have eaten some. You're a helluva pair of watchdogs," I berated them. "You let Chadwick walk right up to a window and peek in. Don't you flat-footed punks realize you're up here to stand guard? What were you doing—playing pinochle?"

"Pinochle, my foot," Patterson flared, his gargantuan frame quivering with indignation. "Me and Lynch haven't eased up for a minute. We saw nothing; we heard nothing—that is, not until some dame in the house let out an awful scream."

"That's right, Lieutenant," Lynch muttered. "Take it from me, if Chadwick walked up here through the park without us seeing or hearing him, he's either the Invisible Man or Tarzan of the Apes."

"Well, all I've got to say is," Regan put in, "it's damn lucky for you Homicide hill billies that Chadwick's threat had nothing to do with pistols. While he stood at that window, he coulda taken a pot shot at Mrs. Partridge." The Sergeant stuck his granite-like jaw in my face. "Get this, Lash," he sneered. "Starting first thing in the morning, I'm putting two of my boys on guard up here. Your flunkies stink out loud."

I said, "Get 'em all up here, I don't care. But when the day comes that a D. A. man can beat a Homicider, I'll use my shield for an ash tray. Comes on, let's blow; it's freezing up here. Besides, nobody's guarding the house."

"There's nothing to worry about," Daniels said. "Every door and window in the joint is locked. I checked when I came on at four, and made the rounds again at eight."

I turned to Frank. "You closed the front door behind you?"

He said, "Yes. And don't worry about Martin having a key to that front door. Or to the back door, for that matter. Jessica called a locksmith this morning and had new locks installed."

Disgruntled, the six of us retraced our steps to Highrock. As we approached the mansion I caught sight of the Webster-Brocton mortuary truck.

"Say, let's have a look at your corpse carrier, Frank," I said, latching onto a hunch and forgetting momentarily that I was flirting with pneumonia. "Maybe Chadwick's using it right now for a hiding place."

"Could be," he muttered. "Especially in the wicker basket."

We hurried to the driveway and moved stealthily toward the truck. A minute later I pulled open the big door in the tail of the car. Instantly two beams of light shot out from behind me.

There was no sign of Chadwick—just a long, low wicker basket, which was empty, and an embalming kit, which contained a small hand pump, a pair of scissors, and a half-gallon bottle of formaldehyde.

Thoroughly disgusted, we crunched out of the driveway and trudged to the south side of the house to examine the ground directly below the latticed window at which Chadwick had appeared. Its outside sill was parallel with my chest. It was easy for me to peek into the study, but Chadwick must have stood on tiptoe to do it. Helen, I noticed, was no longer sitting in the swivel chair. She was pacing the study with a small pearl-handled revolver in her hand. I ducked. In her jittery condition she'd need but one glance at the window to fire that gun.

"No footprints, Lieutenant," Lynch remarked as I squatted down on my haunches beside the men. "Ground's frozen stiff."

"So what?" Regan grunted. "We know it was Chadwick who stood here, and that's what counts. I'd know his face anywhere. I've seen it too many times in the past ten years to make any mistake about it."

"It was Chadwick, all right," I admitted with an involuntary shiver. "And judging from the expression on his face, he means business."

CHAPTER ELEVEN

I was conscious again that I was freezing. My struggle in the park with the undertaker had sweated me up plenty. I looked at Frank and Daniels. Their chattering teeth and stamping feet made me lose no time in putting an end to our outdoor activities. I sent Lynch and Patterson back to their posts and ordered Frank, Daniels, and Regan to return with me to the house. It was exactly ten o'clock when Frank unlocked the front door for us.

As we stepped into the vestibule I looked through the circular pane of glass in the vestibule door and saw Lew Partridge waddling down the stairs. From the dazed look on his pudgy face it was hard to tell whether he was fuzzy from booze or just puzzled as to his wife's whereabouts. A little of each, I suspected.

"Hello there," he called out in a thick voice as we entered the hall. "Looks like Martin gave you fellows the slip." He padded up to us like a seal walking on its fins. "Say, where's my ever-loving wife, Lieutenant?" he asked, swaying slightly on his feet. "Mustn't let anything happen to Helen, you know."

His breath had me swaying a bit on my own feet. With averted face I told him where his wife was.

Handing him the tubular key to the study, I said, "Be sure to lock the door when you let her out, Mr. Partridge. This downstairs floor has got to be absolutely impregnable to Chadwick."

As Lew disappeared under the stairway a phone rang in the hall.

"I'll answer it," Frank said, striding to a marble-topped table that rested against the left wall, close to the sliding doors of the dining room. "It's probably Quinn at the funeral home." He picked up the phone. "Hello . . . Oh, hello, Quinn." There was a long pause. "O.K., I'll be right down." He cradled the phone and marched back to me. "I've got to go to the office, Lieutenant," he said irritably. "Quinn can't find the keys to the filing cabinets, and somebody's down there raising Cain about a transcript. I'll go in the truck and be right back."

When the undertaker was gone, Lew and Helen emerged from the study. Helen, I could see, was no longer toting the pearl-handled revolver.

"Did you lock the door?" I asked the moon-faced man.

Grinning, he tapped the pocket of his suit coat. "Yes indeedy, Lieutenant. Got it right here in my pocket."

I fixed a stern eye on Helen. "What did you do with that revolver, Mrs. Partridge?"

Her face went deathly pale, then was flooded with a look of relief. She'd expected, no doubt, another browbeating in reference to the medallion.

"Oh, that's Philip's revolver," she replied quickly, unable to look me in the eye. "I knew he kept it in the desk. It was certainly comforting to hold it while I was sitting alone in the study. If you want the gun, Lieutenant, you'll find it in the top middle drawer."

"And it's all legal," Lew said with a chuckle. "Philip got a permit the day he made his first dollar." He draped an arm across Regan's shoulders and mine. "Say, you boys look just about frozen." Then coaxingly to Helen, "Think maybe, my dear, you could get Philip to give me the key to his liquor cabinet? These boys could use a good hooker of brandy. Got a little bit of a chill myself," he added with an embarrassed laugh.

But Helen, dammit, turned thumbs down on the idea. "No, you've got to lie down for a while, Lew," she insisted, pulling him toward the stairway. "Besides, you know perfectly well that Philip doesn't want you touching his liquor."

"He's an old miser, that's what he is," Lew mumbled as he permitted his wife to drag him toward the stairs. "Yes indeedy, boys," he called over his shoulder. "The old skinflint embalms every dollar he buries in his pocket."

A complete silence reigned in the hall until the covey of Partridges had reached the second-floor landing. Regan was the first to speak.

He said, "When you gonna give her another workout?"

"There's no rush," I answered. "She knows we're wise about the medallion. It's my guess the next workout will make her produce it." I walked over to the sliding doors of the drawing room and separated them. "Come here, Daniels," I said. He ambled over. "Go down the hall and see if that door to the study is locked. Partridge may have bungled it."

In many respects the drawing room was a duplicate of the dining room across the hall: beamed ceiling, walnut paneling, flagstoned floor, and the same spaciousness. The Sheraton furniture; the gaudy crystal chandelier, which hung like a great stalactite from the rafters; the crackling log fire in the marble fireplace; the Caen stone mantel—all contrived to give the room a distinct atmosphere of formality and stateliness. Yet its grandeur made little or no impression on me, for my eyes couldn't resist the magnetic pull of the flower-banked casket that rested near the curtained French doors that opened out on the veranda. It was a magnificent solid oak half-couch casket trimmed with silver extension handles, with a lining of ivory-colored silk, and it made a perfect setting for the beautiful creature that lay there like the recumbent statue of an angel sculptured in alabaster.

Daniels joined me again at the doorway of the drawing room. He said, "It's locked tight, Lieutenant."

"Good." From one of the tall sliding doors I removed a tubular key, almost a duplicate of the one I'd handed to Lew. Then, sliding the doors shut, I locked them and handed Daniels the key. "Keep it in your pocket," I instructed him. "Apparently nobody wants to sit in there with the corpse, so there's no need to have the doors open. Open them, though, if more flowers are delivered."

"Oh, oh!" I heard Regan say under his breath. "Here comes Philip."

I glanced down the hall. Sure enough, the gaunt, stoop-shouldered undertaker was walking slowly down the stairs. He had on a wine-colored dressing gown at the bottom of which flopped the legs of a striped pair of pajamas. Brown slippers covered his feet.

"Hello, Mr. Brocton," I said as he clopped toward us. "How's that shoulder of yours?"

He snorted as though his wound were the least of his troubles. "Tell me about Martin," he demanded in a voice that was shaking with fear. "Do you mean he was actually prowling around outside?"

I gave him all the details. The more I talked, the more forcibly it was driven home to me that the man was inordinately afraid of Chadwick. His beady eyes had a cringing, hunted look; sweat stood out on his brow; and he chewed his forefinger like a rat trying to gnaw its way out of a trap. I couldn't blame him entirely. After experiencing one dagger thrust, it wasn't likely he'd welcome another.

"To be perfectly frank, Lieutenant Lash, I'm beginning to doubt very much the ability of you and your men," he said incisively. "Martin, apparently, seems to have little or no trouble in evading the police." He fidgeted a bit, glancing down at the floor. "I'm sorry, Lash," he murmured without looking at me, "but I think I owe it to Helen and myself to lodge a complaint with District Attorney Strenz. I'm sure we're entitled to more adequate protection."

"If you want to call him now, Mr. Brocton," Regan put in, throwing me a sly look, "I can give you his home phone number."

Philip shook his head. "No, thank you. I'll wait until the morning. After all, there's little likelihood of Martin's returning here tonight." Frowning, he looked up and down the hall at all the lighted wall fixtures. Then, clip-clopping to the doorway of the dining room, he jerked the doors apart and fairly cringed when he saw the brilliance of the room. "My God!" he exploded, glowering at me. "Who—who turned on all these lights?"

Unperturbed, Daniels said, "I did." He tossed a cough drop into the air and caught it neatly in his mouth. "If the lights weren't on, mister," he added coolly, "it would be a cinch for Chadwick to jimmy one of the windows and sneak in."

"If you fools were really on the job," Philip sneered, "Martin wouldn't be able to get within a hundred yards of a window."

He scuffed toward the vestibule door and began pushing light-switch buttons in the left wall. When he was done, only two small lights remained on, one near the vestibule, the other near the stairway. As he started toward the dining room, I intercepted him. In fact, I grabbed his left arm and marched him double-quick right back to the buttons in the wall.

"These lights stay on, Mr. Brocton," I said authoritatively as I pushed the buttons and flooded the hall with light again. "That goes for every light on this floor. Understand? I'm responsible for the safety of you and your half sister"—I paused to let it sink in—"so don't make my job any harder than it is."

I could see he didn't like the "half sister" crack at all; his eyes raked me inimically.

"Are you also going to pay the electric-light bill?" he inquired with a leer.

I said, "When you talk to Strenz in the morning, tell him to take it out of my salary."

"I still got that phone number, Mr. Brocton," Regan reminded the undertaker.

Philip ignored the Sergeant. "Where's Frank?" he asked me.

I explained.

"Humph!" he snorted. "He couldn't walk there—just a five-minute walk. No, he has to take the car and burn up a lot of gasoline." A disquieting thought must have flashed into his mind. His mouth sagged open, and a stunned expression swept across his pasty face. "Frank was down in the cellar all evening playing with those confounded trains of his," he muttered, almost as if he were speaking to himself. "Yes, and I wouldn't put it past him to leave every blessed light burning down there." He brushed me aside and hurried to the dining room. Pausing in the entrance, he faced me and said in a disdainful tone, "I'm going to the cellar, Lieutenant. Or do you object to my moving around in my house?"

"No. Go ahead," I answered. "I don't care about the lights in the cellar, but make sure you leave the pantry and the kitchen lights alone. And speaking of the kitchen, Mr. Brocton," I said, "how are the chances for our getting Mrs. Partridge to make a pot of coffee? I've a couple of men outside who could use some."

Shocked, Philip drew himself up to his full height. "We're not running a restaurant up here, Lieutenant Lash," he said indignantly. "If you want coffee for your men, send out for it." Grumbling something under his breath about people thinking he was made of money, he clip-clopped out of sight.

Daniels said, "That bastard's so cheap I bet he walks on his hands to save shoe leather."

I walked over to Regan. "What's the matter, Sergeant? Can't you wait to take over?"

"At the rate you're going it's in the bag," he replied. "Can you imagine what Strenz is gonna say when he hears Chadwick gave you the slip tonight?"

"I'll worry about that when it happens. Right now I'd like to know what little Jessica's doing. She's kept clear of us all night. Coming along?"

"Wouldn't miss it for the world, chum. It's my guess she'll bat your brains out."

We left Daniels at his post, climbed the stairs, and knocked on the door of Philip's room. There was no answer. What's more, the door was locked.

"Maybe she's upstairs in the laboratory," I said. "Come on."

Regan blocked my path. "Hey, wait a minute. If Jessica's up there in the bathroom, we can't barge in on her, feller."

"*Laboratory*, not lavatory, you sap," I snarled. "Here, take hold of my hand. You're liable to drink some chemical up there and change into Dr. Jekyll."

There weren't any lights to guide us up to the next landing. But when we finally reached the top, we saw a sliver of light streaming from under a door that was way up at the other end of the house. It wasn't much of a light; still, it did act as a sort of beacon for our faltering footsteps.

It was all of three minutes before my sharp raps on the door brought a response.

"Who is it?" Jessica called irritably through the door. I told her. "Oh, go away," she snapped. "I'm much too busy right now."

I heard her hand touch the key in the lock. Instantly I grasped the doorknob, turned it, and shouldered the door open before the bolt slid home. Her greeting as we entered wasn't at all lady-like. Even Doc Berlinger could have picked up a few new words.

"Well, now that you've forced your way in," she said angrily, "what do you want?"

I studied her for a while. She had an acid-eaten chemist's coat over her black dress, and I wondered whether those gaping holes in the coat had been caused by chemicals or by drops of slaver from her acidulous tongue. More interesting, though, were the many bloodstains on the coat. If Penny hadn't tipped me off that Jessica was working on some sort of blood formula, I'd have sworn this raven-haired beanstalk was employed in a slaughter house. Seeing the bloodstains, I was reminded of Frank's trench coat. I'd planned to call the police lab sometime that evening. However, Chadwick's appearance at the window had Mickey Finned the idea. Funny how things change so quickly. In the early afternoon Frank's trench coat had been a big moment for me. Now I was almost convinced someone had punched him in the nose.

Jessica's lab was a big, neat-looking job. The place was crawling with wooden shelves, and there wasn't an inch of space on the shelves that didn't hold a bottle of some kind. Running the length of the lab was a wide cement work table loaded with test-tube racks, Bunsen burners, retorts, microscopes—everything you'd expect to find only on a chemist's table in some movie serial. In the exact center of the table was a Rube Goldberg contraption of retorts and condensers. Blood-red liquid was boiling in it, with the whole crazy-looking setup plugged in on five different sockets. I thought, if Philip gets a peek at this, he'll have canaries.

"What's cooking, Mrs. Brocton?" I inquired.

"You still haven't told me what you want up here," she said with an air of patience very much tried.

"Just checking up to see if you're O.K.," I explained. "Martin Chadwick was outside a little while ago."

"Yes, I know; Frank told us," she said indifferently, turning her back on us and going to her work table. "But Martin, don't forget, has nothing against me. And as for Philip, he's had the good sense to lock himself in his room."

I sauntered over to the work table to watch Jessica tinker with a stopper in one of the retorts. There was a window behind the table through which I could see a pair of headlights turning into the gravel driveway. Evidently Frank was returning from the funeral home.

"On the contrary, Mrs. Brocton, your husband's down in the cellar," I informed her. "He went there to turn off the lights."

She gazed at me dumbly for a moment, her long arms hanging ludicrously at her sides, her mouth a little open. Then a look of rage contorted her face.

"The fool!" she blurted out, peeling off her coat and flinging it to the floor. "He gave me his word he wouldn't leave his room."

She tore out of the lab, and I made no attempt to stop her. In fact, I was all for it. I'd decided to herd everybody into the dining room. With the five vultures in one room, it would be much easier to keep a protective eye on them. Later, of course, I'd take Helen to the study and get on with that medallion business.

Meanwhile, Regan was examining the retort-condenser affair with avid interest. What fascinated him were the hot drops of red liquid that dripped rhythmically into a beaker.

"You think maybe it's Guinea red?" he asked hopefully.

"I'd leave it alone if I were you, Regan," I advised him, walking to the door. "That is, if you don't want a blood transfusion."

But the Sergeant grunted at me to get lost. So I left the lab, slammed the door behind me, and groped my way down the long dark corridor to the head of the stairs.

When I reached the landing below, I heard a muffled explosion overhead. Then every light in the old mansion went out!

Damn you, Regan, I thought as I whirled and raced upward to the top floor. You stupid, meddlesome lummox.

This time I didn't do any groping in the corridor. I dashed headlong toward the lab with a recklessness that was exceeded only by my eagerness to plant a resounding kick on the seat of Regan's pants. If I could find him in the dark, I'd kick him from here to his Holy Canarsie and twice around the Yankee Stadium.

"Is that you, Lash?" he asked hoarsely as I thundered into, the room. "I musta blown the main fuse," he said with a nervous chuckle. "Stuck my finger in that red stuff and damn near burned it off. Yeah, and when I yanked my hand away, it broke one of them thingumajigs. Then—wham! No kidding, it's a wonder I wasn't electrocuted."

"Come here, Regan," I said in a sirupy voice as I clenched my fist. "Think nothing of it, Sergeant. Just keep your little chin up."

I think Regan suspected what was coming. At any rate he made no movement toward me. But I could hear his heavy breathing, so I edged closer.

"Come here, Regan," I repeated dulcetly. "Nobody's going to—"

The words froze on my lips. From somewhere in the house—from the main floor, as near as I could place it—came a horrible petrifying scream.

CHAPTER TWELVE

Scarcely breathing, I stood transfixed in the darkness of the lab. Icy fingers played a soundless threnody up and down my spine, and my palms oozed cold sweat. A riotous turbulence was going on in my brain. Had Chadwick taken advantage of the fuse situation? Had he broken into Highrock and delivered another hippogriff dagger?

Somehow these appalling questions sent a flood of power into my palsied legs. I lurched to the doorway and pounded swiftly along the corridor until I felt the welcome thump of my hands against the balustrade. At last, thank God, I'd reached the stairs.

Plunging downward, my feet barely touching the steps, I hit the landing below and, swerving to the right, lunged crazily forward. If possible, the darkness here seemed even more impenetrable than it had on the floor above. It was like a black, choking smog that kept closing in thicker and thicker, impervious to straining eyes, invulnerable to flailing arms.

Then the hard thud again of my outstretched hands striking the second-floor balustrade. A swift turn, another downward plunge, and stairs were under my feet again. But gone for the moment was the strength to descend the steps, gone as though somebody had pulled a switch and deprived my legs of all power.

No question about it, hell had broken loose in the main hall below me. I could hear a tumult of threshing bodies; a sickening cacophony of hard fists hitting soft flesh; a din of terror-stricken voices that came saber-toothed out of the blackness and clawed the pit of my stomach.

I thought, Chadwick's down there. He's cutting them to ribbons. They can't find him in the dark.

A tide of insensate fury rose within me, bringing with it a resurgence of power to my legs. Chadwick, damn him, had been making a fool of me these last two days: slipping past my men; leering at me through a window. Now, by God, I'd go down there and wipe up the floor with him.

With a curse rumbling in my throat, with a vague hope in my heart that Chadwick's dagger hadn't yet found its designated victim, I darted down the stairs, raced warily up the hall a short distance, and grappled with the first body I came in contact with. A fist caught me flush on the side of the face, jolting me plenty. I could taste blood in my mouth. Then out went my own five-fingered piece of concrete, straight out like a battering ram. Luckily, it found a target. There was a sharp crack, a groan, a dull thud as though a sack of potatoes had dropped upon the floor. I stooped and ran my hands over the inert body, while around me raged a battle that was reminiscent of my harness days on the Riot Squad. My fingers touched a fat, pudgy face. Oh-oh! I'd landed a haymaker on Lew Partridge.

Suddenly a pair of legs backed into me. In a flash I had my arms around them. I yanked with everything I had. Whoever he was, he hit the floor with a resounding crash, and before he could bounce I was on top of him with my hands at his throat. A fragrance of menthol struck me in the face.

"Daniels!" I yelled, releasing my grip. He gurgled something that sounded like the name of some Polish football player. "Is

Chadwick here?" I shouted at him above the noise of the melee.

"I—don't—know," he shouted back falteringly as I hauled him to his feet. "Lights went out. Everybody started running around like a lunatic."

No sooner had he uttered these words than the hall and the dining room burst into a blaze of light. Someone, thank Heaven, had got down to the fuse box.

With the coming of the dawn, so to speak, the roar of combat died out. An actual hush settled over the arena, while the combatants, disheveled, battered, exhausted, gaped at each other in speechless astonishment. That is, all except Regan.

"Holy Canarsie!" he bellowed, and I observed with sadistic satisfaction that Frank had the Sergeant's head locked neatly in a half nelson. "Why—why, Chadwick ain't here at all!"

A hasty glance revealed the truth of Regan's assertion. There were a lot of people in the hall, but not one of them remotely resembled Martin Chadwick. Whatever disappointment I felt was assuaged by the fact that there weren't any corpses strewn about the floor—just tangled human beings, befuddled yet acutely conscious that they presented a rather ridiculous-looking spectacle. Trying my damnedest not to grin, I studied the tableau.

Frank and Regan, slowly disentangling themselves, were on their knees near the locked sliding doors of the drawing room; Philip, stark terror in his face, cowered behind the marble-topped telephone table; Lew, nursing a bruised jaw, sat in the center of the hall like a Buddha with a toothache; and Jessica, rage and fear fighting for mastery on her face, stood in the doorway of the dining room.

However, up near the vestibule door was an eye-arresting scene that fairly took my breath away. Detective Lynch was sprawled out on the floor, while standing over him, with one foot gladiator-like on the man's chest, and with a broken branch in her hands, was Penny Forbes! Her dinky hat was askew, and her hair looked as if a couple of gamecocks had fought a pitched battle in it.

"Penny!" I cried. "Penny Forbes!" I couldn't help it. Cripes, I couldn't have been more surprised if I'd seen Lady Godiva in a horse blanket.

The screwball blew me a kiss, oblivious of the fact that she'd suddenly become the cynosure of all eyes.

Fortunately, Detective Patterson at that moment hustled into the hall from the dining room and robbed Penny of the spotlight. His sudden appearance made me forget the girl long enough to remember there was work to be done. Penny or no Penny, I had to earn a living.

"Get Lynch off the floor," I ordered Patterson. Then, with Daniels' help, I raised Lew to his feet. It was like lifting a bale of cotton. "Everything O.K., Mr. Partridge?" I inquired with an innocent look.

He was stone sober now. Rubbing his jaw and chuckling a little, he said, "It was, Lieutenant, until somebody opened the front door and let a mule gallop in."

I glanced over at Lynch. He was as wabbly as a tall vase in a parlorful of jitterbugs. "And how about you?" I asked him.

Gingerly he removed his dented hat and touched the bump on the back of his head. "Thought at first the ceiling had caved in," he muttered. "But I see now"—he indicated the wrist-thick branch in Penny's hand—"it was only a telephone pole that hit me."

I gave them all a stern look. "Well?" I growled. "Who started this rumpus?"

There was an immediate outburst of voices, and the crowd converged on me as though I were handing out ten-dollar bills.

"Hold on!" I thundered, holding up a silencing hand. "Quiet, everybody!" I turned to Daniels. "Suppose you tell me," I suggested.

He said he was standing in the center of the hall when all of a sudden he saw Philip come out of the pantry and begin turning off the lights in the dining room. He'd rushed in and ordered Philip to stop. But it was no dice. Then Frank had come home, and when Daniels called him into the dining room to see if he could reason with Philip, Frank had read Philip the riot act and turned on the lights. A little while later Jessica had walked in, and it was then that all the lights had gone out.

"Right away Mr. Brocton started yelling that Chadwick was in the house," Daniels continued. "The next minute I heard everybody skedaddling to the hall. But it was my hunch the main fuse had blown. So I felt my way to the kitchen. Then I heard Patterson pounding on the rear door. So I let him in, opened the trap door in the floor, and told him to go down to the cellar and have a look at the fuse box. But I left him flat when I heard that scream. I ran back to the hall, found a riot going on in the dark, and pitched in because I thought Chadwick was on the loose."

I looked at Jessica. "Was it you who screamed?"

She sniffed contemptuously. "Don't be ridiculous."

"How about you, Penny?" I asked.

"Not me, Christopher dear," she replied demurely. "Jeepers, I haven't screamed since the fleet was in."

Statue-stiff, Jessica eyed the screwball as though somebody had uncovered a garbage can under her nose. "Who *is* this person, Lieutenant?" she demanded. "And what is she doing here?"

"Miss Forbes is a friend of mine," I answered truculently. "I asked her to call for me. Any objection?"

"How rather lovely," Jessica sneered. "But I must insist that she leave at once, Lieutenant. Highrock, you know, is not a trysting place for the Police Department."

"Oh, dry up, Jessica," Frank drawled. "Highrock is wipe-open to the Lieutenant's friends, particularly if they're all as pretty as this one." It gave me a twinge to see the admiring look he bent on Penny.

I was all business again. I said, "Then it must have been Mrs. Partridge who—" Pausing, I looked at Lew. "By the way, where *is* your wife?" I asked him.

"Upstairs, of course," he replied with an assurance that didn't quite ring true. "That is, I think she is," he added hesitantly. "When that scream woke me, I ran downstairs to see what had happened. Thought maybe Helen was down here and had seen Martin again." Really worried now, he produced a handkerchief and mopped his face. "Guess—guess she's still upstairs lying in her bed. Must have slept through it all."

"You'd better go up and see if she's O.K., Mr. Partridge," I told him with a casualness I was far from feeling. Then to Daniels, "Go along with him. If she's all right, ask her to come down."

As they hurried toward the stairs I walked across to Lynch. "How did you get in?" I asked him.

He pointed to Jessica. "Mrs. Brocton let me in the minute she heard me pounding on the front door. She said Chadwick was in the hall; she'd heard him run down the stairs. So I ran in and reached for my flash. But somebody crashed into me, and the flash went spinning out of my hand. About five minutes later"—he pointed sheepishly to Penny's club—"I got konked on the noggin. It was my own fault. If I'd shut the front door behind me, the young lady wouldn't have been able to get in."

Facing the crowd, I said, "In other words, you've all been battling your heads off on account of a fuse blowing out," and I proceeded to tell them of Regan's mishap in the lab.

I expected a tirade of abuse from Jessica. I wasn't disappointed. True, Regan had it coming to him; still, I'd no idea that Jessica would go so completely off her nut. The bitch actually frothed at the mouth. She tore into Regan and me with a tongue-lashing that would have blown the main fuse all over again if she'd been anywhere near the cellar. Philip lit into us, too. Big and brave in the knowledge that Chadwick wasn't on the premises, he called us everything under the sun, from snooping morons to imbecile coffee swillers. Indeed, by the time Philip and Jessica were done with us, poor Regan's face would have made a good cape for a matador. Even the Sergeant's offer to pay for the damage didn't throw any oil on the troubled waters.

"You've ruined months and months of world!" Jessica snarled at him, her voice a reedy shrill. "Are you so utterly stupid that you—"

"Oh, Jessica, shut up!" Frank blasted. "I'm sick of listening to you. You're not fooling anyone with your cockeyed experiments. The only reason you spend your time in that fool lab is because you're just too damn lazy to experiment with a dust rag."

"I won't have you talking to Jessica that way!" Philip cried, rushing over to Frank and shaking a trembling fist under the younger man's nose. "I've had enough of your impertinence— entirely too much. Do you hear me? You'll either apologize to Jessica or you can pack up and get out of here. Yes, and take the Partridges with you. Or maybe you prefer just to take Helen," he added sneeringly.

There was no mistaking the insinuation in his words, and Frank got it as quickly as anyone. His face went white with rage; a muscle twitched in his jaw.

Oh-oh, I thought, here it comes. And it did. No fist, mind you, just the palm of his hand. But it landed on Philip's face with force enough to crack an upper plate.

There was a breathless silence. Philip, his face livid, was the first to speak.

"You'll regret that, Frank," he said slowly in a flat, unnatural voice. "You'll pay for it a thousand times over."

Hurried steps on the stairway put an end to the little drama. Lew and Daniels were pelting down the stairs at breakneck speed. Somehow I didn't like the look on Lew's face as he surged toward me. It was a bit too grave, a shade too pallid. A queasy feeling began to stir my insides.

"She isn't upstairs at all," he blurted out, panting in deep wheezy gasps. "We searched every room. No sign of her." He caught hold of my arm in a frenzied grip. "Lieutenant, you don't think—?"

"Now, don't get excited, Mr. Partridge," I said placatingly. "That goes for everyone here," I added as the crowd began to babble nervously. "Mrs. Partridge is somewhere in the house and we'll find her." I looked at Daniels. "Did you try the top floor?"

He said, "Every room."

That queasiness in my stomach hadn't abated any. "The key to the study, Mr. Partridge—did you turn the key over to your wife, by any chance?" I inquired, working on the angle that Helen, dubious of my protection, might have slipped down to the study to get the pearl-handled revolver.

"Why, no," he answered, fumbling in the pockets of his coat. "I've got it right here." A puzzled expression came into his face. "No, I haven't," he muttered. "It's gone!"

I said, "Mrs. Partridge, no doubt, removed it from your pocket while you were catching those forty winks. Come on, let's go down the hall to that door under the stairway,"

Like the Pied Piper of Hamelin, I marched off with a mob at my heels. They followed me down the hall, tailed me under the stairs, and all but dented my rear bumper when I pulled up abruptly at the door to the study. It was locked, thoroughly and completely, and neither the pounding of my fist on the door nor the discordant entreaties of the mob brought any response. Getting down on one knee, I peeked through the keyhole, hoping to heaven I'd see Helen reading a book or something. All I saw, though, was a well-lighted empty room, sinisterly quiet save for the crackling log fire.

Rising, I said to the crowd, "She may have unlocked the connecting door and stepped into the drawing room. Let me have that key I gave you, Daniels."

With the tubular key in my possession I led the way up the hall to the towering sliding doors of the drawing room. I inserted the key (with a scarcely noticeable trembling, praise be), turned it, and drew the doors apart. The next instant I was pushed bodily into the room by the influx of the crowd behind me, like a hunk of wood on the crest of an incoming wave. Only by throwing wide my arms and putting my back in reverse was I able to stem the tide.

The drawing room was glowing with light. Yet here, too, was that same sinister silence that had seeped so palpably through the keyhole of the study door. It sent a shiver down my back; made me prescient of lurking evil and impending disaster. Even the flames in the fireplace seemed to cower as though they considered it sacrilegious to dance and cavort in the presence of death. And thinking of evil and disaster and death, I turned my head to look at the flower-banked casket.

Someone, I think it was Patterson, beat me to it, "Merciful God!" I heard him cry in a strangled voice. "Look—look over there by the casket!"

On the flagstoned floor of the drawing room, about two feet away from the casket, lay Helen Partridge, her body as lifeless as that of the corpse in the coffin above her. And buried hilt-deep in her bloodstained bosom was a hippogriff dagger!

CHAPTER THIRTEEN

For a dreadful minute or more my eyes refused to swerve from the unspeakable horror that lay near Paula's casket. Behind me, I could hear convulsive sobs and shrieks of terror—all rising to a crescendo bordering on panic. Yet an inexplicable something held my eyes to this new and even more horrible manifestation of Martin Chadwick's murder-twisted mind. Corpses weren't anything new to me; I'd seen scores of them in the course of my police work. But here was a murder victim whom I'd talked with little more than an hour ago, a young woman for whom I'd really gone all out to protect. Maybe it was the sheer impossibility of the murder that was getting me. Maybe it was the fact that this latest of Chadwick's outrages meant for me a swift and inglorious ejection as officer in charge. Whatever it was, it took everything I had to pull my eyes away and get down to the business of being a copper again.

"Clear the room," I ordered the detectives. "Get these people into the dining room and keep them there." I faced the crowd. "Come on, folks, move. Step lively—everybody."

As luck would have it, though, my staccato commands, instead of impelling the crowd to move toward the doorway, succeeded only in awakening what my pop always referred to as "plasma-phobia"—the primitive urge that attracts people to spilled blood the way flies are attracted to sugar. As though a signal had been given, the crowd made a concerted rush toward the corpse on the floor. Trying to stop them would have been as futile as holding back Niagara Falls with an eyecup. Philip literally threw himself upon the corpse, his wails of grief sounding like the caterwauling of a dying cat. Watching him, I had all I could do to keep my temper and supper down.

Regan and the four of us from Homicide pushed and pulled and pleaded until our faces were lathered with sweat. We got Philip off the corpse easily enough; but when we'd get him and the others as far as the doorway, they'd slip loose and tear back to the corpse again. The only one we didn't have the heart to pester was Lew Partridge, who stood near the body of his wife as though carved from stone, tears running unashamedly down his moonlike face. He was staring at her as though his very soul were ebbing away. Then all at once his voice broke into hard sobs of irrepressible anguish; and before anyone could stop him he slumped to the floor and buried his face in the crook of his wife's outstretched arm.

Patterson and I tugged at him to no avail. The harder we tried to pull him up, the more tenaciously he clung to the corpse. Finally, giving it up as a hopeless job, I let Frank, Jessica, and Penny go to work on him. But I held back the cringing Philip, who was now wringing his hands like a distraught woman.

"Come on, Lew," Frank coaxed as the three of them crouched solicitously beside the man. "Look, old boy. I'll get a bottle of Philip's best brandy and you and I can go to the dining room and finish it off. What do you say, Lew?"

It got an immediate response. "Yes—a drink. That's what I need, Frank," Lew moaned, struggling to a sitting position and rocking his head from side to side. "Brandy! Buckets of it—barrels of it. So help me, I never want to draw another sober breath as long as I live."

Frank signaled Patterson to lend him a hand. Together they got the grief-stricken Lew to his feet. Then Frank crossed the room to a liquor cabinet near the connecting door. Finding the cabinet locked, he swung around angrily and strode over to Philip and me. He stuck out his hand with an air that brooked no argument.

"Give me the key, Philip," he said quietly, and the twitching muscle in his jaw was working overtime.

Philip reared like a frightened horse. "I'll do nothing of the kind," he blustered, edging closer to me. "Lew's had more than enough of my brandy. He's been lapping it up all evening. Drink! Drink! Drink! That's all the drunken swine thinks of."

"Give me the key, Philip." Frank's voice was even lower now, but it had a metallic edge to it that made my spine tingle.

"You can't order me around. I won't have it!" Philip cried, bristling with resentment. Yet all the while his hands were groping in his pockets for the key. "A cold-blooded murder has taken place in this house," he went on wretchedly, "but all you've got on your mind is a crazy urge to fill that fat pig with my brandy. Here, take the key. Take it and be damned."

As Frank reached for it, Jessica shot forward and snatched the key from Philip's fingers.

"I'll open the cabinet," she declared, her face dark with fury. "I'll bring out every bottle that's in it."

Heels clicking furiously on the flagstones, she sailed across the room, opened the liquor cabinet, and beckoned Frank to join her. When he was no more than a step or two away, she suddenly stuck her arm into the cabinet and with one fell blow swept the dozen or so bottles onto the floor. The crash of glass sounded as though someone had fallen through a skylight.

"There!" she snarled, pointing to the shattered bottles and spilled liquor. "There's your brandy. And I hope you choke on it."

Her attempt to run from the room was forestalled by a lightning-like move on Frank's part. He sprang after her, caught her savagely by the arm, whirled her about, and all but slapped her teeth out with a series of palm and backhand blows that made her sallow cheeks look like hunks of raw beef. I know I should have stopped him, but I couldn't do that and hold Philip at the same time.

Somehow the breaking of the bottles seemed to break the stubborn streak in the crowd. Patterson, Lynch, and Daniels had no trouble herding them across the hall and into the dining room. Penny was the last to leave. As she prepared to step into the hall I pulled her aside.

"Look, Penny," I said as Regan sauntered over to us, "I haven't time now to question you. But when I do, make darn sure you've got a good explanation for coming here tonight. Now go in there and see to it you behave yourself."

Regan tapped her on the shoulder with mock severity. "And God help you, sugar, if we find a goldfish on Helen Partridge," he warned.

"I'll be good, boys, honest I will," she promised. "Besides"— she cast a quick look at the corpse on the floor—"I'm scared, sort of." With that her eyes swung dreamily to the broken bottles. "You fellows wouldn't happen to have a straw, by any chance, would you?"

I smacked her smartly on the fanny. "Go on, beat it," I growled. "We've got work to do."

With the crowd tucked away safely in the dining room, the three detectives came trooping back. I was waiting for them.

"Patterson," I commanded, "you and Lynch go back to your posts."

"Much good it does," the giant grunted. "If you ask me, there's just no stopping this guy Chadwick. Will somebody tell me how the hell he got into the house?"

"That's what we've got to find out," I answered. "Go ahead— blow." Reluctantly they scrammed. "Daniels, call West Twentieth

Street," I said. "Tell 'em what's happened up here. And when they stop ranting about my inefficiency, tell 'em to notify the M.E.'s office that we've got another corpse up here for them to work on. Then go upstairs and check all the windows. It might also be a good idea to poke around a little in the cellar."

Dismissing Daniels, I closed the sliding doors and began examining the windows in the drawing room. Regan trailed after me, inhaling and exhaling great gobs of alcoholic air.

"Tough break for you, Lash," he said without any tears in his eyes. "Strenz'll cut your gizzard out for this. And you wanna know something? I ain't so damn keen about taking over. If locked windows and doors don't mean a thing to Chadwick, the chances of nabbing him are slim."

"Talk sense," I fired over my shoulder. "There's *got* to be a jimmied window somewhere in this house, and it's my guess it's in here or in the study."

I was all wet: Every window in the drawing room was locked tight. The same went for the French doors that opened onto the veranda. To cap it all, I damn near set myself on fire by attempting to glance up the chimney. One look, however, was enough to convince me that only a midget Santa Claus in an asbestos suit could have squeezed his way down.

Still confident, I opened the connecting door and stepped into the study. I wasn't surprised at finding the door unlocked. It was clear that Helen had unlocked it in order to enter the drawing room from the study. I was flabbergasted, though, to find both windows in the study securely latched.

"See what I mean?" Regan said with a sickly grin. "I tell you, Lash, we're not dealing with a lawyer; we're up against a magician."

"Nuts. Daniels'll find what we're looking for; wait and see."

Regan snapped his fingers. "I've got it! Penny was able to get in on account of Lynch leaving the front door open. So maybe

Chadwick was right behind her when she barged in. It was pitch-dark; nobody would have seen him."

"Now I know you're nuts," I said. "Jessica didn't open the door for Lynch until *after* she heard the scream. That means that Chadwick was already in the drawing room. That blood-curdling scream of Helen's came, no doubt, the instant Chadwick grabbed hold of her in the dark."

"What did she come down for, anyway?"

"I don't know. Maybe to get the pearl-handled revolver. Maybe— Say, wait a minute. The medallion!" I exclaimed. "I bet a week's pay she—"

I broke off and made a dash for the drawing room with Regan lumbering behind me. Reaching the corpse on the floor, I eagerly examined the surrounding area. Then, wrapping a handkerchief around my right hand, I dropped to my knees, slid my covered hand under the body, and ran it slowly over the flagstones. The touch of metal against my fingers brought an exultant cry from my lips.

"Here it is!" I cried, dragging out the medallion from under the corpse and rising to my feet. "This explains, I think, what Helen was doing here. She was afraid we'd go upstairs and search her room for the medallion. So it was up to her to find an almost foolproof hiding place."

"Paula's casket!"

"That's right. But when she got to the casket, she probably heard a noise behind her. Anyway, when she whirled around, Chadwick drove the dagger into her. Helen, of course, immediately let go of the medallion."

"Ain't it kinda funny that Chadwick didn't pick it up and take it with him?" Regan asked.

I wrapped the medallion in my handkerchief and dropped it into my pocket. "Maybe he didn't see it in her hand. Maybe the lights went out before she came in from the study." A thought struck me. I began searching the slit pockets in Helen's black dress. In one was a black-bordered handkerchief; in the other, the tubular key to the study door. "Regan," I said in an awed voice as I looked down at the key in my hand, "you weren't kidding when you said we were up against a magician. Our finding this key in Helen's pocket proves it."

"What's so special about the key?"

"It's incontestable proof that when Helen sneaked into the study, she locked the study door and put the key in her pocket."

"So what?"

"So if all the doors and windows were shut—and we know definitely now that they were—then how the hell, Regan, did Chadwick get in here to commit the murder?"

"He used to live in this house. Maybe he has a duplicate key for every door in the joint."

"I doubt it," I said. "When he turned this place over to his in-laws, he was still on friendly terms with them. Therefore, he wouldn't have held back any keys. Besides, Jessica had the locks changed on the front and the rear door this morning."

"How come Daniels didn't see Helen sneak downstairs?"

"Because Daniels had rushed into the dining room to make Philip stop monkeying with the light switches. We were upstairs in the lab with Jessica; Frank hadn't got home yet; and Lew, if we can take his word for it, was having a snooze for himself. All this, of course, gave Helen a clear field. It's quite possible she heard us go up to the lab when she was in her bedroom." Suddenly with a smothered oath I dropped the key into my pocket and reached for my gun.

Regan jumped about a foot off the floor. "Holy Canarsie, what's wrong?" he demanded, glancing wildly about the room.

I could scarcely control my voice. "Regan, we're a pair of first-class saps," I croaked. "Good God, man! This is it. This is where we take him."

The Sergeant peered at me with a mystified look on his face. "Stop making with the mouth," he pleaded. "Give out, Lash. Make it add up."

"Don't you get it?" I whispered hoarsely. "Chadwick! If it's a miracle how he got in here, then it's also a miracle how he got out. We didn't find any unlatched windows, did we?"

"Why, the bastard's probably right here in this room!" Regan exclaimed. He jerked away from me, pulled out his gun, and faced the banked flowers. "O.K., Chadwick," he snarled, leveling the heater. "Come out of there, you son-of-a-bitch, or I'll blow a cloud of chrysanthemums in your face."

I didn't wait to see whether Regan got any results. I remembered the tall wooden cabinet in the study. A man could easily hide in it. I'd have a look. So I lammed into the study and closed in cautiously on the cabinet, my gun all set to spit a slug. Slowly I reached for the door handle. Then I yanked open the door and braced myself for a hurricane onslaught. But nothing jumped out at me, except the odor of stale tobacco from an old smoking jacket with a long meerschaum sticking out of one pocket.

That's all I could see in the cabinet, just a smoking jacket and a lot of wooden coat hangers.

It didn't take long to complete my search. I looked under the desk, examined the floor for a possible trap door, and unblushingly tapped the walls in an effort to find a secret panel or something. I even examined the two latticed windows again. They were definitely locked, and so was the door that led out under the stairway.

Pooped and discouraged, I returned to the drawing room. I'd heard no roar of a roscoe, so I wasn't surprised to find Regan giving the walls a workout with his knuckles.

Embarrassed, he said, "I ain't playing knock-knock, Lash; I'm looking for a secret panel. All these damn detective stories have 'em, but the only secret panel I've found so far is the one on the rear of my long underwear."

For fifteen minutes Regan and I tapped the walls, but they were as solid as a bride's first batch of biscuits. My knuckles hurt like fury. With all the tap-tapping I'd done, it was a wonder they weren't worn down to my elbow. Still worse, my thirst was terrific. I had half a notion to throw myself down on the broken bottles and lap up a snootful. In a pinch Regan could use his jackknife and handkerchief as a tourniquet.

Fed up with wall-tapping, I drifted back to Helen Partridge. Squatting, I studied the dagger. The business end of it was buried out of sight in her bosom, but the haft was very much in evidence. It was an exact duplicate of the other murder weapon, except that this hippogriff had a sapphire in each eye socket.

I was about to stand up when my eyes fell upon Helen's right hand. It was clenched as though she'd died in a paroxysm of pain or terror. Yet, strangely, her left hand was open. It puzzled me. Was there something in her right hand? Medical examiners raise an awful stink if you monkey with a D.O.A. From the Chief M.E.'s office comes a constant "hands off" admonition. But this was no murder-shrouded-in-mystery squeal. Everybody, including "Doubting Thomas" Christopher Lash, knew who the killer was. Even if I handled or moved this corpse, even if I tied it into a bowknot, the answer would still be the same: Chadwick.

Opening her right hand was like peeling an orange. I had to work on it finger by finger. *Rigor mortis* wasn't by any means complete as yet, but the muscles had already become firmer and more resistant to pressure.

"Whatcha doing now?" Regan inquired as he came toward me. He watched me as I opened her hand.

"This hand was clenched. Thought maybe—"

The hand was wide-open now. I stared at it. Empty. No— wait! I leaner closer. Four strands of hair were lying in the palm. They were short strands, each about two inches in length, yet almost invisible in the glare of light that came from the crystal chandelier. Had I found four strings of priceless pearls, I couldn't have been more elated.

"We've hit the jackpot, Regan," I gloated, and I was trembling with excitement. "These hairs definitely establish the identity of the killer. Helen must have grappled with him when she swung around from the casket. Woman-like, she must have grabbed him by the hair. At any rate, the killer cleared out without knowing he'd left four of his calling cards in her hand."

Regan crouched beside me. "But we know the identity of the killer," he argued. "Dammit all, Lash, how much more proof do you want?"

"But right here in her hand is the clincher, Regan. These hairs belong to the killer. Prove to me they're Chadwick's, and I'll buy you a case of liquor."

The Sergeant bent over and examined the strands like a predacious bird about to pounce on a tasty tidbit of titmouse.

"It's a deal, chum," he chuckled. "And you can pay off right now. These look to me like dark-brown hairs, and Chadwick's mop is browner than a life guard at Coney Island."

"Not so fast, Regan," I said quietly. "Lew has brown hair, what there is of it; and so have Frank and Philip—and Penny."

CHAPTER FOURTEEN

Frowning, Regan ran his thick fingers through his hair. "Yeah, that's right," he muttered. "Guess there's nothing we can do about it till we nab Chadwick. Any suggestions?"

Placing the four strands of hair in one of my little envelopes and penciling a big "X" on it, I said, "All we have to do is go to Chadwick's apartment tomorrow and pick up some hair from his hairbrush. But let's do this thing right. Let's get a specimen of hair from everybody in the house."

"If we walk out there and start scalping them, they'll squawk to high heaven."

"Let 'em squawk," I grunted, taking out a batch of envelopes and removing a small pair of scissors from what I called my "hunting" equipment. "Come on. The sooner we start, the better."

We left the drawing room, locked the sliding doors, and walked across the hall toward the dining room. Daniels met us in the doorway.

"Just this minute came up from the cellar," he informed me. "Everything's airtight down there; no jimmied windows or anything. It's the same story upstairs."

"You called West Twentieth Street?"

"Uh-huh. It knocked them for a loop. Scanlon said he'd call the M.E.'s office, then, notify Neely and Strenz. The whole works ought to be up here in no time."

Regan patted me on the back. "So long, Lash," he said with a chuckle. "It's been nice knowing you."

Paying no attention to the Sergeant, I said to Daniels, "From now on, stick here in the doorway of the dining room. Don't let any of these people out of your sight."

I looked over his shoulder. Lew was sitting at the refectory table with his head buried in his arms; Frank and Penny were standing near the fireplace, conversing in low tones; and Philip, chewing his favorite forefinger, was pacing the room like an expectant father. Jessica was nowhere in sight.

"Where's Mrs. Brocton, Daniels?" I asked.

"In the kitchen. That Webster guy sent her there to make some coffee."

"Good. We can use some. Let's you and I get to work, Regan."

Armed with scissors and the batch of envelopes, I strode to the refectory table, where Lew was hunched over so apathetically. He didn't lift his head when I spoke to him, nor did he give any sign that he heard me. So without any further ado I snipped off a few strands of his hair—there was a little tuft of it above each ear—and placed them in one of the envelopes. An instant later the Sergeant and I headed toward the twosome at the fireplace.

Frank and Penny were so engrossed in each other that I doubt whether they were aware of our presence in the room. I know Philip had seen us walk over to the refectory table—he'd glared at us—but he'd turned his back on us and missed, I think, my little Samson and Delilah performance on Lew.

"Ah! Here's Lieutenant Lash," Frank remarked, and he appeared annoyed that his making time with Penny had to suffer an interruption. "Miss Forbes and I," he added, smiling, "have been having a heated argument over here. Miss Forbes is positive that Martin's innocent. From all I can gather, I think she suspects Jessica."

"Speaking of Jessica," I said, "I hear she's rustling up some coffee. How did you manage it?"

"Philip has a bad case of jitters. I told Jessica a hot cup of coffee would fix him up fine."

"Philip and me both," Penny piped up, shuddering.

"Say, Penny, I didn't know your hair was so beautiful," I said, making my eyes give out with an admiring look. "Why, it's glowing like burnished copper."

"Jeepers!" She jumped away from the fireplace, clamping her hands to her head. "Quick! Somebody get a pail of water!"

"Stop clowning," I snapped. "Honest, Penny, your hair's beautiful tonight."

She stared dreamily at the ceiling. "'Glowing like burnished copper.'" Even more dreamily she stretched out a languid arm. In a queenly voice she said, "You may kiss my hand, Sir Christopher."

I felt like a jackass, what with Regan and Frank looking on, but I took her paw and planted a quick kiss on the fingers. I was surprised not to have a goldfish shoved into my mouth.

"You know what, Penny?" I said. "I'd like to have a strand or two of that hair. No kidding."

She eyed me suspiciously. "Are you planning to stuff a mattress?"

"Don't be silly. I want it for a keepsake. Besides, there's an old superstition in the Lash family that if we carry a girl's lock of hair in our wallet, we'll never want for money."

Up went Penny's hand to her head. When the hand came down, it held several long strands of hair.

"There you are, darling," she cooed, waving her eyelashes at me. "Your only worry now is the Bureau of Internal Revenue." Her face hardened somewhat, though, when she saw me place the strands in an envelope and scribble her name on it. "'Glowing like burnished copper,'" she mimicked. "Huh! I bet that's what you say to all your pennies."

Clicking the scissors. I turned to Frank. "Now let's have some of yours, Mr. Webster."

His lips twisted into an ugly smirk. "Not until you tell me what you want them for. If I need a haircut, I'll go to a barber."

I should have told him, I suppose, but his antagonism at this moment sort of stuck in my craw. Moreover, I could still feel that kink in my back from his half nelson. Then, too, maybe I didn't like his interest in Penny.

I said, "Let's not argue about it, Frank. A murder's been committed in this house, and murder gives me a lot of privileges. I'm sure you don't want to obstruct justice, so let's do this thing quietly," and I lifted the scissors to his head.

Scowling, he shoved my hand away. "Get this straight, Lash," he said through clenched teeth. "I've no desire to obstruct justice or anything else. I just don't like police tactics; I don't like the way you push people around." His smoke-gray eyes now were mere slits, and the muscle in his jaw was twitching me a danger signal. "I've had an antipathy to policemen all my life," he went on in a surly tone. "Maybe it all started when I was a kid. If I played on the grass, they chased me. If I hitched a ride on a trolley, they cuffed me. If I—well, you get the idea, Lieutenant. I just don't like cops."

"Maybe that's because cops aren't so easy to slap in the face," I remarked evenly. "Remove those glasses of yours and I'll do a little slapping around here myself."

"I don't know what this is all about," Philip whined behind me, "but this is certainly no place to settle your differences. Apparently neither one of you has any respect for the dead."

"Shall I hold your glasses, Mr. Webster?" Penny inquired sweetly.

Frank gave her a hard look. Then his face broke into a grin. "On second thought, I'll follow your lead, Miss Forbes." He flicked his hair with a finger. "Go ahead, Lieutenant. Not too short on the sides, if you don't mind."

With Frank's contribution under wraps I turned to Philip. There was no trouble. In fact, he not only let me snip off some of his hair, but he also accompanied Regan and me to the kitchen to help us talk Jessica out of some of hers. Personally, I think he was afraid we might open the icebox and swipe an olive.

Jessica had two eight-cup percolators on the stove when we trooped in. She was standing at a table cutting a fruitcake into slices that were thinner than a postage stamp. A half-pint bottle of cream, a bowlful of sugar, and ten cups and saucers and as many spoons were laid out on a big silver tray.

I let Philip propose the haircut.

"Why do they want a few strands of my hair?" she demanded of him fiercely.

"I—I don't know," he stammered, looking a little foolish.

She brushed him aside and peered at me contemptuously. "What nonsense is this, Lieutenant?" she asked. "What possible bearing can a few strands of my hair have on the capture of Martin Chadwick?"

In no mood to quibble, I picked up the silver tray and started toward the pantry. Instantly Jessica dropped the cake slicer and dashed after me.

"Give me that tray!" she blazed, yanking it from my grasp.

I said. "It's a pleasure, Mrs. Brocton," and with her hands thus occupied, I had no difficulty at all in snipping off some of her hair. I did, however, get a helluva barked shin.

"He tricked me, Philip!" she shrilled. "He deliberately—"

"Thanks, Mrs. Brocton," I cut in, writing her name on the envelope. "Thank you so much."

With a torrent of abuse ringing in our ears, Regan, Philip, and I hit for the pantry. As we entered it Philip paused, then dashed back to the kitchen. Regan and I stopped to watch him. He took the bottle of cream off the tray, put it in the refrigerator, then brought out a can of evaporated milk. When he'd placed the can on the tray, he came hurrying back to us.

Nudging Regan, I said to the undertaker, "It's certainly nice of you and Mrs. Brocton to go to all this trouble—about coffee and cake, I mean. Would two dollars cover our share of it?"

"You misjudge me, Lieutenant," he retorted indignantly. "I admit I'm what you might call a frugal man, but I abhor greediness. Let's see. You, the Sergeant, three of your men, and that Forbes person . . . h'm. Shall we say a dollar?"

"Make it a dollar and a quarter," I said, handing him the money. "I always use three lumps of sugar."

On entering the dining room, I saw Daniels talking to Doc Berlinger in the hall.

"Hello, Lash," the M.E. called out as Regan and I strode toward him. "Why the hell didn't somebody tell me I needed a compass? I've had a helluva time finding this trading post."

Shaking his hand, I said, "Didn't think I'd be seeing you so soon again, Doc. Last night it was Paula Chadwick; now it's her sister."

Berlinger made a wry face. "That means Chadwick has only one more corpse to go. Christ! Maybe I'd better take a room up here until it's all over."

"I see you've got a lot of confidence in us."

"Don't mind me, Lash. After all, if it wasn't for people committing murder, I'd never get a chance to wear off some of this fat. C'mon, where's my meal ticket?"

I told Daniels to stick with the crowd. Then, unlocking the sliding doors of the drawing room, I led Berlinger to the corpse on the floor. Regan closed the doors and toddled behind us.

Putting down his bag, Berlinger dropped his hat and coat upon the floor and knelt beside Helen Partridge.

"Take it from me, Lash," he said, wheezing a bit, "after twelve years of kneeling down like this, it's a wonder I haven't got housemaid's knee."

The sliding doors opened and Daniels stuck his head into the room.

"The big wheels are rolling up, Lieutenant," he said, grinning. "Thought maybe you'd like to know."

"Thanks." I walked to the French doors and peered through the glass panels. Three cars had pulled into the driveway and about a dozen men were heading toward the veranda. "O.K., bring 'em in, Daniels," I ordered. Then to Berlinger, "You can skip the autopsy as far as I'm concerned, Doc. I know the time of death—eleven-forty, two or three minutes either way—and I'm positive she died of an overdose of dagger."

"Suits me," he grunted, flexing Helen's fingers. "You've no idea," he added, "how I hate cutting these beefy babes open from Adam's apple to pelvis. By the time you get all their organs out you feel like you've just completed a five-year concert tour." He dropped Helen's arm, probed under his eye patch for his magnifying glass, and began studying her throat and the nape of her neck. "H'm. Some minor bruises here," he remarked. "Looks like Chadwick grabbed her by the throat with his left hand before slamming the dagger home. No sign of manual strangulation, though. Probably grabbed her by the throat to throttle a scream."

"Would the ultraviolet-ray test with fluorescent powder bring out the fingerprints on her throat?" I asked.

"Sure. That is, if the killer wasn't wearing gloves when he grabbed hold of her. But why waste good powder, Lash? You know who the killer is, same as I do."

I changed the subject. "Get hold of anything else, Doc?"

"Two very interesting things," he answered, nesting his phony glass eye in the socket.

"Yeah, I know," I said. "But what else?"

"Nothing, except that I didn't find any goldfish. How come you boys didn't send me that fish for an autopsy?" he asked with a straight face.

"We knew you wouldn't be interested," I said. "It was masculine gender."

Further discussion was put to flight by Carl Strenz thumping into the room. Behind him were Neely and Chief of Detectives Gilbride, followed by a lot of top brass and reporters. Lolling in the rear were two fingerprint men and a police photographer.

Strenz ignored me completely. Quiet, soft-spoken Gilbride, however, gave me a warm handshake, and Neely patted me on the back as though he were trying to tell me that Staten Island wasn't anything like Siberia.

In no time at all Regan and I had them briefed and in possession of all the facts; that is, all except the part about Regan's blowing the main fuse. I'd laid the blame on Frank's trains; and Regan, anything but a dope, had strung along.

After we finished a Cook's tour of the drawing room and the study I saw Strenz pull Regan and the bigwigs aside for a whispered conference. It didn't last long. Strenz soon signaled me to join them.

"Lieutenant," he said, clearing his throat and brushing some invisible dust off his coat, "I don't as a rule make a practice of interfering with the workings of the Homicide Squad. I don't mind telling you, though, that I'm completely dissatisfied with the way you've handled this case. You've an enviable record, I admit, but apparently this Chadwick affair is a little too big for your britches. To put it bluntly, Lash, I'm relieving you of your duties as officer in charge. If Gilbride and Neely wish you to continue on the case, I've no objection. But as of this instant"—

he indicated the grinning Regan—"Sergeant Regan will assume complete charge. I'm sorry, Lash, but that's the way I feel about it."

"Very good, sir," I said, turning over to him the medallion and managing a Pagliacci smile. Then to Neely, "Mind if I trot along home, Dan? I'm dog-tired."

Neely walked me to the sliding doors and out to the hall. "Don't take it too hard, Chris," he whispered, squeezing my arm. "Regan's a good man, but he doesn't know yoga from nothing. If you want to keep working on the squeal, it's O.K. with me and Gilbride."

"Thanks, Dan. You know, my pop used to say it's only the good detectives who get a kick in the pants. The bad ones are always sitting down on the job. Oh, while I think of it, what did Max have to say about the blood on Frank Webster's trench coat?"

"It didn't match the blood on Paula's evening gown, Chris. As a matter of fact, Max said it was ox blood, and I don't think he meant Regan's."

Heaving a sigh, I said, "This must be my lucky night. Dan, see to it we get a fluorescent-powder test on Helen's throat, will you? The boys might pick up something."

Neely said, "Anything to keep you happy, boy." He grazed my chin playfully with his fist. "G'wan home now and get some sleep," he ordered. "See you in the morning," and he stepped back into the drawing room and closed the doors.

I wriggled into my overcoat, picked up my hat, and pried Penny out of the *kaffeeklatsch* that was going on in the dining room.

"Jeepers, what's the matter with you, Christopher?" she asked, putting on her fur cape and ankling with me to the vestibule door. "Your face looks like something I've seen on a bottle of poison."

I told her about Strenz giving me the heave-ho.

"Why, the nasty old so-and-so," she ripped out. "For two pins I'd go in there and throw a goldfish at the worm." She nudged me and held out her hand. "Go ahead, give me two pins."

"Forget it," I said, grasping her by the shoulders and smiling down at her. "I'm taking you home, Penny—unless, of course, you'd like to stop somewhere and eat."

"Umm. Sounds good. Butter on both sides of the bread?"

"Both sides and the edges. And while we're eating, Penny, you can tell me why you came here tonight."

She straightened my tie and on tiptoes struggled a minute to moisten down my cowlick. Finally she resorted to a bobby pin.

"I wanted to help you, Christopher," she said with disarming simplicity. "Tonight I suddenly remembered something, something very important. At least I think it is. But now that I'm up here I can't for the life of me remember what it was I remembered."

"You're fibbing, Penny," I chided softly. "What you're trying to tell me is that you've changed your mind. You wanted to tell me something; now you're afraid to do it."

"Yes, I— Oh, damn! I don't want to get mixed up in this mess, Christopher. I've got a career to think of."

I said, "I'll make it easy for you, Penny. Tell me what's on your mind, and I promise I'll do everything I can not to involve you in any way."

"Remember, darling, it's a promise." For a minute she stood rigid and silent. At last she asked in a tiny voice, "What time was it when Paula was murdered?"

"Between six-thirty and seven o'clock."

"Would it interest you to know"—I could barely hear her—"the name of the person Paula was with at that time?"

"Yes, very much," I said, trying to keep my voice low. "Who was it?"

"Lew Partridge."

CHAPTER FIFTEEN

When my alarm clock did its rise-and-shine routine at seven-thirty Tuesday morning, it was like pulling teeth to drag myself out of bed. In the wee small hours Penny and I had done away with a couple of thick steaks in some chophouse on upper Broadway. But instead of wiping our mouths and going home, we'd sat for another hour at the table discussing everything under the sun except Lew Partridge's Sunday get-together with Paula. Lord knows I'd tried hard enough to steer her onto the subject, but the mere mention of Lew's name had given her lockjaw. Later, in a taxi, I'd tried another approach: I'd slipped my arm around her and murmured some honeyed words. Cripes, after that I'd forgotten the existence of Lew Partridge.

I had breakfast that bleak, bitter-cold morning in the corner cafeteria. From orange juice to coffee I heard a radio in the rear of the joint blaring out the news of Chadwick's fiendish attack on Helen Partridge. The commentator was spitting out quotes and unquotes like nobody's business. District Attorney Strenz was confident of Chadwick's immediate apprehension; Police Commissioner Farran—blah, blah, blah. Apparently everybody had made a statement except the corpse herself. Strange to say, there was no quote and unquote that Strenz had put Sergeant

Regan at the helm. For that matter, neither was there any mention of it in my morning paper. Could it be possible that Strenz had changed his mind about ousting me?

I took a Seventh Avenue express to 72nd Street, walked west to Riverside Drive, then north to 74th. It was the Commodore himself who opened the main door of the Parkview Towers for me.

"Hello, Lieutenant," he said deferentially. "I see Mr. Chadwick's on the loose again."

"Yeah. But he'll come home soon to change his socks. So make sure you hold onto him."

"Fat chance," he grunted, walking with me to the door of Chadwick's apartment. "Dicks are watching this house every minute of the day."

I dragged out Paula's leather key case and unlocked the door. "You'd better come in with me, feller," I suggested. "I don't want Chadwick to pop up someday and accuse me of taking his kayak."

We padded through the dust and the stifling heat until we reached the lawyer's bedroom. A bed and a chiffonier were in evidence, but the rest of the room was definitely museum.

"Here's what I'm looking for," I said, picking up a pair of military brushes from the chiffonier. "I hope they weren't used by General Grant at some time."

I pulled out a few strands of hair, put them in an envelope, and scribbled Chadwick's name on it. Fifteen minutes later I was back in the subway. Destination: Police lab, 400 Broome Street, Room 701.

Bald-headed Max Weiss, one of the assistant laboratory workers at the police lab under Captain Ragen, is as nice an old duffer as you'd want to meet. He's skyscraper tall and flagpole thin, and has gimlet-like eyes that glare at you as though they can't wait to see what you look like under a microscope. However, when he smiles, the whole lab seems to light up, and before you know it you feel a fill-'em-up, throw-another-log-on-the-fire affection for the man.

"Well, well! Look who's here," he beamed, wiping his hands on his dark-green work coat as he came striding out to the little desk at which I was standing. "Papa Lash's little boy Christopher. What's the matter, Chris?" he inquired, crushing my fingers in his long, bony hand. "You stay away because you owe me money or something?"

"Been awfully busy, Max," I said. "You know how it is."

"Sure. These stinking killers never take a holiday." He wiped his hands on his coat, then placed them upon my shoulders. "How goes the Chadwick business? Not so good, eh? All morning we've been talking about it. Every schlemiel who walks in is asking me if there's some chemical that can make a man invisible."

Producing my batch of envelopes, I said, "Keep it under your hat, Max, but I'm about the only cop in the city who isn't entirely convinced of Chadwick's guilt. Sounds crazy, doesn't it?"

He chuckled. "Sounds more like your papa." Wiping his hands on his coat, he pointed to the envelopes in my hand. "My goodness, what *is* all this?"

As briefly as possible I gave him the particulars and explained what I wanted.

"Simple like anything, Chris," he declared. "Come on inside to the lab."

He swung open the brass rail, and I followed him into an L-shaped lab that was reminiscent of Jessica's on the top floor at Highrock. Its walls were painted a two-toned green, and its windows on the south side looked down on Police Headquarters. The whole place had a clean, cheerful, efficient look about it, like old Max Weiss himself. The three green-coated men at the other end of the lab were too busy with their work even to throw a glance at us.

Max said, "Take off your coat. Make yourself comfortable. I get us a nice comparison microscope." He took me to a large metal table, wiped his hands on his coat, turned on a light. "Now we get to work," he remarked, pointing to a microscope. "First, we take a bit of hair from the Sample 'X' envelope. Sample 'X' are the hairs you found in the hand of the corpse. No?"

"That's right," and I handed him Sample "X."

He wiped his hands, opened the envelope, removed one of the hairs, stained it, then placed it on a glass slide. A moment later he fastened the slide onto one of the two stages of the comparison microscope.

"So!" he grunted, peering into the two eyepieces and fiddling with the elevation knob. "A microscope, Chris, can tell more about a hair than you possibly realize. It tells us from what part of the body the hair comes from; how it was removed from the body; age; nationality—a lot of things. But all we're interested in right now is the bark of the hair. The surface markings will tell the story." He wiped one of his hands on his chest and held it out toward me. "O.K., let's have your first suspect."

I gave him Penny's envelope. As he went about the business of staining and mounting I felt a tenseness growing in me. I thought, Here I am head over heels in love with the babe. If her hair should match with Sample "X"—I quickly erased the thought. But it wriggled back like a snake taking cover, like an undertow slinking away, then returning in the form of an awesome, overpowering wave. This time I didn't fight it. Penny might be the killer, at that. Her goldfish had been found on Paula. What's more, she'd been at Highrock last night. Maybe she'd also killed Chadwick. Maybe she knew the contents of his will; knew she was slated for a share of the estate. With the three Broctons out of the way, she could see to it that Chadwick's body was found, then lay claim to all his possessions. I was sweating profusely now. What the hell was taking Max so long? Why didn't he just

look at the damn hair and tell me yes or no? Why the hell did he
have to stand so motionless? Gripes, to look at him you'd think
he was peeking into Lana Turner's dressing room.

"Chris," he said at long last, lifting his shiny bald head, "you
can give this one a clean bill of health. It doesn't match," and
wiping his hands, he removed the slide and tossed it into a trash
receptacle.

I didn't say a word, but the sigh of relief I heaved must have
sounded like the dying gasp of a ham tragedian. Darling little
Penny was in the clear.

Again Max wiped his hand on his chest and held it out palm
upward. "Now we try the second suspect."

This time I gave him Frank Webster's. With deft fingers he
stained one of the hairs, placed it upon a slide, then mounted the
slide on the second stage of the microscope.

I thought, Here's the guy I've got my money on. Why did he
balk so at giving me a specimen of his hair? But if he's the killer,
what was his motive in killing Paula and Helen? Outwardly he's
tough and sarcastic; down deep, though, he seems a pretty good
egg. An idea stirred in my cranium. Maybe he's a self-appointed
one-man crusade against Chadwick and the Broctons; maybe he's
out to avenge the death of his wife, Barbara.

A crash of splintering glass brought me back to earth. Max
had tossed another slide into the trash receptacle.

"That one's out, too, Chris," he said. "Sample 'X' and your
second suspect have nothing in common."

The next specimen of hair to be mounted on the stage was
Philip Brocton's. As Max studied it through the eyepieces I gave
the undertaker a mental going-over. Philip, for all his nice big
yellow streak, was greedy for money. The lust for lucre has given
many a man a motive for murder; has supplied not only the
motive, but also the intestinal fortitude to go through with it.
But if Philip was the killer, why had he killed Helen? In a vague

sort of way I could see a possibility of his deriving some benefit
from the deaths of Martin and Paula, assuming that Martin was
dead, of course. But Helen's death wouldn't benefit him in the
least. Unless— Oh-oh! Was it possible that he'd killed her to get
possession of the medallion? If so, why hadn't he taken it? Why
had he left it on the floor of the drawing room? Pressed for time?
Couldn't find it in the dark because Helen had fallen on it? With
bated breath I waited for Max to lift his head.

"No good, Chris," he announced. "This one looks nothing
like Sample 'X.'" He caught the look of bewilderment on my
face. "Come, see for yourself." Wiping his hands on his coat, he
reached out and pulled me over to the microscope.

I declined the invitation. "No, thanks," I said. "I'll take your
word for it." With that I wiped my hands on my coat and handed
him Lew Partridge's envelope. Cripes, he had me doing it now!

Lew, I thought, isn't the killer type. But that didn't mean
anything. I've seen plenty of killers, and to look at some of them
you wouldn't think butter would melt in their mouths. Lew, I
remembered, had said something about having worked at one
time for the Universal Insurance Company. H'm. Lots of murders are inspired by fat insurance policies. Maybe Little Boy Lew
had peddled some double indemnities to Paula and Helen; had
wangled a place for himself in the beneficiary's seat. Could be.
After all, unless Penny was pulling my leg, Lew had been the last
person to see Paula.

I kept my eyes riveted on Max's face as he bent over the microscope. It was expressionless. Had it suddenly lighted up, I
think I would have turned a somersault. As the seconds flew
by, however, the wrinkled face began to take on a gloomy cast.
Therefore, I wasn't at all surprised to see the slide go into the
trash can. I even managed to grin a little.

"Bah! Another fizzle," Max muttered. Then, as I handed him
Jessica's envelope, he gave me one of his three-hundred-watt

smiles and said with a chuckle, "Your papa didn't mind fizzles, either."

I said, "Hell, no. Once I asked him why they called a detective a dick. You know what he said, Max? Said it was just a nickname for Richard the Lionhearted."

While I waited for Max to set up the Jessica Brocton slide, I ruminated a bit on the possibility of Jessica's being the killer. She was a quick-tempered bitch, cold-blooded and plenty smart. Furthermore, there'd been no love lost between her and Helen, and maybe a similar dislike of each other had existed between her and Paula. It was Jessica who had found the empty dagger box in Chadwick's apartment on Sunday night. But was the box empty when she found it? Old Vinegar Face might have found the two hippogriff daggers in it and concealed them on her person.

The sound of breaking glass told me that Max had reached a verdict. This time it wasn't so easy to force a smile on my lips. With Jessica in the clear, my Chadwick-is-innocent hunch was just so much hooey. Dammit, all of them had a clean bill of health: Penny, Frank, Philip, and Jessica. Not a killer in a carload. All clean and pure and stamped with approval.

"Well, that's that," I said, shrugging my shoulders.

"Ach! Don't be discouraged, Chris." He wiped his hand on his chest and took the remaining envelope away from me. "Now we make the final test. No?"

He removed one of Chadwick's hairs from the envelope. When it was stained and mounted, he studied it for a few minutes through the eyepieces. Finally he straightened up and said, "A perfect match; like two peas in a pot. Here"—he pulled me over to the microscope—"take a look. Seeing is believing."

I squinted through the eyepieces of the microscope and saw what looked like a pair of fancy golf stockings, minus the feet. Max murmured about "pith" and "medulla" in my ear, but I didn't pay any attention. The pair of golf stockings was perfectly matched, and all the pith and medulla in the world couldn't put my Humpty Dumpty hopes together again. I made a mental note: One case of liquor for Sergeant Regan.

"Well, at any rate, Max," I said, rummaging through the envelopes, "I know now where I stand. From now on I can concentrate on nabbing Chadwick without having any confounded hunches crimping my style." Finding the envelope marked "X," I put it in my pocket. Then, picking up my wraps, I held out my hand. "Thanks a million, Max; you're a prince. By the way, I understand it was ox blood you found on that trench coat Dan Neely sent here yesterday. Tell me, would ox blood play any part in the making of human blood?"

"Yes, but nobody's got anywhere with it. It doesn't work."

"Well, thanks again, Max," I said.

It was ten-thirty when I left the police lab. It was a few minutes shy of eleven when I climbed to the third floor of 320 West 20th Street, entered my eight-by-eight cubicle, and plunked myself down at my heel-marked, cigarette-burned desk. The desk, surprisingly enough, had no cake of soap on it. A cake of soap on your desk denotes you're washed up on a squeal; and if you bellyache to the boys that you didn't get the breaks, you're liable to find a towel with the soap.

What I did find, though, was a batch of interdepartmental reports on top of three large manila envelopes. The envelopes, I discovered, contained correspondence, miscellaneous papers, memorandum pads, and a stack of canceled checks—all from Chadwick's office.

I flipped through the checks, looking at all the "Pay to Bearer" lines for the name of Penny Forbes. I didn't find any, thank goodness. Nor did I find any with Paula's name on it. Beginning with the month of June, however, and working backward through the one- and two-year-old checks, I found plenty of evidence that Chadwick had been a first-class sucker for the Partridges, the

Broctons, and Webster. They'd hit him for telephone numbers, and the more I studied the checks, the more I appreciated the rumor that Chadwick's legal fees were never under twenty-five grand.

The memo pads were those ordinary two-ringed gimmicks that give you a day-by-day scribbling area. Instead of ripping out your day's doodling, you lift the sheet and run it over the rings, thus preserving it for future reference. Chadwick evidently thought a great deal of his doodling; the memo pads went back as far as 1940.

I picked up the pad for the current year. The last penciled scribbling had been made on Friday, the fourth of December. I studied it carefully. In the center of the page was: "Call J. B. —$25,000 tops." Then came some doodling: a sketch of three tiny watches, all of them giving the same time, seven o'clock. J. B., of course, could be anybody. Yet J. B. *might* stand for Jessica Brocton. As for the three little watches—well, Paula had been murdered sometime around seven o'clock. . . . Truthfully, I didn't work myself into a lather over it. Max and his microscope had proved to me beyond a doubt that Chadwick was the killer. From now on, dammit, I'd follow the crowd and stop fiddling with hunches.

By chance I happened to pick up a two-year-old memo pad. Beginning with the first of January, I leafed through the entire month. When I hit the first of February, though, I found a notation that made me sit up and take notice. It said: "Helen Partridge's birthday, February 9. Money? Jewelry? Ask Paula for suggestions."

Good God, I thought. Here's the first decent break I've had. To hell with Max. To hell with Strenz. Here's definite proof that Chadwick's innocent!

CHAPTER SIXTEEN

The door of my cubicle burst open and disclosed the scrawny figure of Dan Neely. His eyes were bloodshot and bleary, as though they'd been open all night, yet there was a broad smile on his seamed face.

"Well! It's nice knowing you thought enough of us to come to work," he said with exaggerated gruffness. "Where you been, Chris?" he added. "Called you three times last night. No answer. You and the goldfish again?"

I made like I didn't hear him. I told him everything I'd done that morning: the hair-picking at Chadwick's apartment; the visit to the police lab. I particularly stressed the fact that the hairs I'd found in Helen's hand were Chadwick's.

Neely's smile broadened. He clapped me on the back. "So you've finally come home to Jesus, eh? Good! Maybe now we'll make some progress on this squeal."

I said, "You can say that again, Dan. Effective immediately, I'm out to get the real killer."

Neely glanced at the ceiling, appealing to higher powers, I think, to hold back their bolts of lightning. Thrusting his face savagely into mine, he said in a trembling voice, "You're out of your mind, Chris. You don't know what you're saying. Too much goldfishing, that's what. One minute you admit Chadwick's the killer, the next minute you're sounding off about somebody else." He picked up my phone. "Get me the psychopathic ward at Bellevue;" he barked at our switchboard operator.

I jumped up, yanked the phone out of his grasp, and pushed him into the chair at the side of my desk. "Now you listen to me," I ordered, cradling the phone and wagging my finger in his face.

"No, you listen to me!" he roared, pouncing from the chair. "Strenz washed you out last night; gave you the bum's rush. It would have stuck, too, except that Jessica Brocton had to open her big mouth about Regan blowing the fuse. Anyway, the upshot was that Gilbride and I went to work on Strenz and got him to put you back in the driver's seat."

"Looks like you're going to get a case of liquor for Christmas, Dan," I said, smiling.

"Common sense is all I want from you," he snapped. "You're in charge again, Chris. So for the love of Mike don't let Gilbride and me down by following up these crackpot ideas of yours."

Gently I pushed him into the chair. "Have I ever let you down?" I asked. He was silent. "Well, have I?"

"No. But there's always a first time."

"Look, Dan. I can prove that Chadwick's innocent. And the proof is right here," I said, tapping the two-year-old memo pad.

Interest flickered in his eyes. I could see that something was urging him to let me explain, while at the same time a strong disinclination to be taken in by my fantasies was holding him back.

"O.K., show me," he finally surrendered. "But it had better be good, brother. I read Lynch's report on all that junk, and he said it didn't amount to beans."

I handed him the memo pad. "Read what it says on that sheet for the first of February," I said, planting myself on the edge of the desk and lighting a cigarette. "Read it, Dan, and tell me if it makes anything tick."

Neely studied the scribbling. At last he said, "Maybe I'm dumb. All I get is that Chadwick wanted to buy Helen a birthday present and couldn't quite make up his mind what to get her. Looks like he was going to ask Paula to suggest something."

"That's right. But doesn't the fact that Helen was born in the month of February mean anything to you?"

"Not particularly."

"Do you know the birthstone for February?"

"No." A glint of amusement sparkled in Neely's eyes. "Let me guess. A tombstone?"

"No, Dan, the amethyst. Did you take a good look at that murder weapon last night?"

"Uh-huh."

"What kind of stones were in the eye sockets of the hippogriff?"

"Gilbride said they were sapphires. Say, what are you leading up to?"

"Just this: The amethyst, not the sapphire, is the birthstone for February. To put it another way, the killer used the wrong dagger. Chadwick, I assure you, wouldn't have made that mistake."

"Maybe Chadwick didn't have time to be choosy. It was pitch-dark in the drawing room. Maybe when he reached for the daggers, he couldn't tell which was amethyst and which was sapphire. So he took a gamble, that's all. Personally, Chris, I think you're making a mountain out of a molehill. For my money, your theory stinks."

"Thanks. My pop used to say—"

"You and your pop give me a pain in the rear end," he interrupted brusquely. "If I were you, Chris, I'd go to a spiritualist tonight and see if you can get your old man to tell us how Chadwick got into that locked drawing room. In the meantime, get to work on these reports and stop making an ass of yourself." And tossing the memo pad onto my desk, he rose from the chair and slammed away to his own cubicle.

A lot of people, particularly readers of detective stories, have an idea that when a Homicide man is put officially in charge of a murder squeal, it's up to him to run his fanny off in an effort to bring the culprit to justice. According to the misinformed, this would-be Sherlock Holmes does practically all the legwork, interviews suspects singlehandedly, and then, after squeaking out a couple of tunes on his fiddle, comes up with all the right answers. Taxpayers, it ain't so; and if anybody tells you different, he's either a whodunit addict or he's taking a home correspondence course in How to Be a Detective.

As for playing the fiddle—well, that's no exaggeration. I've yet to meet a Homicide man who didn't play second fiddle to heavy brass. It's teamwork that solves murders, and each branch of the police department is a member of the team, whether it's ballistics or a platoon of patrolmen from a local precinct. The captain of the team is the guy who's officially in charge of the squeal. It's his job to correlate the various branches into a formidable fact-finding unit. He's the human clearinghouse of every report, official or otherwise, that pertains to the squeal. In other words, from the assemblage of reports submitted he separates the chaff from the wheat and prepares an interpretive report that goes to his immediate superior, who in turn sends it on to the bigwigs. If the report shows a lack of progress, a conference is called, which is merely another way of saying that the bigwigs put on a nice little inquisition for the littlewigs. Not only do they call you up on the carpet, but nine times out of ten they carry you out on it.

The Chadwick squeal, of course, didn't come under the heading of a squeal to be solved. With the exception of myself, everybody from the commissioner down to the bat boy on our baseball team knew the killer was Martin Chadwick. For that matter, thanks to the newspapers and radio commentators, everybody in the five boroughs knew it, including all points north, south, east, and Westchester. The only riddle in the squeal was how a prominent public figure such as Chadwick could still be wandering around loose without anybody spotting him.

It was a riddle, all right, and the newspapers were making the most of it. One editorial writer said the police department was stone-blind, and suggested that the commissioner equip every man on the force with a seeing-eye dog. A columnist for one of the tabloids even took a lulu of a pot shot at me. He said in his column, "Instead of man-hunting, Lieutenant Christopher Lash, heretofore a pretty smart copper, is spending his A.M.'S and P.M.'S with a musical comedy cutie. It's a penny-wise, pound-foolish practice, Lieutenant."

For five straight hours I sat at my desk, taking only a thirty-minute breather for lunch. I caught up on all the reports, and even managed to boil them down to a three-page condensation. The midnight-to-eight shift reported an uneventful night at Highrock, and the same held true for the two boys on guard at the Webster-Brocton Funeral Home. The fingerprint men had found no prints on the murder weapon except Martin Chadwick's. But the medallion had plenty: Chadwick's, Helen's, and Frank Webster's. At first I got a little excited about Frank's prints being on the medallion, until I remembered that he'd stood toying with it on Sunday night in Chadwick's apartment. The biggest disappointment, though, was the report on the silver-nitrate test. The fingerprint men hadn't found a single print on Helen's throat, and it was their combined opinion that Martin Chadwick had held her by the throat with a gloved hand.

Before knocking off for lunch I'd sent a couple of experts up to Highrock to test the walls and the floors of the drawing room and the study. If there were any secret panels or trap doors up there, they'd find them pronto. I'd also instructed them to examine the doors. If they found nothing unusual, they were to take the tubular keys and make the rounds of the local locksmiths. Somewhere in that neighborhood they might find a locksmith who'd made duplicates of those keys for someone in Highrock. And I didn't intend to confine the detectives to local locksmiths. If they reported failure, I'd institute a citywide search.

After lunch I made two phone calls: one to Highrock, one to Sam Willis' wife. The Highrock call was just a routine check on my men stationed up there, but the call to the cabbie's wife was really important. Sam, she told me, was out cruising in his hack. She didn't expect him home until seven o'clock.

"Will you tell him to stick close to home this evening?" I asked. "Tell him Lieutenant Lash will call for him about seven-thirty."

Shortly after three o'clock I got a call from Penny. Her sultry voice was music in my ears.

"How you doing, angel?" I asked.

"Chris darling, I'm literally frazzled," she complained. "Will you believe it? I've been shopping all day for a fire hydrant."

"A what?"

"Fire hydrant," she repeated. "You know—one of those canine comfort stations. Jeepers, don't people have dogs any more? Chris, I tried all the big department stores, and the best they could offer me was a silly old umbrella stand. Finally got one, though, in a junk shop. Was Cuspidor happy! Why, the little darling kicked up his heels the minute he saw it."

"How did you get the hydrant home?"

"In a taxi, of course. The junk-shop man didn't have any paper to wrap it in. So I rolled it to the curb, stood it up, and waited for a taxi. Then something awful happened.

"Don't tell me a dog—"

"Good gracious, no. There was a car parked at the curb, and a policeman came along, saw the fire hydrant, and gave the poor driver a ticket. Oh, it was awful, Chris."

I clucked my tongue sympathetically. "What you need, Penny, is another steak dinner," I suggested. "How about celebrating with me?" And I told her of my ascension to the throne again.

But she turned down the suggestion. She was tired, needed a shower, all that sort of thing. She promised, however, to call for me at Highrock; that is, if she could get the stage manager to let her skip the second act again.

"Last night I told him I was going to have a baby," she explained. "Tonight I'll have to tell him I'm going to get married." She popped me a kiss. "'Bye now, darling. Oh, Chris, before I forget it, do send Cuspidor a little something for his birthday. He's so terribly sensitive, the little darling."

"How about a bag of assorted cuffs?" I asked.

There was a tinkling laugh at the other end of the line; then a click, and silence.

What with one thing and another, I didn't get out of my cubicle until six o'clock. I strolled up to 23rd Street, stepped into a retail liquor store, and shelled out fifty skins for a case of rye, which the proprietor promised to deliver to Sergeant Regan's place in West 18th Street. If Regan's old man wasn't home, there was every possibility that the Sergeant would see some of the bottles.

I grabbed a bite in an Italian spaghetti house, and half an hour later I walked out with a full stomach and a sore wrist. I'd laid off the slivers of garlic, though. If Penny called for me at Highrock, there'd be a long taxi ride to 97th Street.

At seven-thirty sharp I arrived at Sam Willis' dump on the corner of 49th and Third. I shook his hand and bowed to his straggly-haired wife.

"Jeez, Lieutenant," he said, ushering me into a parlorful of squawking kids. "When the old lady said you was comin' to pick me up, I thought maybe it was a pinch or somethin'."

"Nothing like that, Sam. I'm here to ask a favor. Frankly, I need your help."

"All ya gotta do is name it, Lieutenant."

"I want you to go uptown and hide in a closet."

Sam swallowed hard. "Jeez, what's the angle?" he croaked.

"If you were to hear again the voice of our friend Mr. Trench Coat, would you recognize it?"

"I—I don't know. Maybe I would, maybe I wouldn't."

"Like to try? I'll make it worth your while, Sam."

"Brother, you've got yourself a partner."

I said, "Good!" Then, reaching for a handful of change, I said to the brood: "O.K., kids, bring out your piggy banks."

CHAPTER SEVENTEEN

It was eight-twenty when Sam maneuvered his cab into the drive-way at Highrock and parked behind a car that I recognized as Regan's jalopy. The mansion was ablaze with lights, yet seeming-ly no amount of illumination could dispel the spectral appear-ance of the place.

"Jeez, this joint gives you the creeps," Sam whispered as I alighted from the cab. "Whatever you do, pal," he added with a shudder, "don't forget to send for me."

"Stop worrying. I'll have you inside in no time. Just sit tight until Lynch gives you the word."

I left him and headed toward the veranda. Before I'd gone half the distance Lynch stepped out from behind a tree and beamed his flashlight in my face.

"Oh, hello, Lieutenant," he said, switching off the light.

"Everything shipshape?"

"Not even a polar bear prowling around." He jerked a thumb over his shoulder, "Sergeant Regan's inside." His voice dropped to a whisper. "Look out for him, Lieutenant; he's plenty burned up."

Lowering my own voice, I said, "About fifteen minutes from now, Lynch, go over to that cab and take the driver around to the side of the house. Stop at the study window. I'll open it and let him in."

He chuckled. "Dirty work at the crossroads, eh? O.K. Fifteen minutes."

I stepped onto the veranda.

"Where's our little band of vultures?" I asked Daniels as I entered the hall.

"Frank's down in the cellar with his trains, Jessica's up in the lab, and Philip and Lew are in the drawing room. Regan's with them. Have a cough drop?"

"No," I grunted. Then I said quietly, "For the next hour or two stick in the drawing room, Daniels, and make sure nobody gets an earful at that connecting door. Let's go, boy."

I led the way to the sliding doors, separated them, and stepped into the drawing room. Daniels was right behind me.

The room, for all its brilliance of light, was terrifyingly gloomy. Indeed, the gloom was so oppressive I felt a shiver run through me, particularly when I saw the two caskets near the French doors. So startling was the resemblance of one corpse to the other that for an instant I half suspected that the undertaker had placed Paula's casket against a mirror. As for the flowers— well, for a minute I thought I was in a florist shop.

Lew, I noticed, was standing at Helen's coffin like a huge dog with its front paws on the edge of a water trough. His face was convulsed with anguish, and his lips moved soundlessly as though he were entreating his wife to open her eyes and speak to him. It wasn't a pleasant sight. For once it was almost a pleasure to fix my eyes on the pasty, frightened face of Philip Brocton, who was sitting beside Regan at the far end of the drawing room.

As Daniels and I walked over I could see the Sergeant's frame begin to bristle. Lynch was right. Regan was burned up over the officer-in-charge deal, and judging from the way he looked at me, I was an out-and-out arsonist.

"Hello, Regan. Hello, Mr. Brocton," I said.

Philip offered me his tapioca-pudding hand, which I shook under duress, while Regan grunted something unintelligible.

"Come into the study, Sergeant," I went on, eying him significantly. "There's something I want to discuss with you."

Springing to his feet, Philip grasped my arm. "You're—you're not going to leave me alone in this room, are you?" he gasped, green around the gills.

It was tough keeping a sneer out of my voice. I said, "No. Daniels'll stay with you." Then to the detective, "Give him a cough drop; it'll steady his nerves."

Regan and I went into the study. When I closed the connecting door behind us, the Sergeant told me in a surly tone to speak my piece and let him get back to some fresh air.

"Snap out of it, Regan," I said. "If anyone should be down in the mouth around here, it's me. On account of you, feller, I had to shell out fifty skins tonight for a case of rye."

His face lighted up. "Y'mean those hairs we found in Helen's hand were Chadwick's?"

"Nothing else but."

Regan's bellicose manner disappeared like a Murphy bed. "Guess now you'll string along with the rest of us, eh?" he inquired with a laugh.

"Nope. I still say Chadwick's innocent."

"In the face of all the evidence we've got?" He wagged his head mournfully. "Man, you're screwier than a ship with six propellers. Unless, of course, you've"—he gave me a shrewd look—"latched onto something I don't know I about."

"Why don't you hang around and see?"

"Chum, I wouldn't go home now even if I knew the name of the Mystery Melody and knew I was gonna get a phone call from the sponsors."

A pair of knuckles rapped on the glass of one of the latticed windows. It came so unexpectedly that Regan not only jumped a foot high but actually reached for his gun.

"Take it easy, Regan," I cautioned. "It's only Lynch."

"Phew! For a minute there I thought it was Chadwick. You know, it's just like that bastard to knock on the window and thumb his nose at us."

I hurried to window and unlatched it. "O.K., Lynch," I whispered. "Boost him in."

Noiselessly, Sam scrambled into the study.

"Say, I know this guy," Regan declared as I locked the window. "He's the feller who found Paula in his cab. What's the gimmick, Lash?"

I draped an arm across Sam's shoulders. "Sam's going to hide in that cabinet over there, while you and I question Lew, Frank, and the Broctons," I explained. "Sam, don't forget, heard the killer say, 'Take me to the Allison Theatre, and don't spare the horses.' So if we're lucky, Sam may be able to recognize that voice tonight."

"The hell he will," Regan scoffed. "Not unless we can coax Chadwick to drop in and say a few words. But go ahead, Lash. Don't let me stop you. I'll ride along just for the laughs."

"You ready, Sam?" I asked.

"Sure thing, Lieutenant."

I took him to the wooden cabinet, opened the door, and motioned him to step inside.

"You'd better sit down," I advised. "This may take longer than I think. Whatever you do, Sam, don't make any noise. Don't do anything but keep your ears open and wait for me to tell you to come out. If you wedge a piece of paper in the door, you'll be able to see and hear and breathe without any trouble."

When Sam was all set, I placed a chair in front of the desk, parked myself in the swivel chair, and asked Regan to bring in Philip Brocton.

"Sit down, Mr. Brocton," I said when he and the Sergeant walked into the room. "We have a few questions we'd like to ask."

Nervously he fumbled into the chair. "Yes—of course," he said, nibbling what was left of his forefinger. "If there's anything I can do to—"

"First of all," I interrupted, "how's that shoulder of yours getting along?"

"That fracas in the hall last night didn't help any," he whined. Then, gritting his teeth as though he lay shattered and bleeding beneath Old Glory on some battlefield, he added heroically, "But I'm not complaining, Lieutenant. Frankly, I'm grateful the good Lord saw fit to spare me."

Sometimes, I suppose, even the good Lord gets tired and makes mistakes.

"Mr. Brocton, give us a brief account of what you did last Sunday evening," I said, taking out my notebook and pencil. "What I'd particularly like to know is where you were between six-thirty and seven o'clock. Let me advise you to stick rigidly to the truth. We'll check every statement you make, and if we find any discrepancies, we'll haul you down to headquarters for a real going-over."

He remained silent for a time, peering at me with his beady eyes, endeavoring, I think, to find in my face some explanation for this uncalled-for quiz session. I think he would have voiced a protest, except that my menacing expression frightened him somewhat.

At last he said, "If you can possibly avoid repeating any of this to Frank or Lew, I'd appreciate it. It's a personal matter, and I've no desire to have it reach the ears of my brothers-in-law."

I told him we'd keep everything in strict confidence.

Sagging with relief, he murmured a faint "Thank you." Then, glancing cautiously at the connecting door behind him, he leaned forward and said in a confidential tone, "I needn't tell you that ever since last July, Martin has done everything in his power to hurt us. He was instrumental in having Lew thrown out of Universal Insurance, and he did everything possible to put Frank and me out of business. I admit it was Martin's money that set us up in our present establishment. But from the moment he turned against us he began demanding that we make good on our promissory notes. To top it all, he even demanded an exorbitant rental on Highrock; threatened eviction if I didn't pay it."

"What's all this leading up to?" I asked irritably.

"It explains," he answered in a scarcely audible voice, "why I went to see Martin last Sunday."

I sat bolt upright in the swivel chair. Even Regan must have been jolted, for he grabbed a chair, pulled it up quickly to the side of the desk, and sat down, his eyes fixed eagerly on the undertaker's face.

"And did you see him?" I inquired.

Philip took another fleeting look at the connecting door and another bite out of his forefinger. "Yes," he answered. "And if I must say so, it was anything but a pleasant meeting."

"Tell us about it."

"When Paula informed us that she was in a family way," he went on, "we took it for granted that Martin would ease up with his outrageous demands. He didn't. Furthermore, even Paula refused to intercede for us. None of us, of course, had nerve enough to approach Martin. That is, not until last Sunday afternoon, when I decided to phone him and make an appointment to see him Monday morning in his office."

"What did he say when you called? Was he friendly?"

"No; very aloof, in fact. Said I most certainly couldn't visit his office. If I wanted to see him, I could meet him at three that afternoon in the lobby of the Eastern Hotel on Fifty-seventh Street. He had to meet a client there at three-thirty. Well, to make a long story short, I arrived at the hotel at three and had a ten-minute talk with Martin. He was quite un-co-operative. And when I pleaded with him to extend the time on our notes, he said he'd see us in hell first. There was no point in arguing with him, so I walked out."

I made a few notations in my notebook. "And was that the last time you saw him Sunday?"

"Not exactly," he said hesitantly. "Halfway to the subway I decided to go back and have another try at Martin. But as I approached the hotel I saw him shoot out of the door and into his car. The next minute he was scooting uptown."

"That business about meeting a client there at three-thirty must have been a lot of hooey," I remarked.

"Definitely, Lieutenant. Personally, I think Martin—I haven't any right to say this, of course—but I think Martin had a date that afternoon with some woman. Don't ask me why; it's just a hunch of mine. His having to meet a client, no doubt, was simply an excuse to get away from the apartment without arousing Paula's suspicions."

"Did he mention the name of the client, by any chance?"

"No."

"What did you do after he drove away?"

"I—I called Paula. I admit it wasn't a very nice thing to do. But Martin had treated me shabbily. So I told Paula what had happened and even voiced an opinion as to what I thought Martin was up to."

"How did Paula take it?"

"Surprisingly calmly," he replied. "In fact"—two spots of red stained his pasty cheeks—"she told me to mind my own business and leave Martin alone."

"What happened next?"

"I decided to enter the lobby of the hotel and remain there for a while. I thought perhaps Martin would return and I'd have another chance to talk with him."

You're a liar, mister, I thought. I bet anything you figured Chadwick might return with a dame on his arm. Then you'd really go to work on him; you'd make him do anything to keep your mouth shut.

"And did he come back?" I inquired.

"No; and I waited until almost six o'clock. Then I walked to the subway, took an uptown express, and got home around six-forty-five."

"Who was here when you returned?"

His beady eyes wavered and fell. "Helen," he mumbled, studying his hands.

"Where was your wife? And what about Frank and Lew?"

"Jessica was out taking a walk. Frank, I believe, was at the movies. As for Lew—I couldn't say; he didn't tell me. However, I could make a good guess. He was probably sitting in some gin mill."

I made some more notations. "O.K., Mr. Brocton, that's all," I said. Then to Regan, "Take him out, Sergeant, and bring in Lew Partridge."

Three or four minutes elapsed before Regan completed his delivery. When the Sergeant finally returned to the study with the little roly-poly in tow, Lew shuffled in like a man suddenly bereft of his eyesight.

Now that I was face to face with him, I was shocked by the change in his appearance. No mistake about it, Helen's untimely death had done things to poor Lew. What once had been a rotund, jovial-looking face was now a shrunken blob of clay. Moreover, he appeared to have lost considerable weight. Maybe it was my imagination, but his heretofore blubbery figure seemed incredibly shriveled and deflated. Of one thing I was sure: It wasn't going to be pleasant putting the screws on a guy whose heart was so obviously breaking.

He came to a halt in front of the desk, peering at me with dazed, bloodshot eyes. "You sent for me?" he asked in a listless voice.

"Yes. Sit down, Lew," I said affably. "This won't take long. Just a few routine questions I want to get off my chest."

He sank into the chair and stared vacuously at the fire in the grate. Suddenly he faced me and said in a voice thick with emotion, "I've some questions for you, too, Lash. When are they going to get Martin? How long do I have to wait before I can see that bastard burn?" He buried his face in his hands. "So help me, Lash, if I ever lay hands on him, I'll tear him to pieces."

I hate to harp on this, but it sticks in your craw, this business of kicking a man when he's bent over a barrel of trouble. Nevertheless, you soon learn in this racket that when a guy is in a bent-over position, your foot has a better chance of reaching its target. Gripes, I didn't want to bear down on this guy, no more than I'd wanted to browbeat his wife. Still, there was no way out of it. As my pop used to say, "In this business, son, it pays to leave your heart home on the mantelpiece. If you don't you'll forget your handcuffs someday and find it's damn hard tying up a killer with heartstrings."

"Lew, we happen to know you saw Martin and Paula Chadwick on Sunday," I said, ignoring his questions. "Do you want to tell us about it? Or would you rather go downtown and have them push you around a bit?"

Slowly Lew raised his head and gave me a searching look. "How did you know?" he asked, making an effort to keep his voice from showing the intensity of his feeling. "Did—did Helen tell you?"

"We have our methods," I informed him. "Don't forget, there's always someone who sees what he shouldn't see. Want to tell us your side of it?"

After a long deliberation he nodded his head. "Why not?" he muttered. "I didn't do anything I shouldn't have." He sighed heavily and hunched himself closer to the desk. "Along toward five o'clock in the afternoon," he began, "I told Helen and Jessica I was going down to the funeral parlor to chew the fat with Quinn. Quinn's the night man. On Sundays he takes over from four until closing time."

"Where were Frank and Philip?"

"Frank, I believe, went to the movies as soon as Quinn relieved him at four. He always goes to the movies on Sunday. And Philip left here at two o'clock to attend a meeting of the church elders."

"What time was it when you reached the funeral parlor?"

"I didn't go there. It was just an excuse to get out of the house. You see, I had an appointment at six-thirty to see Martin and Paula at their apartment. I'd been phoning them constantly for a week or two, and they'd finally consented to see me."

"Why did you want to see them?"

"I felt sure I could persuade Martin to get me back my job with Universal Insurance. Helen knew I had the appointment, but not Jessica. That's why I had to pull that gag about seeing Quinn."

I said, "O.K. Get on with your story."

Lew nodded, his eyes shifting again to the fire in the grate. Staring at the flames, he said, "I took Philip's car out of the garage—Jessica raised hell about it, of course—and immediately started down to Seventy-fourth Street."

"Just a minute, Lew. Why didn't Philip use the car? Wasn't it raining cats and dogs?"

"Philip's deathly afraid to drive in the rain, afraid the car'll go into a skid. Then, too"—this with a faint smile—"he thinks gasoline is entirely too expensive."

"What time was it when you got to the Parkview Towers?"

"Exactly five-forty-five—much too early for my appointment. I knew Martin hated people who didn't keep on-the-dot appointments, so I decided to pull away from the house and kill a little time in some nearby bar." He was silent for a while. Then, moistening his thick lips as though he were lubricating them to make easy passage for some difficult words, he turned to me and said, "But I never got to the bar. The minute I started the motor I saw Paula dash out of the front entrance. I could see she was terribly upset about something. When I called to her, she ran over to the car, opened the door, and jumped in."

I pushed my pack of cigarettes across the desk. Lew's hand trembled as he took one. My own hand trembled a bit as I clicked my lighter and held it toward him.

"Did she give you any idea, any inkling as to what the trouble was?" I asked.

He puffed on the cigarette as though he'd been submerged in water for a minute and was gulping in great gobs of air. "No," he answered, squinting at me through the smoke. "All she said was, 'Lew, take me as fast as you can to Eighty-third Street.' With that she burst out crying. I could see she was in no condition to answer a lot of questions, so I shot up to Eight-third and Riverside Drive. She made me stop the car there. She jumped out and ran halfway up the block toward West End Avenue. At first I thought I'd follow her. But all of a sudden she ran up a flight of stairs and disappeared into one of the houses, an old brownstone that was all boarded up. It was then that I saw Martin's car at the curb. A few minutes later—I think it was then about six-fifteen—Martin and Paula came out of the house, got into the car, and drove off toward West End Avenue."

"You're positive it was Martin Chadwick?"

"I didn't see his face clearly; I was half a block away. He was wearing his trench coat and black fedora. Oh, it was Martin, all right. I'm sure of it."

"That boarded-up brownstone—do you know who owns it?"

"No."

"What's the number of the house?"

"I couldn't say. When I saw Martin and Paula drive off, I returned home by way of Riverside Drive. I decided not to keep the appointment. I figured if Martin and Paula were having one of their arguments, it wouldn't do me any good to break in on it."

"What time did you get home?"

"Not until eight o'clock. I stopped off at a neighborhood bar to toss off a few drinks. A place called the Wigwam, on Thayer Street and Sherman Avenue."

For a few minutes I was busy with my notebook. At last I said, and I tried to make it sound unimportant, "Did Mrs. Partridge have any insurance?"

Not a muscle in his face moved. A look of dull obstinacy clouded his eyes. "That's none of your business, Lash," he declared sullenly. "You've absolutely no—" He broke off, shrugged his shoulders. "Doesn't matter anyway," he went on in a lugubrious voice. "Nothing matters any more. Sure, I'll tell you, Lash," he cried, scrambling to his feet. "Thanks to Martin, I'll have something like twenty grand to jingle in my pocket. And you know what? Oh, this'll kill you, Lash. Helen was the beneficiary on Paula's policy." He threw back his head, laughed mirthlessly. "Think of it! I'll be a rich man—crawling with money—lousy with it! You know what I'm going to do with it?" he demanded, leaning over the desk and pushing his face close to mine "No, you're wrong. Horses and liquor won't get a penny of it. I'm going to have some real fun. Yes, indeedy. Every day, Lash, I'm going to burn a pile of it in front of Philip and Jessica. It'll kill 'em!" He swung away from the desk and lurched to the connecting door. "It'll drive 'em stark, raving mad, I tell you." And with a laugh that made my flesh crawl, he opened the door and stumbled into the drawing room.

"Well, what are we waiting for?" Regan asked me, his face quivering with excitement. "Holy Canarsie, Lash, didn'tcha hear that part about the boarded-up brownstone? Bet you a case of rye that's where Chadwick's hiding out."

"Not so fast. One thing at a time, Regan," I cautioned. "Remember, Sam Willis has yet to hear Frank and Jessica. Besides, if Chadwick's using that brownstone for a hideout, he won't be leaving it in a hurry."

At that instant somebody knocked on the connecting door. It opened, and Daniels stuck his head into the study.

He said, "That Forbes dame is here, Lieutenant. You want to see her?"

"Yeah. Show her in."

"Boy, you got it bad," Regan observed when Daniels was gone. "Penny's a swell dish, I admit, but swell dishes like that, chum, don't belong in a lieutenant's china closet."

I had it on the tip of my tongue to answer that crack. I would have, too, if Penny hadn't breezed in at that moment. She looked extra-delectable that night. A small beaver hat sat jauntily on her head, and under a beaver jacket was a green velvet dinner gown with a neckline that seemed to be taking a suicidal plunge. It was all of sixty seconds before I could look her in the face.

"Hi, Penny," I said, rising and waving her to the chair in front of the desk. "Sit down, angel, and rest your wings."

"Gee, Penny," Regan drooled, "you look scrumptious tonight in that dress, like a jewel box or something."

She was too busy admiring the room to pay any attention to us. Finally she ambled over to the bust of Shakespeare, wrapped an arm around it, and said to me:

"Quote: 'How now, mad spirit? What night-rule now about this haunted grove?' Unquote."

"We're playing a little game, Penny," I said, walking over to her and leading her to the chair in front of the desk. "You want to play?"

She squirmed out of her jacket, threw it on the back of the chair, and reached into her handbag. Pulling out a five-dollar bill, she tossed it upon the desk. "Sure thing, darling," she chirped. "I'm shooting five. Give me the dice."

"Not that kind of game," I remonstrated as I picked up her fin and shoved it into her handbag. "Sit down, Penny, and I'll tell you about it."

Ignoring the chair, she perched herself prettily upon the desk and crossed her legs. "O.K., Chris. Let's hear it."

"Can you say, 'Take me to the Allison Theatre, and don't spare the horses'?"

The impish smile on her face disappeared like a cockroach in a roomful of DDT bombs. "Is this a gag?" she asked, throwing Regan and me a shrewd look.

I said, "Don't be silly. The object of the game is to see which one of us can hit the lowest key." In a deep bass voice I rumbled, "Take me to the Allison Theatre, and don't spare the horses. . . . See what I mean?" I said in my natural voice. "Now you try it, angel."

She said it, all right. By God, her voice sounded so masculine I had to look at her gams to convince myself she wasn't wearing trousers.

CHAPTER EIGHTEEN

"Nice going, Mr. Forbes," I said with a laugh. Not that I felt much like laughing. I thought, You worry the heart out of me, Penny. Why the devil does that little head of yours keep bobbing up in this squeal? Aloud I said, "You win, angel. The—"

"Oh, stop it, Chris," she cut in petulantly. "Do I look that dumb?"

"What do you mean?"

She slid off the desk, tripped to the wooden cabinet, and yanked open the door. "O.K., groundhog," she said to Sam Willis, "you can come out now."

I sprang toward the cabinet, shut the door, and pulled Penny away. "Blast you," I fumed. "How did you know he was there?"

"Are you kidding?" she asked. "Look, darling. There's an empty cab standing in the driveway. What's more, there wasn't a newspaper in town that didn't play up that 'Take me to the Allison Theatre' business."

"Well, smarty, you march right out to the drawing room and stay there until I send for you," I said huffily. "And don't breathe a word of this. Understand?"

Pouting, she picked up her jacket and lolled over to Shakespeare. With her hand on the Bard's shoulder she said, "Quote:

'I would speak blasphemy ere bid you fly: But fly you must; uncurable discomfort reigns in the hearts of all our present parts. Away, my lord, away!'" And with a hammish gesture of infinite despair she flung the jacket across her chest, strode to the connecting door, and out. But the door had scarcely closed when it popped open and Penny stuck her head into the room. "Unquote," she said, and pulling her head out, slammed the door.

"She's nuts, I tell you," Regan remarked, grinning. He pointed to the bust. "It's a wonder Benjamin Franklin didn't tell her to go fly a kite."

I didn't correct him. Like Doc Berlinger, Regan wasn't interested in bronze busts, anyway.

"Go down to the cellar and get Frank Webster up here," I told him. "And if you think you can't handle him, take Daniels along."

Regan hitched his trousers a trifle. "He's coming up even if I have to shove him through the floor."

Much to my surprise, Regan returned to the study in one piece. Even more surprising, he had Frank with him.

"Have a chair, Frank," I said in a friendly manner. "You and I have some unfinished business to attend to. I still want to hear where you were and what you were doing on Sunday evening between six-thirty and seven."

"You mean you dragged me upstairs for a fool thing like that?" he drawled through twisted lips as he dropped into the chair in front of the desk and slung a leg languidly over the arm of it. "I don't get it, Lash. Is Martin the man behind these murders? Or do you suspect me of having something to do with them?"

"I'll put my cards on the table," I said candidly. "I doubt very much that Chadwick's the killer. Oh, I admit there's a preponderance of evidence against him. In fact, I'm probably a damn fool for not accepting it. But until I feel differently about the whole thing, I'm going to keep hammering at you people."

"At least you're honest about it," he returned, helping himself to one of my cigarettes, which I lighted for him. "But I'm damned if I can see where any of us fits the bill as a good suspect." He blew a stream of smoke through his nostrils. "Take Philip, for example," he continued. "Philip hasn't guts enough to commit a murder."

"What about Jessica?"

He chuckled. "Jessica has the guts and the brains, all right, and I don't doubt she despised Helen. As for murdering Paula, though, that's absolutely out. Jessica isn't capable of loving anyone too deeply, but she came close to it in her affection for Paula. It was Paula who persuaded Martin to set up that lab for Jessica."

"How about Lew?"

"Definitely a softie. Furthermore, he worshiped Helen. You know that as well as I do."

"Which leaves me only one suspect—you."

Again he chuckled. "I can appreciate your singling me out, Lash," he said complacently. "In your book I meet all the requirements, I suppose. I'm a hard-crusted, devil-may-care sort of guy, and rubbing out a couple of human beings wouldn't faze me too much—not after having seen so many of them shot to hell in the Bulge." He paused and flung his cigarette into the fireplace, where the flames went at it like a dog gnawing a bone. "There's just one thing missing—motive," he went on. "Why the hell would I want to kill Paula and Helen? I was damn fond of them."

"I'm not so much concerned with motive, Frank, as I am with opportunity."

Unblinkingly serene, his smoke-gray eyes peered at me. "In other words, Frank," he said, smiling, "where were you on the night of December sixth?"

"I'll settle for the evening of December sixth," I told him. "Between six-thirty and seven."

He added another leg to the arm of the chair and leaned back with knees clasped in his hands, an indolent picture of solid comfort.

"At that time, Lieutenant," he said musingly, "I was in the balcony of the Allison Theatre. Let's see. Quinn relieved me at four, so it must have been about four-twenty when I stepped out of the bus and entered the theatre. It was almost seven-thirty when I came out."

"What time did you get home?"

"About twenty after eight. It wasn't raining when I came out of the Allison, so I decided to walk home; thought I'd grab a little fresh air."

"What movies did you see?"

Up went his eyebrows. "You mean I'm supposed to remember the titles?"

"That's only half of it," I said grimly. "I also want to hear what those pictures were about. It so happens," I added, grinning, "that I was in the Allison on Sunday. So make it good, feller, I'm all ears."

He returned the grin. "Right now I'm a little hazy about the titles," he confessed. "But they'll come to me, I'm sure. The feature picture was a story about Adolf Hitler and his escape from Germany. Suffering from amnesia, he comes to America as a stow-away, and years later becomes American ambassador to Israel. The 'B' picture was a stinker: cowboys, rustlers, and a city gal with a big ranch on her hands. Then the newsreel and a Pinky the Polar Bear animated cartoon."

For ten minutes I plied him with questions. When I was done with him, I hadn't the slightest doubt that on the sixth of December he'd spent the late afternoon and part of the evening in the Allison Theatre. He'd even recalled the titles of the pictures and the names of the stars.

"H'm. Looks like I've lost my pet suspect," I muttered with a gesture of resignation.

"You're forgetting something, Lash," he said with a mild sneer. "The show at the Allison opens on Wednesday and plays through to Sunday. They don't change the program down there until Monday. So it's quite possible I went to the Allison some-time between Wednesday and Saturday. If I were you, I'd do a little extra checking on my pet suspect."

"Thanks, I will. By the way, Frank, how did that ox blood get on your trench coat?"

He made no effort to conceal his amazement. "Say, you're all right, Lash," he said admiringly. "I had to go downtown Saturday morning to pick up some transcripts, so Philip asked me to stop off on the way back and pick up some ox blood for Jessica at a slaughterhouse on Eleventh Avenue. One of the bottles broke and christened me plenty. I had to throw the coat away."

"Frank, I'd like some information about the funeral tomor-row. I want to have some men tag along to keep an eye on Philip."

He said, "It's to be a double funeral, you know. Services in our chapel at two o'clock, then on to Cedar Palms Cemetery up near Riverdale. Paula and Helen are to be placed in a mausole-um." He saw my eyebrows go up. "That's right, a mausoleum," he added gloomily. "When my wife and her folks had that ter-rible—" He paused, jerked his head toward the drawing room. "Did they tell you about it?" he asked.

"Yes. The plane cracked up."

"Well, when it happened, Philip prevailed on Martin to buy a mausoleum. Gave him a swell sales talk about how nice it would be for all of us to be together someday. I was in the Army at the time, but I suspect Philip got a whale of a commission out of the deal."

"One more question. Philip insinuated last night that your feelings toward Helen were perhaps a little more affectionate than they had a right to be. Were you in love with—"

I didn't have time to finish the sentence. I saw him spring from the chair, saw his right hand coming toward me with the speed of an express train. If I hadn't hastily thrust my arm upward, I would have taken a blistering crack on the face. Again he swung at me viciously. But by this time I was on my feet and poised for action. I caught the flying arm and with a quick downward movement twisted it so suddenly that Frank sprawled over the desk like a drunk groveling on a bar. Releasing him, I shoved him none too gently into his chair.

"That mitt of yours needs a muzzle," I reprimanded him. "And the same goes, I guess, for my big mouth. If I've offended you—"

Face inscrutable, he got up, straightened his tie, walked to the connecting door, and opened it. "Lew, will you come here a minute, please?" he called into the drawing room.

There was an awkward minute of silence before the roly-poly figure of Lew Partridge appeared in the doorway.

"What is it, Frank?" he inquired as the undertaker closed the door.

Taking him by the arm, Frank brought him up to the desk. "Lew, tell this lug what the score is," he demanded, and his voice was the epitome of calmness. "Lieutenant Lash is under the impression that I was carrying the torch for Helen; that possibly behind your back I was having an affair."

Lew looked at me and shook his head. "Nothing of the kind, Lieutenant," he said, placing his arm across Frank's shoulders. "If Philip put that bug in your head, it's because he's burned up that Frank is always battling with Jessica. Why, if it hadn't been for Frank, my marriage would have busted up long ago. Helen used to get fed up with my gambling and drinking. Two or three times she threatened to leave me. She would have done it, too, if Frank hadn't convinced her to give me another chance."

Impulsively, I stuck out my hand. "I'm sorry, Frank," I said, and I meant it. "I sincerely apologize."

With equal impulsiveness he grasped my hand. "Forget it, Lash. Water under the bridge. Coming, Lew?" Together they entered the drawing room.

"And now for Jessica," I said. "Think you can handle a tigress, Regan?"

"Where is she—up in the lab?"

I nodded my head.

"O.K.," he said. "But if I ain't back in ten minutes, come up-stairs and look for me in one of her glass tubes."

As I expected, Jessica stormed into the study with scorn and defiance written all over her unbecoming map. Behind her—far behind her—was Regan, his face lathered with sweat, his chest heaving like a canoe in the wake of a ferry boat.

"Well, what is it now?" she demanded, marching up to the desk and raking me with her cold, piercing eyes. "You and this red-headed ape," she added wrathfully, "seem to have an idea I've nothing to do around here except twiddle my fingers."

I looked at her for a minute. Not that I derived any pleasure from it. At best she was nothing to feast one's eyes upon. Fur-thermore, her black dress hung sloppily on her beanstalk frame, and her chemist's coat appeared bloodier and more acid-eaten than ever. Irrelevantly I wondered what Philip had seen in her. So far as I could see she had no sex appeal: homely face, drain-pipe figure, and a chest that in Doc Berlinger's book would have been classified as a fortress without cannon. Yet there was no doubt she had brains; it showed in her eyes like a fleck of gold peeking out from a pan of gravel.

"Have a chair, Mrs. Brocton," I said placidly.

"You can dispense with the social amenities, Lieutenant. I prefer to stand," she told me with frozen-faced austerity. "Come to the point. Why did you send for me?"

"I've some questions I'd like you to answer. For instance, where were you on Sunday evening between six-thirty and seven?"

She threw back her head and gave vent to a laugh. It was the first time I'd heard her laugh, and it sounded like someone buttering toast.

"You amuse me, Lieutenant," she leered. "As officer in charge of this case, you certainly believe in concentrating on the unimportant. Tell me, are you interested in capturing Martin Chadwick? Or do you simply come up here to keep out of the cold?"

"Very funny, Mrs. Brocton," I said. "But I still insist on knowing where you were between six-thirty and seven. The chairs at headquarters aren't the most comfortable in the world, but people do get very conversational in them."

She took the hint. "Very well, let's get it over with. I went for a walk," she informed me sullenly. "I'd been working in the lab most of the day, so I left here about five-thirty to get some air. Didn't get back until about eight o'clock."

"It was raining pretty hard at five-thirty."

She said, "I like to walk in the rain."

"Where did you walk to?"

"I crossed the 207th Street bridge and walked as far as the Grand Concourse in the Bronx. Then I walked north to Mosholu Park."

"Quite a walk, isn't it?"

"Yes. But I always take a long walk when I've a chemical problem to solve. Walking stimulates the mind. Apparently you don't walk very much, Lieutenant," she added curtly.

"Did you stop off somewhere?"

"No. And I didn't meet anybody."

"H'm. Not a very concrete alibi, Mrs. Brocton."

"Perhaps. But it's the truth."

I decided to throw her a low curve. I said, "Today when I was going through Chadwick's papers, I found something rather interesting. I was amazed to learn that Chadwick had a phone conversation with you last Friday."

She gave me a sharp look. After a long pause she said with a sneer, "That is amazing, particularly since I haven't seen or spoken to Martin since last July."

"Let me refresh your memory. The phone call concerned a sum of money—twenty-five thousand dollars, to be exact."

Again she emitted an unpleasant laugh. "Frankly, Lieutenant, I don't know what you're talking about."

"You deny that Chadwick called you on the phone?"

"I certainly do," she spat at me.

I jotted down some notes in the notebook. "That's all, Mrs. Brocton," I said. "Except that I don't want you to go upstairs to your lab right away. Stay in the drawing room for a while. I may want to talk with you again."

She eyed Regan and me suspiciously. "If you're planning to go snooping in the lab—"

I told her that the Sergeant and I had other plans; that her lab wasn't of any particular importance to us at the moment. She must have believed me. Without saying another word she turned on her heel and walked into the drawing room. Miraculously, she didn't even slam the door.

The moment she was gone I sprang up, dashed to the connecting door, and turned the key in the lock. Then I crossed to the wooden cabinet.

"O.K., Sam," I said quietly as I opened the door. "Come on out."

Eyes blinking like a pair of sharp-turn signal lights, the cabbie stepped out of the cabinet and began rubbing his numb legs.

"Well?" I demanded, grasping him by the shoulders and shaking him a bit. "Which one—which voice did you recognize?" I shook him harder. "For Pete's sake, talk."

"Jeez, Lieutenant," he muttered, and I felt a slight shudder under my hands. "None of them sounded like that guy in the trench coat. Nope, not even the babe who opened the door and peeked in at me."

I felt as if I could have done him some violence— slapped
him, punched him maybe. Instead, I pulled him up close to me
and fixed him with a fierce look. Meanwhile, Regan was having
a helluva good laugh for himself.

"Sam, think hard," I pleaded. "Don't let me down, feller. You
heard them all. Surely one of them must have sounded like the
man you heard on Sunday night."

"Jeez, I'm sorry," he croaked. "I'd give my right arm to help
you, honest I would. But it's no go, Lieutenant. They just didn't
sound like him."

A towering rage took possession of me. I could feel hot blood
surging into my face like steam rising in a radiator. I was trembling with anger. All I could see in my mind's eye was the grinning, leering face of the killer—a face that had Philip's beady
eyes, Lew's pudgy cheeks, Frank's twisted lips, and Jessica's re-
pulsive ugliness: a composite picture of a face that was split from
ear to ear with a mocking grin, as though it were laughing at my
puny efforts to track down a killer.

Suddenly, losing all control of myself, I shoved Sam away
from me, barged into the drawing room, and bore down on the
crowd with my fists clenched and my jaw outthrust. God knows
what I looked like, maybe like a ham actor in some blood-and-
thunder melodrama, but there must have been a dangerous glint
in my eye, for the soft drone of voices ceased immediately, and
everyone backed away as though I were some spectral figure from
Beyond, an avenging angel about to wreak vengeance on the ungodly.

I lost my head completely. "Oh, you're diabolically clever,
Mr. Killer," I ranted, coming to a halt and glaring at each one in
the crowd. "You're a cold, calculating murderer. But I'll get you,
Mr. Killer. Do you hear me?" Again I looked at each member of
the group. "So help me, I'll get you if it's the last thing I ever
do."

For a minute or two a tomblike silence came over the vast room. Half the crowd peered at me with terror-stricken eyes; the other half looked on with amused, somewhat bewildered expressions on their faces. Then Daniels and Regan were beside me. I felt them tugging me backward toward the study. I didn't protest. I was suddenly tired and dispirited: a beaten, confused man.

"Holy Canarsie, what got into you, Lash?" Regan inquired as he and Daniels plunked me into the swivel chair behind the desk. "No kidding, this squeal is cracking you up, chum. A coupla more nights up here and you'll be keeping Penny company in a snake pit."

I signaled Daniels to get back to the drawing room. "I sure blew my top," I groaned when the detective was gone. "But I couldn't help it, Regan. There's a killer out there, I tell you. And right now he's laughing his head off at us."

"Steady now, feller," Regan cooed, patting my shoulder. "Just sit quiet-like. Attaboy." He turned to Sam Willis. "Let's get him out to your cab, Sam. We'll take him home and put him to bed." With that he cocked an ear. "Just listen to 'em out there," he said, chuckling. "They're as mad as hops."

Regan wasn't fooling. The roar of angry voices in the drawing room was terrific. Evidently, now that the grim hunter had departed from their midst, the jackals were baring their fangs and snarling defiance. It was then that the connecting door opened and Penny sailed in.

"You were wonderful, darling," she said to me, straightening my tie and fussing with my rumpled collar. The kiss she planted on my forehead could be heard, I bet, as far away as Glintz's livery stable. I had half a notion to call her down.

Suddenly the connecting door opened and Daniels raced up to the desk. I didn't have to look twice at him. to see that something was amiss. I began to feel that old-time queasiness in my stomach.

"Come outside on the double, Lieutenant!" he exclaimed. "Boy-oh-boy, have I got something to show you!"

All of us scrambled out of the study and streamed into the drawing room. The room, I noticed, was deserted.

"Where are they all?" I asked Daniels.

He said, "I chased them into the dining room. The minute I saw what it was I figured I'd better clear them all out so you'd have a little elbow room. Come over here and I'll show you." He guided us to a small mahogany library table that had been placed near the two half-couch caskets in order to accommodate some of the smaller floral pieces. "Go ahead," he added peremptorily, "take a peek at that table."

We crowded closer. All at once Penny clutched my arm and gave a half-stifled cry of amazement.

"Look!" she cried. "Look what's on top of the table!"

At first I saw only the sprays of flowers. Then my eyes fell upon a serpentine row of small metal letters. They were letters of the alphabet, pronged metal letters that are used on announcement and bulletin boards. Bending over to examine the damn things, I was dumfounded to discover that the metal letters conveyed a message:

ITS A BET LASH

For a long interval everything in the room appeared to swim crazily in a mist. Finally my eyes cleared and I found my voice. "Good God," I gasped. "The killer—the killer has answered my challenge!

CHAPTER NINETEEN

After that I was a new man. I began to feel alive, refreshed, ready for anything. My weariness was gone, and my self-confidence, like the circus, was back again bigger and better than ever.

The killer had answered my challenge! I'd stung his vanity; I'd pierced that impregnable armor of his; I'd made him come out into the open for a moment and reveal his fine Italian hand. Lord, it felt good for a change to be standing in front of the eight ball instead of behind it.

"Go on home, Sam," I said to the cabbie as I slipped a sawbuck into his hand. "Thanks for coming up," and turning a deaf ear to his protestations, I turned him over to Daniels and told the detective to show him to the front door.

"Well, what have you got to say for yourself, Regan?" I asked, teetering cockily on the balls of my feet. "Who's crazy now, feller?" I demanded. "Didn't I tell you Chadwick had nothing to do with these murders?"

Poor Regan looked about as happy as a mother with five gold stars in the window. "I can't believe it," he muttered. "Why, this means the killer's right here in the house."

"Uh-huh. If you walk across the hall," I said, "you'll find him in the dining room." The sliding doors opened, and Daniels was back. "Come here, Daniels. Who was standing at this table?" I asked him.

He shrugged his shoulders and popped a cough drop into his mouth. "Couldn't say, Lieutenant. Must have been done while I was in the study with you and the Sergeant."

"How about you, Penny?" I inquired. "Did you see anybody near this table?"

She glanced up at me, little slit trenches creasing her brow. "N-no, Chris, I didn't," she replied slowly. "Truthfully, darling, I was too busy watching the liquor cabinet."

"Never mind. We'll try another angle. Daniels," I said, facing the detective, "go to the dining room and bring in that barber-shop quartet. Maybe we can get one of them to sing about what he saw in here."

But it didn't work. I talked, myself blue in the face. I coaxed, threatened—all to no avail. Neither Philip nor Jessica nor Frank nor Lew had seen anyone standing at the table; and none, of course, admitted authorship of the message. However, I did learn where the pronged metal letters had come from. Philip had purchased them on Saturday night. He had placed them in the drawer of the library table, but in all the excitement of the last few days he had forgotten to take them to the funeral home.

With Jehu Regan at the wheel, the trip that night to 97th Street was made in almost nothing flat. Of the three of us, I was the only one in good spirits. Penny was unusually quiet, almost to the point of glumness, and Regan was tight-lipped and moody.

"What's wrong, Penny?" I asked as we drew up to the Sheldon Arms. "You've been terribly quiet all the way down." I stepped onto the sidewalk and helped her slide out of the front seat. "Anything I've said or done?"

She patted my cheek. "Don't be silly. It's just—" She bit her lip, and I was startled to see her eyes brimming with tears. "Oh, Chris, I—" She paused and wriggled the fingers of her right hand—a signal, I gathered, that she wanted a handkerchief.

I thought, This is a fine how-do-you-do. In the movies some big lug always has a hankie in his pocket when the little doll needs it. But mine has a lot of metal letters in it. I did the next best thing; I gave her the end of my tie. And damned if she didn't even wipe her pretty little nose with it.

"Now, what's this all about?" I demanded, lifting her chin and gazing fondly into her eyes.

"Oh, Chris darling, please try to understand," she pleaded, clinging to me. "I—I just wanted to get even for that 'Take me to the Allison' trick you played on me."

"What are you talking about?"

"That message on the table. I—I did it, Chris," she blubbered, using the tie again. "I found that box of letters in the drawer and— Oh, I'm a horrible little brat, darling. If it wasn't so cold, I'd tell you to take me across your knees and whale the devil out of me," and sobbing, she broke away and tore into the house.

Gone was all my confidence. Gone was that new-man, raring-to-go feeling that I'd felt so strongly at Highrock and all the way downtown. Just a beaten, discouraged guy again, only this time something new had been added: disillusionment and bitterness.

How could you do this to me, Penny? I thought. My God, angel, you and your screwball tricks have made a monkey of me. Here I was thinking I was hot on the killer's trail, and I wake up and find I'm right back where started.

I fumbled into the car and sat down, acutely conscious that the dead silence of the night was being rudely shattered by Regan's uproarious guffaws. Dumbly I looked at him. Tears were coursing down his cheeks, and his hairy fists were pounding the wheel in a paroxysm of laughter.

"This is killing me," he gasped, controlling his merriment for a moment. "Just wait till I tell Strenz. 'It's a bet, Lash.' Oh, brother!" And off he went again into another paroxysm.

Just before I let him have it I thought, quote: "There's no time like the present." Unquote.

The following morning, Wednesday, the ninth of December, I found my desk at West 20th Street blanketed with paper. The top of the old desk looked like lower Broadway on the day Charles Lindbergh received his rousing scrap-paper reception. With the exception of a few official reports, the bulk of the reading matter was from old John Q. Public himself. Scores of people had written in that they'd seen Martin Chadwick during the last few days. On Monday, for example, seventeen different people had seen him in seventeen different states. One crazy galoot claimed he'd seen the lawyer in Times Square in a Santa Claus suit.

Every big murder squeal inspires a deluge of these crank letters. And, believe it or not, we don't ignore them, despite the fact that we know in our hearts that 95 per cent of them are written by crackpots and limelight hunters. After all, there's always that slim possibility that one of them might be the McCoy. And wonder of wonders, I found one.

It was from a dame who lived on 83rd Street. She'd been sitting at her window last Sunday about five-forty-five when suddenly a big green sedan had pulled up in front of the old brownstone across the street. A man in a trench coat and black fedora had entered the house, followed fifteen minutes later by a young woman in a mink coat.

That's all she'd seen. She'd gone from the window to sit down to supper. But her letter included the address of the brownstone, plus the interesting information that the house was owned by Jonathan Barrett.

Jonathan Barrett! That was Chadwick's multimillionaire friend, the guy on whose yacht Chadwick had thrown that would-be birthday party for Paula last July. Another thought struck me: Surer than hell, those initials "J. B." on Chadwick's memo pad referred to Jonathan Barrett and not Jessica Brocton. Oh, well, just another boot in the rear. I was used to them by now. Anyway, I detailed Dorsey and O'Connor to go up to 83rd and keep an eye on the house. Later I'd call Regan, and the two of us would explore the joint from top to bottom.

Grabbing my phone, I had a call put through to Andy Huestis, who was doing the eight-to-four shift at Chadwick's office in Chambers Street.

"Andy, did Chadwick's secretary report for work this morning?" I asked.

"Yeah, she's right here, Lieutenant. Says her salary's paid to the fifteenth."

"Put her on."

I asked the babe for an explanation of the "J. B.—$25,000 tops" notation I'd found on Chadwick's memo pad. I got it. Chadwick's friend Jonathan Barrett had gone to Florida three months ago. Barrett, like Chadwick, was something of an art collector, and before leaving for Florida had given Chadwick the keys to his house, with explicit instructions to sell all or part of the Barrett collection. Chadwick had disposed of some of the things, and on Friday had received an offer of twenty-five grand for Barrett's three Tompion watches. Chadwick had told his secretary that he'd call Barrett at seven o'clock that night, but she wasn't positive, she informed me, that Chadwick had done so. She'd left the office at five.

So that was that. "J. B." was definitely not Jessica Brocton.

Presently I got around to reading the reports. The two experts I'd sent to Highrock to examine the drawing room and the study reported a dismal lack of success in finding any secret panels or trap doors. Nor had their examination of the door under the stairway been any too successful. The lock, a Jeremiah Hobbs affair, showed absolutely no signs of having been tampered with. As for their visits to the local locksmiths, they'd covered them all from Spuyten Duyvil to Washington Heights, and none had remembered ever making a duplicate of the tubular keys the detectives had shown them.

At noon I phoned Regan, and a short while later he picked me up in his jalopy. As we whizzed uptown I gave him a detailed account of my morning's activities.

"And what have you been doing?" I asked.

He said, "I was working on that magic-door business. Remember when Penny told us about being introduced to Chadwick while she was playing in *Son of the Sultan?* Well, I took myself up to Actors Equity this morning and asked them to check over their list of magicians and tell me if any of them had ever played in *Son of the Sultan.* I figured maybe Chadwick had met the whole cast and taken a special shine to the magician in the show—if there was one. So help me, Lash, they found one, a Jap by the name of Mokato the Mystic."

"Did you contact this Mokato and have a talk with him?"

"Sure. But I didn't mention Chadwick's name. I just asked him if he knew how to get in and out of a locked room without using a key."

I sat up straight. "Then what?"

"He walks into a closet and tells me to lock him in. So I lock the door and hold the key in my hand. The next thing I know I find him standing behind me with a big grin on his face."

"Good God, Regan!" I cried. "That's it! This Mokato must have taught Chadwick the trick."

"That's what I thought. But when I asked the guy to tell me how he did it, he takes the key out of my hand, opens the closet door, and drags out his twin brother. Christ!"

At 83rd Street Regan stopped the car in front of a three-story brownstone that was sandwiched between a pair of ultramodern apartment buildings. From basement to roof the doors and windows of this architectural anachronism were shrouded by slabs of weather-beaten boards. It didn't look at all inviting. In fact, its high front stoop gave me the impression that the old joint was sticking its tongue out at us.

I signaled Detective Dorsey. He crawled out of his squad car, walked across the street to our jalopy, and put his foot on the running board.

"Anything stirring?" I asked him.

He said nobody had gone into the house; nobody had come out. O'Connor, he added, was guarding the rear.

"Hey, Lash," Regan piped up. "How we gonna get into this dump? Break down a door, maybe?"

"No, I'm pretty sure I've got keys for it." I showed him Paula's key case. "Lew told us that Paula entered this house on Sunday, didn't he? Well, she couldn't have done it without keys."

"Chadwick coulda let her in."

"But he didn't. That woman who lives across the street said in her letter that the girl in the mink coat unlocked the storm door herself." I turned to Dorsey. "Tip O'Connor off that the Sergeant and I are going in," I instructed him. "Then stay out here and grab anyone who tries to sneak out."

Regan and I walked up the stoop. For a few minutes I experimented with Paula's keys before I found one that opened the storm door. Then I had to experiment all over again to find the right key for the main door. I finally got it.

With our flashlights beaming, we stepped into a dingy foyer from which we proceeded into a narrow hall. The silence was oppressive in this dungeon-like brownstone, and the foul, musty air sort of beckoned to my lunch to make a return trip on the alimentary canal.

I played the beam of my flashlight on the wall. "There's a light switch, Regan," I said. "Try it. Maybe Barrett didn't have the electric company turn off the juice."

Regan flicked the switch, and the foyer was flooded with light.

"That's a break," I muttered. "It'll make our job a lot easier."

On our left was a pair of doors opening into a long, narrow living room. The room was bursting at the seams with *objets d'art,* and so closely did they approximate the junk in Chadwick's living room that I was not a little surprised to find there was no Eskimo kayak. At first I was too busy eying the Barrett collection to pay much attention to the room itself, but as we edged toward the center we came upon two overturned chairs and a smashed hourglass. The glass had evidently been knocked off the mantelpiece. In any event, it had fallen upon the strip of marble in front of the gas-burning fireplace, where it lay shattered amid countless grains of bright purple sand.

"Chadwick and Paula musta had a hell of a battle in here before they walked out to the car," Regan observed as he studied the overturned chairs and the remains of the hourglass. "If it wasn't for the fact that they walked out together, I'd say Chadwick made an attempt to bump her off in this room."

For at least three hours we explored the brownstone, room after room, closet after closet. We looked in the kitchen-to-dining-room dumb-waiter shaft, crawled out on the roof, and even went down to the cellar to peek into the furnace. If Martin Chadwick has hiding in Barrett's house, then there was only one logical explanation: He was definitely hiding in Mrs. Barrett's sewing room. I hadn't bothered to examine the thimbles up there. Furthermore, as extra proof that Chadwick wasn't using the brownstone as a hideout, there was no mussed-up bed, no scraps of food.

At four-ten we walked out of the place like a couple of men in deep-sea divers' shoes. Every bone in my body ached, and so great was my weariness that if I hadn't looked at my hand I would have sworn I was carrying a .75 millimeter gun instead of a flashlight.

"I'm worn to a frazzle," Regan complained as we joined Dorsey on the sidewalk. "My legs are so sore from getting down and looking under beds and bureaus I bet I won't be able to attend Mass for a month."

"You and O'Connor can call it a day," I told Dorsey, sinking into the front seat of the Sergeant's car. "I'll send up a new shift as soon as I get downtown."

Regan dropped me off at West 20th Street, and I climbed laboriously upstairs to my cubicle. Neely barged in the instant he heard me plop into my chair.

"Chris, that goldfish dame of yours has been calling up all afternoon," he growled.

"Don't talk to me about that screwball," I snapped. "She and I are washed up."

"Good. At last you're getting some sense. How did you and Regan make out this afternoon?"

I brought him up to date.

He said, "We got in touch with Jonathan Barrett. He's in Florida, all right, and says it's true that Chadwick called him on Friday at seven o'clock. He's all busted up over the murders. Says he's sure Chadwick's innocent."

"Did you find out where his yacht is? If it's anchored anywhere in the Hudson, Chadwick may be—"

"Forget it," Neely broke in. "The yacht's been tied up near Miami since October. By the way, Chris, that double funeral went off without a hitch. Donovan said he stuck like a leech to Philip Brocton."

When Neely was gone, I detailed a night team to watch Barrett's brownstone, front and back. Then my phone rang. A very contrite Penny was on the wire.

"Chris darling," she cooed in a sackcloth-and-ashes voice, "please don't be angry with me." I didn't say a word. "Jeepers, can't you take a joke?" I still maintained a dead silence. "Chris, do come up and have dinner with me," she pleaded. "Honest, I'm cooking your favorite dish. Incidentally, what is your favorite dish?"

"Blondes!" I roared into the phone, and hung up.

One minute . . . two minutes. . . . The phone rang again.

"As I was saying, Chris," Penny said as though nothing had happened, "I'm cooking your favorite dish, platinum bleached garnished with ash. Dinner's at six o'clock and—"

"Look here, Penny," I interrupted with all the severity I could muster. "I don't want any dinner; I don't want to see you; and I don't—" I suddenly found myself biting my tongue. I shrugged. "Oh, what's the use? O.K., sugar. Six sharp."

I arrived at Penny's door with a five-pound box of candy in one hand and in the other a bag of assorted cuffs for Cuspidor. Luckily I'd found a tailor who was willing to make up half a dozen cuffs without asking too many questions.

"Chris! You've come back to me," Penny said huskily when the "Call to the Post" had sounded and she appeared at her door. "Oh, Chris, I can't tell you how happy I am." She pulled me into the living room, then spied the candy and the paper bag. "For me?" she inquired, looking up through her lashes.

"You and Cuspidor," I said, handing them over.

She peeked into the paper bag and gave a squeal of delight. "Cuspidor!" she cried, turning to the mutt, who was eying my cuffs hungrily. "Look what Mr. Lash brought you—a big, big box of candy. And look what he brought me." She let him look into the bag. "All these lovely cuffs! Jeepers, darling," she said, throwing her arms around my neck. "Just what I wanted!"

We sat down to a dinner that was positively delicious. In fact, everything was perfect. Penny was sweetness personified in a confection of a dress that she said brought out the color of her eyes. (It brought out mine, too, but not the color.) Even Cuspidor behaved himself, and the fumes of kerosene from the farmer's lamp on the table were dissipated by the heady fragrance of Penny's perfume. Best of all, I enjoyed the thirty minutes we sat together on the sofa. It was the first time I'd ever kissed Penny; yet the moment our lips met, I knew the boys at West 20th Street would soon be shelling out for a set of flat silverware.

At seven-thirty Penny began making preparations for her departure to the theatre. Suddenly a loud wail came from the kitchen.

"Chris, that's Cuspidor!" Penny exclaimed. "Something's happened to him!"

Dashing into the kitchen, we found the pooch had imprisoned himself under the refrigerator. He had wedged himself in so tightly that there was no possibility of wriggling loose.

"Be calm, darling," Penny called to him as we got down on our knees. "Mr. Lash will get you out, just wait and see. Oh, hurry, Chris. Hurry."

I slid my arm under the refrigerator, grasped the damn hound by the hide, and pulled for all I was worth. He yelped plenty, but I finally got him out. Immediately Penny cuddled him in her arms, and while she murmured sweet nothings into his ear, I got to my feet. I was about to brush the knees of my trousers when I discovered I had quite a number of Cuspidor's hairs in my hand. I began brushing them off. Then my whole body stiffened, and I looked at the hairs as though I held a winning ticket on the daily double at Tropical Park.

Unnerved, Penny put the dog down. "Chris, did he bite you?" Still kneeling, she looked up at me, her face pinched with alarm. "Chris, speak to me. Say something. Please, if it's hydrophobia— Oh, darling, if you can't talk, at least froth at the mouth—anything, Chris, so I'll know."

Penny's voice sounded miles away. My ears were ringing; my heart was pounding; and behind my staring eyes a hundred and

one kaleidoscopic thoughts were tumbling and falling and sliding, yet rapidly forming a brilliantly clear picture of something
that heretofore had been so dishearteningly obscure.

Still staring at my hand, I walked dazedly into Penny's bedroom. Like an automaton, I picked up the phone and dialed
Regan's home number.

"Get into your car, Regan, and pick me up in front of the
Sheldon Arms," I said to him in a voice that I scarcely recognized
as my own.

"What's cooking, chum?" he demanded.

I said softly, "We're going to meet Martin Chadwick."

CHAPTER TWENTY

Not until I was out on the sidewalk, with my back braced against the cold bricks at the side of the entrance to the apartment building, did I realize that I'd cleared out of the Sheldon Arms without so much as saying a parting word to Penny. I'd simply put down the phone, grabbed my hat and coat, and dashed out to the elevator.

It felt good standing there in the cold. Scudding clouds were overhead, and a biting wind tugged fretfully at my overcoat as if it wanted me to move on so it could romp again with the scraps of paper in the street. Curiously, I welcomed the bluster of the wind. It cooled my fevered brow, blew from my eyes the last cobwebs of doubt.

A battered sedan drew up to the curb. A rusty voice hailed me.

"O.K., Lash, give," Regan entreated as I slid in beside him. "Did Penny finally break down and tell you where Chadwick's hiding?"

"No. Cuspidor gave me the answer," I retorted, smiling. "A lot of answers, in fact."

Regan leaned over and smelled my breath. "I know bloodhounds can run down a criminal," he remarked, "but I never heard of a Spitz doing it. Honest, the country's going to the dogs." He caught my sharp look. "O.K., where to?"

"Cedar Palms Cemetery near Riverdale. But stop at the first drugstore we come to. I want to make a phone call,"

"Cedar Palms Cemetery?" he echoed. "That's where they took Paula and Helen today." He grabbed me by the arm. "I get it! Chadwick's using that Mussolini up there as a hideout. No wonder we couldn't find him."

Three blocks later we stopped at a drugstore. In ten minutes I was back in the car.

"Everything's all set," I told the Sergeant. "I called the Riverdale precinct. They'll contact the cemetery officials and see that we get in."

Despite the fact that I'd been given complete directions to the cemetery, Regan and I had a job trying to find it. We meandered on every highway and byway in that section of the Bronx.

"Why the hell didn'tcha bring Cuspidor along to tell us the way?" Regan griped as we came to a dead end overlooking the Hudson.

"I wanted to," I snapped, "but he's making a speech tonight at Town Hall."

At last, however, we found it, a sprawling, God-forsaken encampment of the dead, with hundreds of marble ghosts standing rigidly on guard. I'd never had occasion to enter a cemetery at night, but now that the opportunity was at hand I didn't think I was going to relish it.

Regan stopped his cement mixer in front of a church-like building from the windows of which came a soft glow of light. There were two cars parked ahead of us, one a squad car, the other a snazzy convertible.

"Good. They're ready for us," I said, getting out. "Bring along your flashlight, Regan."

As we walked toward the entrance a thickset man opened the door.

"Finally made it, eh?" he inquired in a friendly voice. "I'm Detective Happel, Fiftieth Precinct."

There were introductions and handshakes. Then Happel took us into a small office, where three men were sitting in a cloud of tobacco smoke.

"This is Hanson, my sidekick," Happel said, indicating a sober-faced, gray-haired chap. "This is Rankin, the night watchman for Cedar Palms, and this is Mr. Sahner, the general manager."

More introductions, more handshakes.

"Have you a key to Chadwick's mausoleum?" I asked the manager.

Sahner, a thin, middle-aged man, said, "Yes, Lieutenant. We have keys for every mausoleum in the cemetery."

"Is that the customary practice?"

"Yes. We make periodic inspections of the mausoleums on account of blowouts."

I asked what he meant. He explained that occasionally, owing to poor embalming, corpses in unventilated mausoleums fill up with gas and explode in the crypts, thus blowing out the cemented slabs.

"May I ask the reason for this exhumation order?" the manager inquired.

"I have reason to believe," I said quietly, "that Martin Chadwick's body is entombed with that of his wife."

Regan, the precinct detectives, and the night watchman let out a roar of astonishment. Instantly Sahner held up a silencing hand. "Impossible, Lieutenant," he countered. "There's just room enough in each crypt for one coffin. And I don't have to tell you that one coffin will not accommodate two adults."

"Nevertheless, I insist that we have a look."

"I've no objection. I simply believe you're wasting your time, that's all. Come, we'll need tools."

Equipped with chisels, hammers, and screw drivers, we climbed into our cars and drove through the high wrought-iron gate that the night watchman swung open for us. Then, with Sahner leading the way in his convertible, our little cavalcade of cars began rolling along a gravel driveway. Suddenly he stopped in front of something grim and white that bulked a short distance off the driveway. In the gleam of our headlights I could see it was a fairly large mausoleum made of square-cut Italian marble, with a beautiful bronze door and tiny windows of stained glass.

"Let's have the keys, Mr. Sahner," I said when the six of us had formed a little group near the convertible. He handed them over. "O.K., boys, let's go."

I led the way up a gravel path to the mausoleum. With each crunching step I could feel my heart increase its pounding. Tiny shivers began to run through my body, icy currents that I attributed to the rawness of the wind, but which I knew were only nerve vibrations. Not that fear was jangling my nerves. It was something more emotional, something deeper, more devastating: a sickening dread that my feet might after all be leading me into a blind alley. It wouldn't be the first time that cold logic had played me false. Well, sink or swim, win or lose, the next hour or two would give me the answer.

The key clanked in the lock of the bronze door. A twist to the left, the squeaking of hinges, then another key; another twist to the left, and a glass door swung open soundlessly. Behind me I heard the click of flashlights; ahead I saw their beams tear gaping holes in the darkness.

Snatching the Sergeant's flashlight from his hand, I stepped into the mausoleum. The reverberation of my footsteps sounded like faraway tom-toms, and I was aware that even my labored breathing echoed and re-echoed in the awesome silence that pervaded the tomb.

This, I saw, was a twelve-chambered mausoleum, six chambers or crypts on each side, like two gigantic bureaus with large square drawers. At the rear, facing the doors, was a marble bench.

As my companions filed in I began examining the marble slabs on the left. Three of them were sealed and bore the inscriptions *Michael James Brocton, Amelia Cole Brocton, Barbara Brocton Webster.* The remaining three were unsealed and bore no inscriptions.

On the right only two of the slabs were sealed, and by the freshness of the cement I knew that behind them were Paula Chadwick, Helen Partridge, and, unless two and two no longer added up to four, Martin Chadwick. As yet, of course, no stonecutter's chisel had carved any inscriptions.

If I live to be a hundred, I'll never forget that weird night: six men in a mausoleum, chiseling, hammering, hacking at two cemented slabs, while outside, as though protesting this desecration, the wind moaned a dirge that all but raised the hair on my head. We worked in pairs, two at each slab, with the third pair holding the flashlights. Occasionally we alternated.

There were three sections of crypts, two crypts to a section. According to Sahner, Paula was in the right-hand middle section, lower crypt; Helen diagonally to the left. It was all of two hours, though, before the last of the cement was chipped away and the screws removed.

Sweat running into my eyes and down my back, hands blistered and bleeding, I helped Happel and Hanson remove the marble slab from Helen's crypt. It took all six of us, however, to slide out the coffin and lower it to the floor.

"You—you know more about these things than I do, Sahner," I panted. "You open it."

With the flashlights trained on the coffin, Sahner sank to his haunches and unfastened the latches. Then slowly he raised both sections of the lid. Except for the wailing of the wind and our loud breathing, there was utter silence in the tomb. No one made any pretense of calmness. All eyes waited for that lid to complete its seemingly endless journey.

A groan went up. Helen Partridge, as beautiful in death as she'd been in life, lay undisturbed, sleeping her everlasting sleep. No human hands had defiled or violated the sanctity of her coffin. Everything was as it should be.

"I told you this was a waste of time," Sahner said to me pettishly as he lowered the lid and fastened the latches. "And I was dragged away from a houseful of guests to come here."

"We've still got another casket to examine," I reminded him. "Let's put this one back where it belongs."

We raised the coffin, slid it into its crypt, and replaced the slabs and the screws. Ten minutes later we had Paula's coffin on the floor, with Sahner down on his haunches ready again to take care of the unlatching.

This time I could scarcely wait for the man to raise the sections of the lid. I wanted to push him aside and tackle the lid myself; yank it up viciously, get it over with. Every nerve in my body was tingling, and blood beat in my ears until I could barely hear the wind outside. Hurry, hurry, I kept telling him silently. For God's sake, man, lift that lid. This is the moment I've waited for all night. This is it. This is—

The roar that rent the silence in the tomb was earsplitting. In unison we pulled back, recoiling as though a bomb had exploded in our faces. Not a pair of living eyes present didn't bulge in unbelieving horror; not a living face didn't blanch at the ghoulish thing that lay at Paula's feet.

"Godamighty!" Regan bleated as we leaped toward the coffin again for a second look. "It's—it's Martin Chadwick's head!"

Flashlight in hand, I sank to my knees, fighting down the revulsion that urged me to turn away. With minute care I examined the grisly head. It rested face up on a crushed black fedora hat. The eyes were wide open, protruding horribly from their sockets, and the face had a purplish tint to it. Running horizontally across the throat, an inch above the decapitation line, was a purplish-black welt. This welt, plus the purplish face and the protruding eyes, all added up to death by manual strangulation. I wasn't positive, of course. To be absolutely sure, I'd have to find the remaining parts of the body. Not that it would be difficult to find them. Frankly, I hadn't the slightest doubt where they were.

Slowly I rose to my feet. I looked at the tense, sickly faces that surrounded me. "Anybody got a bag or something?" I asked in a matter-of-fact tone. "I want to take this thing down to headquarters."

Happel dashed out and came back a minute later with a small burlap bag. With gloved hands I lifted the head and the hat from the coffin. As I raised them I noticed that the head gave off a strong odor of formaldehyde. Apparently the killer had embalmed the severed head. I noticed something else: Two brass screws had been screwed halfway into the head, one in each temple. From the projecting end of each screw dangled an inch-long strand of copper wire.

"Let me caution you people," I said to Sahner, Rankin, and the precinct detectives, "to keep absolutely quiet about this. Remember, we still don't know who the killer is. So whatever you do, don't let the newspapers in on it. One word in print about this and we're liable to have the killer take a powder on us."

They promised that the matter would be kept secret. Praying to Allah that they meant it, I suggested that we slide Paula's casket into its crypt and replace the marble slab. I also made the suggestion that Sahner have the slabs resealed.

It was midnight before we got back to the little office in the churchlike building, where I immediately phoned Neely to collect the bigwigs and meet Regan and me at headquarters. If Regan didn't hit a telephone pole, I told the little hellion, we'd be there at one o'clock sharp. Neely didn't ask any questions.

He knew by my voice, I think, that a big break had come in the Chadwick squeal.

"I gotta hand it to you, Lash," Regan said admiringly as we thundered away from Cedar Palms. "You were on the right track from the very start. But Holy Canarsie, Lash, how the hell did you latch onto the idea that Chadwick was in Paula's coffin?"

I told him how Cuspidor had got himself wedged under Penny's refrigerator and how I'd hauled him out and discovered the dog's hairs in my hand.

"When I saw those hairs," I explained, "it reminded me of the hairs we'd found in Helen's hand. Right away a crazy idea sprang into my head. Maybe, I told myself, Chadwick sneaked into Highrock on Monday night while we were looking for him in the park. Maybe he sneaked in and concealed himself in Paula's casket. I knew it was physically impossible, yet the more I thought about it, the more I liked it. First, it eliminated the hocus-pocus of Chadwick's getting in and out of the locked study door. Secondly, it tied in nicely with those hairs in Helen's hand. If I was right about Chadwick's hiding in the casket, then Helen, in reaching under the closed section of the coffin to find a hiding spot for the medallion, must have touched Chadwick's head, realized who it was, and, screaming bloody murder, grabbed hold of his hair.

"But common sense told me that Chadwick was much too big a man to hide in that coffin. Then I remembered the broken hourglass and those overturned chairs in Barrett's brownstone, and I began toying with the idea that perhaps Chadwick had been killed in that living room before Paula had arrived there; that the killer had dismembered Chadwick's body and subsequently hidden some of the parts at the foot of Paula's casket. Wow! That was the match that set off the firecracker, Regan. When I worked from that angle, everything suddenly became crystal-clear. It answered so many questions that were puzzling us that I knew beyond all question of a doubt that if we opened Paula's casket, we'd find Chadwick's decapitated head."

"You ain't kidding, chum," Regan said excitedly. "I'm beginning to see daylight myself."

"Attaboy! And the first thing it answered was that little stabbing affair in the casket room of the funeral home."

"Wait, Lash. See if I can do it," Regan pleaded. "If I figured Chadwick was murdered on Sunday, and separated from his noodle, I'd ask myself how, then, he could have stabbed Philip on Monday. The answer's a cinch: The killer sneaked into the casket room, opened the door of the embalming room a little bit, then stuck Chadwick's head past the door, just enough so Philip could get a quick look at it. Then the killer shut the door and waited for Philip to come tearing into the casket room."

I thumped him on the back. "Nice going. And when Philip shot by, the killer purposely stabbed him in the shoulder. The whole idea, you see, was to make Philip think that Chadwick had attempted to kill him. The news of Chadwick's attack would not only build additional evidence against the lawyer, but at the same time prevent anyone from suspecting that Martin Chadwick himself had been murdered. But still the killer wasn't satisfied. Above everything else, Regan, I think he wanted the police to see Chadwick. If the cops, particularly Sergeant Regan and Lieutenant Lash, could get a peek at Chadwick, the killer would know for a certainty that his worries were over. Did you notice those two brass screws in Chadwick's head?"

"Yeah. One in each temple. They had pieces of wire hanging down. They—" In his excitement Regan almost let go of the wheel. "My God, Lash!" he bellowed. "Chadwick didn't come up to the study window on Monday night and glare in at us. That was just his head we saw! Why, it's as plain as anything. The killer fastened a long wire to each screw, then leaned out of a window right above the study window and lowered Chadwick's head down the side of the house. Then he moved it over and brought it up to the sill, just high enough so that we'd spot it and think Chadwick was prowling around the grounds."

"That's the way I add it up, too, Regan," I said. "And when our shouts tipped him off that we'd seen Chadwick at the window, the killer lowered the head, moved it over, then hauled it up as fast as he could. It was then, I'm sure, that he cut the wires from the screws and decided to hide Chadwick's head in Paula's casket. His work was done, so it was time to get permanently rid of his ghoulish toy. You, Daniels, Frank, and I were running ourselves bowlegged in the park. Helen was in the study, and the rest of the crowd was scattered around upstairs. So the coast was clear for him to come down to the drawing room and hide the head at Paula's feet."

"What makes you so sure that the killer hid the head at that time?" Regan asked.

"Because Helen was murdered a little while later, and if Chadwick's head hadn't already been placed in the casket, Helen wouldn't have been found with Chadwick's hairs in her hand. Personally, Regan, I doubt very much whether the killer had planned to kill Helen. Somehow I've a hunch it wasn't on his schedule."

"What d'you mean?"

"This is only guesswork; maybe I'm miles off the target. But I think it was just by pure chance that the killer happened to see Helen sneaking downstairs with the medallion. He must have guessed that she intended to hide it in Paula's casket, and was afraid that if she did that, she'd discover Chadwick's head in the coffin. Then a great stroke of luck hit him. The lights blew out. Immediately he ran to the door under the stairs, entered the study, then stood at the connecting door and watched Helen. I know it was pitch-dark throughout the house, but I'm sure enough light came from the fireplace to enable him to see what

Helen was doing. That scream of hers must have come at the moment she touched Chadwick's head. Anyway, she was probably attempting to haul it out by the hair when the killer closed in on her and drove the dagger into her breast."

"It sounds O.K.," Regan grunted, "except for one very important thing. You know and I know that the killer couldn't have got into the drawing room. The sliding doors were locked, and so was the door under the stairs. Helen herself had locked it. Didn't we find the key in her pocket?"

"Look, Regan. I told you that when I started working from the angle that Chadwick's head was in Paula's casket, it gave me the answers to a lot of things. And the answer to that magic business of the locked study door was one of them."

Again the Sergeant almost let go of the wheel. "This I gotta hear!" he exclaimed. "I tell you I haven't had a decent night's sleep cracking my head over that one. Go on, chum, give. I'm all ears."

"The explanation's so simple you'll bust a rib laughing," I said.

"I don't care; it'll be worth it. Give, brother, give.'

"When Helen sneaked into the study, she was too eager to get to the casket to bother about a little thing like locking a door behind her. After all, the business of hiding the medallion in the casket would require only a few minutes' time. But after the killer had followed her in and committed the murder, he came out of the study door under the stairs, locked the door, and put the key in his pocket. In the meantime the battle had started in the hall, so he sneaked forward in the dark, grabbed the first person he bumped into, and joined in the fight. Then the lights went on, and ten or fifteen minutes later we discovered that Helen had been murdered. Tell me, Regan, what happened when the crowd saw Helen stretched out on the floor?"

"They all ran in and made a big to-do over the corpse. Philip threw himself over the body; Lew toppled down; then Frank and the dames gathered around and— Oh-oh. I see what you mean, chum. With everybody mooning and moaning around the corpse, it was a cinch for the killer to take the key out of his pocket and slip it into Helen's."

"And there, Sergeant," I said, "is your answer to the riddle of the locked door."

We rode for a while in silence, each busy with his thoughts. At last Regan came up with another question.

"If you were so sure about Chadwick's head being in the coffin," he inquired, "why did we have to open Helen's?"

"I thought maybe we'd find some dismembered parts of Chadwick's body in it."

"Maybe we shoulda opened all the coffins in that Mussolini—Barbara Webster's and the old couple's."

I said, "No. I examined those slabs carefully. One look at the sealing cement and I knew the slabs hadn't been disturbed."

"Any idea where the parts are?"

"Yes. But it's going to take a couple of exhumation orders to get them. If I remember correctly, the Webster-Brocton funeral outfit had two funerals scheduled for this morning. It's my hunch that when we dig those bodies out of their graves, we'll find the rest of Martin Chadwick."

Regan cleared his throat. "Give it to me straight, Lash. Which one of them bastards is the killer? Frank? Philip? Or are they in on this together?"

"I honestly don't know who the killer is," I confessed. "At first I was sure it was either Frank or Philip. Now I'm not so sure."

"Well, it can't be Philip. The killer, don't forget, stabbed him in the shoulder."

"Maybe, maybe not," I mused. "Philip, you know, could have stabbed himself. He could have made up that story about seeing Chadwick."

"So it still adds up to Frank or Philip. They're undertakers, ain't they? And only an undertaker coulda embalmed that head of Chadwick's. Maybe you didn't notice it, Lash, but that head we got on the rear seat is loaded with formaldehyde." He jerked a thumb at the burlap bag behind us. "Christ, I can even smell it from here."

"You're forgetting what Penny told us, Regan," I said. "Lew and Jessica can also do embalming. I don't think they're licensed embalmers, but when the Broctons were operating their old man's undertaking business, Lew and Jessica pitched in and learned everything there was to learn. And as for cutting up Chadwick's body—hell, anyone who's ever worked in an embalming room soon picks up a pretty fair knowledge of human anatomy."

Regan said, "I can see where Lew had an opportunity to stuff the rest of Chadwick in the coffins of those two stiffs who were buried this morning—Lew works in the Webster-Brocton joint. But what about Jessica? Seems to me she spends all her time in that lab at Highrock."

"The funeral home closes at one o'clock in the morning," I told him. "Quinn, the night man, locks up at that time and goes home. So it's quite possible that Jessica paid a visit there early Monday morning and distributed the parts. At any rate, it explains that jimmied fire-exit door that leads out of the casket room. We were all sure that Chadwick had jimmied it. But it might well have been Jessica. Frank, Philip, and Lew have keys to the funeral home. They wouldn't have had to break into the place."

"You know what, Lash? I think your hunch is right—about Chadwick being killed in Barrett's living room, I mean. I think that after the killer murdered Chadwick there, he put on Chadwick's trench coat and fedora so he could walk out of the brownstone and drive Chadwick's car away. But up the stoop and into the house comes Paula, so he tells her some whopping lie about Chadwick and gets her to walk out with him and into the car. They drive off, and a little while later Paula smells a rat, jumps out of the car, and runs like hell to a taxi she sees on the corner. But she jumps into the cab before she realizes it ain't got a driver. Then the killer climbs in and lets go with the dagger. Later he gets that bright idea about putting the blame on Chadwick. So he comes back to the cab and pulls his little disappearing act."

"You're O.K., Regan," I said with a chuckle. "As soon as we check all those alibis we picked up at Highrock, I think we'll know definitely who the killer is."

"But what if we can't break 'em?" Regan asked.

"In that case, I've got a little surprise for the killer, a nice little trap to spring on him."

CHAPTER TWENTY-ONE

A light snow was beginning to fall, sprinkling the mound of earth that with each passing minute rose higher and higher beside the grave near which I was standing. Only the heads of the gravediggers were visible now, rising and falling like two corks in a fishing pond.

Dan Neely's elbow dug into my ribs. "Here they come, Chris," he said. "Strenz and the whole bunch of 'em."

Two official police cars rolled into the cemetery and parked in the roadway directly opposite our little group of half-frozen Homicide men. Strenz, Gilbride, and six high-ranking officials poured out—the very same group I'd met at headquarters at one o'clock that morning. They'd pumped my hand off and congratulated me profusely. Now they were doing it all over again, with Strenz even going so far as to wrap a friendly arm across my snow-coated shoulders.

"Lash, I've got news for you," he said, beaming. "Thought you might like to know that Sergeant Regan and his boys have completed their work at St. Thomas Cemetery in Brooklyn."

Eagerly I grasped his arm. "And?"

He nodded grimly. "Both legs, both arms—and all embalmed. They were wrapped separately in Chadwick's clothing. Even his shoes and socks were in the coffin. But no trench coat."

I glanced at the gravediggers. They had climbed out of the grave and were standing at their hoisting machine watching the casket slowly rise to the surface.

I said, "Unless I'm mistaken, we'll find it in that casket."

"Wrapped around a torso," Neely put in with a shudder.

I asked Strenz whether our morning's operations here at Laurel Cemetery in Queens and Regan's casket-raising at St. Thomas had been kept from the newspapermen.

The D.A. and the other bigwigs had promised me at headquarters that under no circumstances would any details concerning the finding of Chadwick's dismembered body be revealed to the press.

"Have no worry on that score, Lash," he reassured me. "We're maintaining the utmost secrecy on this thing. And"—he threw a look at the encircling faces—"God help anyone in the department who lets the cat out of the bag."

We carried the boxed casket to an improvised canvas shelter that had been erected near the grave. Three Homicide men removed the top of the box, but stood deferentially aside when it came time to open the casket. It was their way of telling me, I think, that the honor of lifting the lid was all mine.

Bending over, I stuck both hands into the box and unfastened the latches on the coffin. There was a shuffling of feet as the men crowded closer. Then I lifted both sections of the lid.

A shout went up that panicked a pair of starlings and sent a lone squirrel spiraling up a tree. Frankly, I think some of us had an urge to join him.

Resting between the legs of the corpse—John H. Dodd, according to the name plate on the coffin lid—was a bulky something, something wrapped in a trench coat, which I raised from the coffin and placed gingerly upon the ground. As I unwound the trench coat a strong whiff of formaldehyde assailed my nostrils. Seconds later a naked torso was revealed to our eyes, a torso unmarked by any dagger or bullet wounds.

I began rummaging through the side pockets of the trench coat. From one pocket I pulled out a pair of men's kid gloves and a silk scarf with a knot tied in the middle. In the other pocket, however, I found the torments of hell—something that sent a chill through my body, a dagger thrust into my heart; something that made the old cemetery spin around me like a whirling dervish. In the palm of my hand was a goldfish.

It was close to four that Thursday afternoon before Regan and I got a verification from the M.E.'s office that Chadwick had been strangled to death. There was little doubt in the M.E.'s mind that the murder weapon was the silk scarf with the knot tied in the middle. On the heels of this came the report on the fluorescent powder and ultraviolet-ray tests. No prints had been found on Chadwick's body or on Helen Partridge's throat, but in the cuffs of Chadwick's trousers the boys had found numerous grains of purple sand.

Purple sand. The words electrified me.

"Purple sand in his cuffs, Regan!" I cried. "That means our hunch about Chadwick being killed in Barrett's living room is right in the groove. Remember that broken hourglass and purple sand we found on the floor?"

Regan was almost as excited as I was. "It's all adding up!" he exclaimed.

"And that isn't all, feller. That purple sand may lead us right to the killer."

"How come?"

"The hourglass must have been knocked off the mantelpiece while Chadwick and the killer were struggling in the living room. If purple sand fell into Chadwick's trouser cuffs, then it stands to reason that some of the sand must also have fallen into the killer's cuffs too."

"By God, that's it, Lash!" Regan yelped, leaping off my desk and pacing the room excitedly. "All we gotta do now is go to Highrock and—" Abruptly he came to a standstill and wagged his head negatively. "Naw, it's no good, chum," he went on. "The killer woulda got rid of his suit—even if he didn't know about the sand in his cuffs. He stabbed Paula, didn't he? So why should a smart guy like him hold onto a suit that maybe had bloodstains on it? No, Lash, the only thing we can do now is wait for our boys to bust up one of them alibis."

I said, "They've been checking up since twelve o'clock. So far, the reports don't smell too good." I consulted my notebook. "Lew Partridge told us he left the corner of Eighty-third and Riverside Drive around six-fifteen on Sunday; that he didn't get home until eight because he stopped off at a place called the Wigwam to have a few drinks. Maybe he did. But Dorsey reports that the proprietor of the place doesn't remember serving anyone answering to Lew's description."

Regan sat down again on the edge of my desk. "I can see where Lew had a motive for killing Chadwick," he said. "Chadwick got him fired from Universal Insurance. But I can't think of any reason for him to bump off Paula and Helen. Especially Helen. Lew and his wife struck me as being kinda lovey-dovey."

"Incidentally, Donovan went to the offices of Universal Insurance at one o'clock and picked up some interesting information," I informed the Sergeant. "It was Chadwick who got Lew the job. Lew made terrific commissions—something to do with establishing trust funds. Anyway, all his contacts were made through Chadwick. Chadwick, I understand, advised a lot of his wealthy friends and clients to set up trust funds, paving the way for Lew, of course. But Lew got mixed up with slow horses and suddenly found himself up to his ears in debt. Then he began pulling phony insurance deals on Chadwick's friends, until finally Chadwick got wise and had him kicked out of Universal."

"You say, Lash, that none of the first checkups smell too good. What about Philip's alibi?"

"Huestis went to the Eastern Hotel this afternoon. He found a couple of bellhops who remembered seeing Chadwick and a tall, thin man sitting together in the lobby on Sunday sometime between three and three-thirty. But they swear they didn't see Chadwick's friend from then on. Yet Philip told us he went back to the lobby and waited for Chadwick until almost six o'clock."

"Any luck with Frank's?"

I said, "It adds up to a big zero. The box-office girl and the ticket taker at the Allison told Foley they couldn't possibly remember the people who entered the theatre last Sunday. And Ciano got the same thing from the bus drivers who made southbound runs between four and four-thirty. They told Ciano they're too busy making with the pennies and nickels to pay any attention to who gets on and off their busses. The checkup on Jessica, though, is the real back-breaker. Twelve men are working on that one. So far they've got nothing but sore throats and blistered feet. Little Jessica took a helluva long walk on Sunday. Finding anyone who saw her that night is going to be like looking for a needle in a nudist camp."

"We'll just have to be patient, I guess."

"Not me, Regan. I told you I had a little trap for the killer. Well, tonight's as good a time as any to spring it."

"Mind letting me in on it?"

"No. In fact, I'm counting on you for help. Tonight we'll go to Highrock on the pretense of throwing some more questions at them. Then, just as we're about to leave, I want you to ask me why we never thought of looking for Chadwick in Paula's casket. I'll tell you it's a crazy idea. But you keep on yapping that we ought to have a look; that maybe Chadwick's been cut up into little pieces. I'll finally agree to go with you to the mausoleum first thing in the morning."

Chuckling, Regan said, "It oughta work like a charm. When the killer hears we're gonna open Paula's casket in the morning, he'll do everything he can to see to it we don't find Chadwick's head in the coffin."

"Right. Sometime during the night he'll make it his business to get up to Cedar Palms Cemetery. But we'll be waiting for him, Regan."

My phone rang. It was Strenz on the wire.

"I've got that information you wanted, Lash," he said. "We found Chadwick's will in his safe-deposit box. His secretary gave us the key. The will, by the way, was drawn up about a month ago."

"Did the will—" My voice stuck in my throat.

"He didn't leave a red cent to his in-laws. The art treasures go to various museums, but the bulk of the estate was to go to Paula and the expected heir. There's just one special bequest—twenty-five thousand dollars and an Eskimo kayak to Penelope Forbes."

I thanked Strenz and hung up. Then I got to my feet and reached for my hat and coat. As I put them on I told Regan about the will.

"What a break for Penny!" he said. "But with Paula out of the picture, who'll come into the big moolah?"

"Her next of kin, I guess—Philip Brocton."

Regan's eyes narrowed. "Oh-oh. Looks like we've got our man, Lash."

I shook my head. "I've got a better idea. Let's go to the Sheldon Arms and have a little talk with Penny. And just before we leave her apartment, Regan, I want you to spring that business about looking in Paula's casket tomorrow morning."

The Sergeant looked at me in a bewildered sort of way. "Hey! You talk like you suspected Penny."

"I don't know what to think," I said, and everything inside me seemed to form a hollow into which my wrecked hopes were tumbling. "I know this much: Penny saw Chadwick on Sunday," and I told the Sergeant about the goldfish I'd found in the pocket of Chadwick's trench coat.

He gazed at me dumbly for a moment, his brow creased with lines of worry. "I—I can't believe it, Lash," he said falteringly. Suddenly his brow cleared and he said, "But it can't be Penny. Penny doesn't know the first thing about embalming."

"How do we know she doesn't? I tell you, Regan, Penny fits into the picture as much as any of those vultures up at Highrock. We keep telling ourselves that Chadwick's head was lowered down the side of the house. But isn't it quite possible that Penny sneaked up to the study window and held that head against the pane? Maybe Frank Webster only thought he closed the front door; maybe it didn't lock when he pulled it behind him. Penny, therefore, could have walked into the house. She could have hidden Chadwick's head in the casket, and skipped out before we got back from the park."

"But what about Philip getting stabbed? Penny was in the Sheldon Arms when that happened."

"I still say Philip might have done that little job himself. Maybe he was so scared that Chadwick would get him that he figured the stab wound would give him a good excuse to stay home behind a locked door."

"Well, Penny may be nuts, but she ain't no killer," Regan insisted.

"I hope to God you're right, feller. Just don't forget to do what I told you."

CHAPTER TWENTY-TWO

We went downstairs, piled into the jalopy, and headed north. It had stopped snowing sometime around noon, yet there was still enough snow on the streets to make even Regan drive with one eye open. I didn't like the look of the sky. It seemed sullen and threatening. And dark clouds were putting their heads together as though conspiring to let go with a blizzard.

Penny was prompt in answering the "Call to the Post" chimes. I was startled to see that she seemed to be dressed in mourning: severe black dress, black shoes, no jewelry. My astonishment was as nothing, though, compared with hers. On seeing me, she recoiled a step and leaned weakly against the wall. Then, with a sob that seemed to rack her entire body, she threw herself into my arms.

"Oh, Chris darling!" she cried joyously. "You're alive! You're alive!"

I pried her loose. "Say, what is this?" I demanded. "Of course I'm alive. Never felt better in my life."

"But they told me you were dead, Chris," she sobbed, reaching for my tie. "And I believed it. I knew Cuspidor had bitten you last night, so I thought sure you'd died of hydrophobia."

I caught her by the shoulders. "Who told you I was dead?"

"Some nasty man who answered your phone at the office this morning. I said, 'Let me talk with Lieutenant Lash, please.' And right away he said, 'You can't talk with him, lady. They took him this morning to Laurel Cemetery.' Oh, Chris, you've no idea how I've suffered," and she was back again in my arms.

Somehow I managed to get her into the living room and into a chair. I wouldn't have made it, though, if Regan hadn't unhinged Cuspidor's jaws from my trouser cuff.

"Penny, it's come to a showdown," I said in my sternest voice. "This isn't going to be pleasant for you, but Regan and I aren't leaving here until you answer a few important questions. You may not know it, Penny, but at this particular moment there's a lot of circumstantial evidence sitting on your little shoulders."

Hugging her knees, she looked up at us. It was a slow, searching look. At last she sighed, nodded her head, and said quietly: "I take it, gentlemen, you're going to—what is it they say?—grill me."

"A third degree you won't forget in a hurry," I told her grimly.

Her face lighted up. "Jeepers! This is going to be fun," she exulted. "Oh-oh! Wait, I'll fix the lights." She dragged a bridge lamp closer to her chair and adjusted the lamp shade so that the light beamed full on her face. "There! That's more like it," she bubbled. Then to Regan, "There's a rubber hose in the bathroom, Sergeant."

I kept my patience. "May I proceed now?" I asked sweetly.

She folded her hands in her lap. "Let her rip, Lieutenant. Gad! What a story for my grandchildren!"

"Penny, why didn't you tell me you saw Chadwick last Sunday?" I asked.

Her eyes flashed fire; her hands gripped the arms of the chair. "Who said I saw him?" she snapped. "Whoever said a thing like that is a big—"

"Stop lying, Penny," I cut in through clenched teeth. "Don't make this any tougher for me than it is. We found Chadwick's trench coat today, and in one of the pockets was one of your confounded goldfish."

She attempted to rise, but I shoved her back into the chair. Pale and shaken, she stared at me. "You struck me, Christopher," she said accusingly. "And—and"—she was sobbing quietly—"right in front of my own grandchildren."

"That's only a sample of what's coming," I told her. "Now, where did you say you met Chadwick on Sunday?"

A look of weariness came over her face, and a grim, mirthless smile drew her flame-tinted lips into a thin line.

"I didn't say," she murmured. Then pleadingly, "Please, Chris, I don't want to get mixed up in this mess. There was a movie scout at the matinee yesterday afternoon, and—well, I don't want to ruin everything I've worked for, that's all."

I said, winking at the Sergeant, "O.K., Regan, put the cuffs on her. We're going down to headquarters."

Regan pulled out his handcuffs. "These bracelets ain't from Tiffany's, baby, but on you they're gonna look good."

"Christopher." She said it slowly, putting a world of sultry seduction into it. "I'll—I'll talk now, darling." Suddenly she turned her head a bit to the right, and from her mouth came the voice of a dim-witted boy. It said, "Gee, Grandma, what a big mouth you've got."

I pulled up a chair and sat down. "Where and at what time did you see Chadwick?" I asked without any preamble.

Staring at the floor, she said, "He arrived here about a quarter to four. Believe me, Chris, it was the first time he ever came to my apartment." She lifted her head and looked me unflinchingly in the eye. "That's the truth, Chris."

"Is it?" I couldn't keep the skepticism out of my voice. "The hall attendant said you didn't have any visitors on Sunday afternoon."

"Martin didn't come in the front entrance. He said something about coming up the elevator by way of the basement."

"Why would he do a thing like that?"

"Something about Philip. Martin said he'd met him that afternoon; that Philip was a terrible snoop and had probably followed him uptown. By coming in the delivery entrance, Martin felt sure he'd shaken Philip off his trail."

"Why did Chadwick want to see you?"

"For over a month he'd been begging me to meet Paula. He wanted me to become chummy with her. He had an idea that if Paula had a girl friend to occupy her time, she'd get her mind off her precious family. But I had always refused. I told him it wouldn't work; that Paula would naturally resent a thing like that. She'd assume that Martin and I were more than mere friends. But Martin wouldn't give up. In fact, that was the purpose of his visit. He said he'd reserved a table at the Sabre Club and wouldn't take no for an answer. He said he and Paula would call for me at seven-thirty."

"Did you tell him you'd go?"

"Yes. Then he asked if he could use my phone. He said he'd like to call Paula and tell her the good news. But after he'd dialed the number and said hello, he didn't say another word—just stood there listening to Paula. I couldn't hear what she was saying, but somehow I got the impression she was very angry."

"What time was it when Chadwick made the call?"

"I know it was after four-thirty; four-thirty-five, I'd say. And when he hung up, his face was as white as a sheet. Oh, he looked terrible, Chris—like a man who had suddenly heard some frightful news."

"He didn't tell you what was wrong?"

"No. All he said was that I should forget about our date at the Sabre Club. Then he walked out of the bedroom and put on his hat and coat. Just before he left, though, he said to me, 'Penny, someday I'm going to erect a monument to Alexander Graham

Bell.' With that he walked out. And that's the last time I saw him, Chris—honest."

"When did you put that goldfish in his pocket?"

"When I helped him on with his coat. I slipped two of them into one of the side pockets. Martin always got a laugh out of my doing it, so I thought they'd cheer him up if he should find them later."

I eyed her steadily for a minute. "Tell me something, Penny. Did Chadwick ever drop a hint that he'd remember you in his will?"

"Yes, but only jokingly. He said if he were to die, I'd find myself in possession of a beautiful Eskimo kayak, whatever that is."

Reaching out, I patted her on the cheek. "Thanks, Grandma," I said, rising. "You've been a big help." Then to the Sergeant, "Come on, Regan, let's get up to Highrock."

Penny jumped out of her chair. "Oh, must you, Chris? Why don't you and the Sergeant stay and have supper with me?"

Suddenly Regan slapped his thigh. "Say, Lash, I just thought of something. You know what? We never thought of looking for Chadwick in Paula's casket."

"Talk sense," I growled. "How could Paula and Chadwick fit into one casket?"

"I know it sounds crazy," he protested, "but somebody coulda killed Chadwick, cut him up into little pieces, and stuffed some of the pieces at the foot of the coffin."

"That's ridiculous," Penny said with a hollow laugh, and I noticed she had gone pale. "I never heard anything so silly as that in my life."

"On the contrary," I said hesitantly, "maybe Regan's got something." I turned to the Sergeant. "Tell you what, feller. Tomorrow, first thing in the morning, we'll get an exhumation order and have a look at Paula's casket."

Penny escorted us to the door. "Sure you won't stay and have dinner with me, boys?" she asked. "Cuspidor and I are having sliced Holland Tunnel."

Regan said, "Never heard of it, Penny. What is it?"

"Fresh bagels," she said, and she shut the door just in time.

As we jalopied uptown, Regan and I discussed the strange phone call that Chadwick had made in Penny's apartment.

"What d'you think happened, Lash?" the Sergeant asked.

"I've got a hunch knocking around in my head that Paula didn't know she was talking to her husband. All Chadwick said was 'Hello,' and Paula went on from there."

"I can't buy that. Paula wouldn'ta gone into a spiel without first finding out who she was talking to."

"Let me ask you something, Regan. If somebody called you on the phone two or three times in succession and you weren't particularly interested in talking with that person, what would you do if the phone rang again?"

Regan chuckled. "I'd grab the phone and tell that person off like nobody's business. Wouldn't even wait to near who it was, I'd be so sure it was the pest again."

"Exactly. And I think that's what happened on Sunday, except that Paula was telling off the wrong man. Evidently Chadwick got an earful of something he wasn't supposed to hear. That's why he made that remark to Penny about erecting a monument to Alexander Graham Bell."

"Bell invented the telephone, didn't he?"

"Uh-huh. And thanks to Bell's invention, Chadwick learned something of tremendous importance."

"Penny said she put two goldfish in Chadwick's pocket. How come you only found one?"

"That's easy, Regan. When the killer got into the cab with Paula, the dagger and the two goldfish must have been in the same pocket of the trench coat."

"Yeah, and when he yanked out the dagger, one of the gold-fish musta popped out of the pocket and fallen between Paula's pyramids."

At Dyckman Street and Broadway I made Regan stop at a cigar store. I needed cigarettes, but most of all I wanted to call Neely. I knew he'd never forgive me if I didn't let him in on my little plan to snare the killer.

"Sounds great, Chris," he said enthusiastically. "You and Regan go ahead and do your stuff at Highrock. In the meantime, I'll get some of the boys and hit for Cedar Palms. And don't worry about getting into that cemetery. I'll make all the arrangements. See you later, boy."

I knew it was much too early to go to Highrock; they were probably having dinner right now. So I suggested to Regan that we go somewhere on Dyckman Street and knock off a good meal. With the prospect of standing half the night in a freezing cemetery, I didn't want to run the chance of perishing up there.

Highrock was gloomier-looking than ever when we rolled into the driveway at seven-thirty that night. For one thing, there were scarcely any lights showing. With the exception of the dining-room windows, not a window in the mansion showed a glimmer of light. Apparently Philip's miserliness was running rampant again.

As usual, Detective Lynch accosted us before we were halfway to the veranda.

"Everything's jake," he reported. "Still no Chadwick and still no polar bears."

When Daniels let us into the vestibule, he told us that our four vultures had been scrapping all through dinner.

"Philip and Lew had a devil of a row over Helen's insurance," he informed us. "Philip demanded that Lew fork up for the funeral expenses, but the little guy told him to go chase himself. You could have heard them from here to the Battery."

Our appearance in the doorway of the dining room stifled whatever conversation was going on at the table. An immediate hush came over the room, and I could tell by the four pairs of eyes that glowered at us that our presence wasn't at all desired. Frank and Lew made a pretense of welcoming us, but Philip and Jessica were downright inimical.

For half an hour or so I badgered them, collectively and separately, in reference to their alibis. I particularly hammered at Jessica. Then I opened up a general discussion as to the whereabouts of Martin Chadwick. I even dropped a few hints that I suspected Chadwick had met with foul play, which was Regan's cue, of course, to drag out the Chadwick-in-Paula's-casket gimmick.

"You'll do nothing of the kind," Philip stormed when I'd finished telling the Sergeant that we'd have a look at the coffin first thing in the morning. "Why, the whole idea is preposterous."

"Philip's right, Lieutenant," Frank said after a moment's thought. "It couldn't be done. There isn't room enough in a casket to hold a pair of corpses, even if one of them is dismembered."

"Keep your hands off the dead, Lash," Lew put in sullenly.

Jessica's contribution was the sharpest of the lot. "I'd advise you, Lieutenant, to keep out of that mausoleum," she said threateningly. "If you think we're going to permit Paula's casket to be opened, you're sadly mistaken. If you'd put as much energy in really getting out and looking for Martin as you do in thinking up idiotic ideas, you'd have located him long ago."

"Nevertheless, Mrs. Brockton, whether you approve or not, I intend to open that casket tomorrow," I said, and added, "There are such things as exhumation orders, you know," and signaling Regan to follow me, I strode out of the room.

It began snowing again when we hit the outskirts of Riverdale. This time we had no trouble at all in finding Cedar Palms.

But as we swung into the road that ran past the cemetery a man suddenly appeared out of nowhere and flagged us down with a flashlight. It was Detective Happel.

"We've been expecting you, Lieutenant," he explained, stepping on the running board. "Captain Neely ordered me to stop you. He doesn't want any cars parked at the entrance—too much of a give-away."

"Good idea. O.K., where to?"

"Pull in here on the right."

Regan maneuvered the jalopy off the road and into a clump of trees, where we found a couple of cars already parked. Then Happel led us down the road, through the swirling snow to the churchlike building, which tonight was in complete darkness.

"Where's Neely?" I asked the detective as he beamed us into the little office and out again through a rear door into the cemetery itself.

"The Captain said he'd be waiting for you directly opposite Chadwick's mausoleum."

The three of us tramped along the snow-covered driveway until finally Happel's flashlight picked out the lawyer's marble heap. Instantly a voice hailed us, a voice that I recognized as Neely's.

"Over this way, Chris," he called out. "Over here to the left."

We found Neely standing on the steps of a big mausoleum that in the glare of the flashlight looked something like the public library on Fifth Avenue. It was on the left side of the driveway opposite Chadwick's mausoleum. But the cemetery was so dark that when Happel switched off his flash, I couldn't see my hand in front of my face, let alone a heap of marble across the road.

"Everything all set at Highrock, Chris?" Neely asked, shaking my hand.

"We dropped the bait, all right. Here's hoping we don't have to wait all night for the killer to show up."

"Well, we're ready for him, whoever he is," Neely said grimly. "We've got Chadwick's mausoleum surrounded, and there's a man hiding at each side of the cemetery. The moment a car stops near Cedar Palms we'll get a signal—two quick flashes."

For the first thirty minutes of our vigil I was totally unmindful of any physical discomforts. Gradually, however, a numbing pain began to steal into my legs, and for the first time that night I realized how damnably cold it was. I stamped my feet, waved my arms, blew into my gloved hands. But nothing, it seemed, could shake off the confounded chill I was feeling.

Finally, after several hours of waiting, a flashlight blinked twice, quite some distance away. It was like seeing an oasis in the desert, a port in a storm, a row of cherries in a slot machine. The killer had grabbed at the bait! The wily, calculating fox had come out of his lair. Unknowingly, the evil genius had picked up the gauntlet I'd thrown at his feet.

"He's coming!" I heard Neely say in a tense whisper. "Quick! Let's get closer to that mausoleum."

We stumbled down the steps, raced across the driveway, and threw ourselves prone upon the ground like four soldiers under a barrage of gunfire. I had no idea, of course, how close we were to Chadwick's mausoleum. All I knew was that we were close enough to swoop down on the killer without the slightest possibility of missing him. There was only one remote chance of his escaping: The killer was certain to have a flashlight with him. If, in approaching the tomb, he should happen to throw a beam of light on our outstretched forms—well, he'd have to do some tall sprinting to evade us.

I'd been numb with cold on the steps. Now, oddly enough, I felt spidery rivulets of sweat trickling down my face. What's more, I didn't feel a pain or an ache: I never felt more comfortable in my life, as though I were lying on a feather bed instead of a blanket of snow. I thought, This is solid comfort; so restful, so relaxing. I must try this sometime when I get home after a tough day at West 20th Street.

A hand reached out in the dark and a mittful of fingers dug into my arm.

"He's coming, all right," Neely whispered softly. "Look down the road."

On the driveway, a good hundred yards ahead of us, I saw a beam of light pierce the inky blackness. Then the light went out, and minutes later I could hear approaching footsteps crunching in the snow. They came slowly, hesitantly. Occasionally they petered out completely, as though the killer were pausing in the driveway to strain his ears for any suspicious sounds.

By now I was breathless with suspense. The footsteps, the intermittent flashes of light were building inside me an unbearable tenseness, a bomb of pent-up emotion that was liable to explode at any moment if swift, two-fisted, red-blooded action didn't soon come to my rescue.

The crunching in the snow was close now, very close. Then from the driveway, midway between the two mausoleums, a beam of light stabbed a hole in the darkness, throwing a circular glow on the somber squares of Italian marble. I buried my right cheek in the snow, straining my eyes to catch a glimpse of the man behind the flashlight. But all I caught was a glimpse of falling snowflakes and something black and bulky and ominous. Then complete darkness again, followed by swift oncoming footsteps that crunched not more than a yard or two from our heads.

Unseen hands were fumbling now at the bronze door. Then suddenly there was a deadly silence.

Good God! I thought. Does he hear us breathing? Is that sixth sense of his warning him of danger?

My heart leaped into my throat. Momentarily I felt a paralysis sweep over me. Were my ears deceiving me? No! So help me God, the killer had taken to his heels! He was running toward the driveway with incredible speed. I could hear him tearing past us, his flying feet kicking a spray of snow into our faces. Then I sprang into action and hurled myself headlong toward the drive-way, a flying-tackle leap that plunged me forward like a plane taking off from a runway. It was strictly a hit-or-miss tackle. I had nothing to go by except the sound of crunching snow. Yet for once the gods were with me. My outstretched arms locked around a pair of legs, and the killer and I hit the ground with a bone-shattering crash.

For a few seconds I lay there with the breath knocked out of me, clinging desperately to the threshing legs, while running feet and beaming flashlights converged on us. I could hear excited voices. Then suddenly a ray of light fell upon us.

"Holy Mother in Heaven!" I heard Regan exclaim. "Look who it is!"

I looked, and died a thousand deaths. It was Penny Forbes.

CHAPTER TWENTY-THREE

On the Homicide detail I've helped to break some pretty tough squeals. I've been awarded a couple of citations, a service revolver, a couple of boosts in rank. But I'd have traded them all for an eyebrow tweezer if the crumpled form at my feet had been anyone but Penny Forbes. This Chadwick squeal had been the biggest and toughest of them all. Yet now that it was broken, I felt no jubilation, no inward glow of having done a good job. Instead, I felt sick and heavyhearted. Why in hell had fate sent Penny across my path? I'd fallen for her like a ton of bricks. Her sultry voice, her face and figure, her harum-scarum antics had done something to me that no girl had ever done before. Why, I'd even planned, come the final breaking of the squeal, to ask the girl to marry me. Indeed, I'd convinced myself that my existence hereafter would be meaningless unless I could come home to the little ivy-covered cottage of my dreams and find Penny and Cuspidor waiting for me in the living room, a living room replete with goldfish and fire hydrants. But tonight had shattered all that. The dream was gone. Nothing remained but a murderess.

They yanked her off the ground. For a minute they had all they could do to hold her, a veritable wildcat, scratching, kicking, twisting. Suddenly she ceased struggling, and as they dragged her away toward the office I heard her call out in that throaty voice of hers, "O.K., boys. But don't think for one minute this isn't going to reach the ears of the Racing Commission."

A heavy hand fell upon my shoulder. It was Regan's. "Well, you've one consolation, Lash. They'll never send her to the chair," he said softly. "Penny'll win an insanity plea hands down. Holy Canarsie, I still can't get it through my thick skull that she's the killer. How the hell did she manage to saw Chadwick into pieces and—"

"Give me that flashlight, Regan."

He passed it to me. Without saying a word I played the light over the trampled snow until its beam rested on two objects: Penny's flashlight and alligator purse. Picking them up, I walked over to the bronze door of the mausoleum and examined the lock. There was no key in it. Then I got down on my haunches and studied practically every inch of ground between the bronze door and the place where I'd tackled the girl. Finally I took a peek at the contents of the purse.

"What are you looking for?" Regan demanded.

I handed him his flashlight, ran down to the driveway, swung left, and headed toward the main gate. "Hey, Regan!" I yelled over my shoulder. "How would you like to be best man at my wedding?"

By the time I got to the little office in the churchlike building, Neely had Penny seated at the desk and was firing a volley of questions at her. Blue-lipped from exposure to the cold, he stood menacingly in front of her, his incisive voice rising and falling in scathing denunciation, his fist pounding the desk for emphasis. As for Penny, in deep mourning and fox cape, she was serenity itself. In fact, as I pushed my way through the crowd of precinct and Homicide men, who were taking it all in with amused expressions, I saw that Penny was busy making paper airplanes—and flying them.

"Hold on, Dan," I said, grasping his arm. "There's been—"

"Chris!" Penny leaped from the chair and hurled herself into my arms. "Oh, Chris!" she cried. "Tell this"—she indicated Neely—"this character what page he's on."

I tilted her chin and smiled down at her. "Hello, beautiful," I whispered.

"What is it, Chris?" Neely barked.

I said, "We've made a mistake, Dan. Miss Forbes is not the killer."

Gasps of amazement came from the lips of the detectives, and Neely's jaw unhinged in stark incredulity.

"What are you trying to hand us?" he demanded stridently.

"It's true, Dan," I insisted. "I don't know why Miss Forbes came here, but I do know it had nothing to do with breaking open Paula's crypt. It takes tools to break open a crypt, and Miss Forbes didn't bring along so much as a nail file. Furthermore"—I showed him the alligator purse—"she didn't even have a key to the mausoleum."

"How do you know she didn't drop them in the snow?"

"Because I examined every inch of ground between the mausoleum and where we finally cornered her."

"That's right, Dan," Regan piped up as he plowed through the crowd. "All Lash could find was her flashlight and pocketbook."

I turned to Penny. "It's your turn to talk, angel. And make it good," I added in an undertone.

Disappointment had put Neely in a nasty mood. "Go on, talk," he growled at her. "Did you come up here to pick flowers? Or was it to put a goldfish on somebody's grave?"

The way Penny's little foot was tapping, I was afraid she was about to put a bump on somebody's head. So I nudged her in the back as a signal to keep everything under control.

Facing me, she said, "When I left the theatre I decided to go to Highrock and meet you. But when I got there, one of the

guards outside told me that you and the Sergeant had left. I
knew, of course, that you'd gone to Cedar Palms Cemetery."

"How could you possibly know we—"

"Chris darling, don't be so dense," she chided me. "Didn't
you tell me at the apartment that you and Regan were going to
Martin's mausoleum in the morning?"

"Yes, but—"

"Well, when the guard told me you'd left Highrock so soon,
I figured you'd gone to the cemetery tonight instead of waiting
till morning. And since Martin Chadwick is a very dear friend
of mine, I wanted to be with you, Chris, to see if Regan's hunch
was correct about—well, you know what."

"How did you manage to climb over the wall?" I asked. "And
where did you get the flashlight?"

"I came here in a cab. The cab driver boosted me to the top
of the wall and gave me his flashlight—all for a five-dollar tip."

"How did you know where to find Chadwick's mausoleum?"

"My goodness, darling, Martin brought me here any number
of times," she explained. "We used to come on Sundays and walk
through the cemetery."

"Why did you suddenly run away from the mausoleum?"

"Are you kidding, Chris? Jeepers, when I saw that you and
Regan weren't there, I was scared to death. All I could think of
was to get out of the cemetery while the getting was good."

A silence came over the office. It was finally broken by Neely.

"Well, what are you waiting for?" he snarled at the detectives.
"Get back to your posts out there, and don't let me hear a peep
out of you. For all we know, the killer may be hacking away at
the crypt right now."

But the men had hardly stirred themselves when the phone
on the desk rang. Holding up a silencing hand, Neely answered
the call. At first his leathery face remained absolutely impassive.
Then gradually a wide grin cut a swath across the weather-beaten
features.

"Thanks, Larry," he said. "Thanks for calling." Then, putting down the phone, he cleared his throat noisily and said in a voice that trembled ever so slightly, "It's all over, boys. The squeal's broken. You can go home now."

I grasped his arm. "What's happened, Dan?" I inquired, and now my own voice was trembling a little.

Neely beckoned Regan and me to step closer, which he did. "That bait you boys tossed around at Highrock tonight sure paid off," he told us quietly. "Guess the killer figured the jig was up. At any rate, he committed suicide about thirty minutes ago. Took a dose of potassium cyanide."

My stiff lips could barely form the words. "Who—who was it, Dan?"

"Lew Partridge. They found him on the floor of his bedroom with one of Chadwick's daggers lying beside him. You'd better get down there and take over before the newspapers get wise to what's happened. If you don't, somebody from the tabloids will be dragging the body downtown to pose for next Sunday's magazine cover. I'll keep in touch with you."

Five minutes later Regan's jalopy was racing through the snowstorm to Highrock. This time, with Penny sitting between us, every rut in the road was a pleasure.

Detective Lynch greeted us almost with open arms. "Well, it's all over, Lieutenant," he said happily as he halted us midway to the veranda. "Night after night I've been freezing my pants off out here, and all the time the killer was right there in the house."

Even Daniels was enthusiastic. "No more Highrock for me, boys," he chortled, his mouth exuding menthol. "From now on I go back to civilization."

As the four of us entered the dimly lighted hall, Philip came out of the drawing room. He was deathly pale, yet for once his beady eyes and gaunt face didn't have that cringing, frightened look. There was something smug about his manner, as though he'd known all along that Lew Partridge was the culprit.

"Congratulations, Lieutenant," he said with overbearing friendliness as he walked toward us. "I think the Police Department may well be proud of you. It's incredible that with all the evidence pointing to Martin you still had the courage to—"

I interrupted him. His hogwash was making me sick. "Let's all go into the drawing room," I suggested curtly. "I'd like to hear all the particulars before I go upstairs."

"But of course!"

Fawning a little, he led us to the sliding doors on the right and ushered us into the drawing room. The vast room was in semidarkness with only a couple of wall lights lit, and quite a few seconds elapsed before I discovered that Jessica and Frank were present. Jessica was sitting primly on a large sofa; Frank was standing near the fireplace, gazing moodily at the flames. He barely acknowledged our entrance.

With an extravagance that must have made Philip's heart skip a beat, I switched on the mammoth chandelier.

"Thank heaven we'll soon have some privacy around here," Jessica said, glaring at me. Her eyebrows went up as she spied Penny in deep mourning. "A death in the family, Miss Forbes?"

Penny slipped off her cape and sat down beside the woman. "No, nothing like that, Mrs. Brocton," she replied, raising her veil. "Lieutenant Lash and I plan to have an early breakfast, that's all."

There was an awkward silence, which I hurriedly broke by asking Philip to give me the lowdown on Lew.

"Lew seemed terribly morose after you and the Sergeant had gone," he explained. "He sat in the dining room, staring off into space. He was still sitting here when Jessica, Frank, and I went upstairs to our rooms."

I turned to Daniels. "How long did he stay there?"

"Till almost eleven. When he came out to the hall, he started toward the stairs, then turned around and came in here. I saw him walk over to that liquor cabinet, but he walked out to the hall again when he found the cabinet was locked. 'Guess I'll have to use my own brandy,' he said to me. Then he went upstairs to his room." Daniels popped a cough drop into his mouth. "About eleven-thirty—I was sitting near the dining-room doors at that time—I heard a heavy thud over my head. Lew's room is above the dining room, so I figured the little guy must have guzzled too much brandy and toppled dead-drunk onto the floor. Then I got worried. Maybe, I said to myself, Chadwick got into Lew's room and bumped him off." He passed around the box of cough drops. "Anybody want a cough drop?"

"No. Get on with it," I said irritably.

"Well, I ran upstairs, and the minute I got to Lew's door I could hear him moaning. But the door was locked. So I yelled for help, and Mr. Webster and Mrs. Brocton came out of their rooms to see what was the matter. It was Mr. Webster who helped me break open Lew's door. But the little guy was dead when we got to him."

I looked at Philip. "Why didn't you come out to help?"

He flushed a bright red and nibbled his forefinger. "I thought Martin was in the house. I begged Jessica not to go out of the room, but she wouldn't listen to me." He bridled a bit. "Don't forget, Lieutenant"—he touched his shoulder—"I had reason to fear Martin."

A sneer curled my lip. I had sense enough, though, to keep my mouth shut. Turning away, I said to Daniels, "What happened after you discovered Lew was dead?"

"I sent Mr. Webster and Mrs. Brocton back to their rooms. Then I took a look at the corpse. It didn't take long to see that it was a clear case of suicide. There was a bottle of potassium cyanide capsules on the floor near the corpse, and near the bottle was one of those goofy-looking daggers. Oh, brother, when I found that dagger beside him, I knew we'd finally caught up with the right pigeon. Then I ran downstairs and called West Twentieth Street. Larry said he'd have the M.E. and all the works up here as fast as he could. After that I made these people come downstairs. We've been here ever since."

Frank turned away from the fireplace and came over to me. There was a dazed look on his face, yet something hard and ugly glittered in his smoke-gray eyes.

"Maybe I'm not too bright, Lieutenant," he drawled, "but what makes everybody so damn sure that Lew murdered Paula and Helen?"

"Keep out of this, Frank," Jessica warned him acidly. "Nobody asked for your opinion. Besides, I'm sure the police know what they're doing."

"No, let him talk," I said. "Go ahead, Frank."

He jammed his hands into his trousers pockets and stared momentarily at the floor. At last he said, "How do we know that Chadwick didn't poison Lew and place that hippogriff dagger beside him?"

Jessica took it upon herself to answer him. "Because Lew had locked his door, stupid. Didn't you have to break it open to get in?"

"You've a poor memory, Jessica dear," he said, leering at her. "I distinctly recall that Helen also was behind locked doors. But Martin got her, didn't he?"

"No," I said, and I paused to let the three vultures drink it in. "For your information, Chadwick himself was murdered. He was strangled to death last Sunday about an hour before Paula was killed."

The only one present whose eyes didn't pop was Regan. But before they could swamp me with questions, I signaled Daniels and the Sergeant to follow me out to the hall.

"Take us up to the corpse, Daniels," I ordered the detective. "Let's have a look at the little bastard."

We mounted the stairs, turned left, and walked along the second-floor landing. Finally Daniels stopped us near the very end of the corridor and pushed open a door on the right-hand side.

The room we entered was glowing with light. It was an exceptionally large room, tastefully furnished in maple, with four casement windows. It was the floor space between the twin beds, though, that interested me the most, for lying face down on that part of the carpeted floor was Lew Partridge. Even an inexperienced eye could see that the pudgy little man had died in agony. His legs were drawn up toward the trunk of his body, and his arms were coiled over his head like a couple of serpents.

"Everything's just the way I found it," Daniels said as I squatted beside the corpse.

I glanced at the small bottle on the floor. It was labeled potassium cyanide and contained about twenty or twenty-five white capsules. Then I looked at the dagger that was about two feet away from Lew's head, a dagger with an amethyst-eyed hippogriff. I picked it up with my handkerchief and placed it upon the night table. There was something else on the table: a half-filled pint bottle of brandy. Using my handkerchief, I turned the bottle upside down. The sediment I saw on the bottom of the bottle told its own grim story. Lew, apparently, had dosed the brandy with potassium cyanide. Replacing the bottle, and again using my handkerchief, I picked up the bottle of capsules from the floor and placed it upon the night table.

"Get Frank and the Broctons up here," I commanded Daniels. "But tell Miss Forbes to remain where she is."

Daniels was back in less than five minutes. He ushered Jessica, Frank, and Philip into the room.

"Mrs. Brocton, don't touch anything, but take a look at this bottle of potassium cyanide," I said, escorting her over to the night table. "Did you ever see it before?"

She stepped across Lew's legs with about as much emotion as if she were stepping across a threshold.

"Yes, I've had it for some time on one of the shelves in my lab," she answered indifferently. "In fact, I've many deadly poisons up there—if you'd care for any," she added with a nasty smirk.

"Don't you lock the door of your lab when you leave it?" I asked.

"No. That is, not unless the Sergeant"—she threw a significant look at Regan—"happens to be in the house."

"Then it's obvious that while you people were in your rooms tonight, Lew stole up to the lab and helped himself to that bottle. One thing more, Mrs. Brocton. Look at this suit on Lew. Do you happen to know if he wore it last Sunday?"

Jessica was amused. "Humph! It happens to be the only suit he had to his name. Of course he wore it."

"Thanks." I squatted down beside the corpse again and this time turned my attention to the cuffs on his trousers. However, when I turned them inside out, there wasn't so much as a grain of purple sand in them. "Think hard, Mrs. Brocton. Did Lew send this suit out to the cleaners any time this week?"

"Don't be absurd," she retorted. "If he had sent it out to be dry cleaned or pressed, he would have had to work in his pajamas."

"What were you looking for in his cuffs, Lieutenant?" Philip asked.

He was standing so close to me I couldn't resist the temptation. In a flash I reached out and turned down both cuffs on his trousers. There was plenty of lint in them, but no purple sand. Then I looked up at Frank. He smiled at me.

"I'm next, I suppose," he said. "Lord knows what you're looking for, but go ahead," and he stepped closer to me.

He didn't have to extend a second invitation. Quickly I turned down his cuffs. Again I drew a blank.

Suddenly from downstairs came on ungodly pounding at the front door. Then silence. A minute or two later I heard the heavy tread of many feet on the stairs.

"Here I am again, goddammit," Doc Berlinger panted as he thumped into the room, followed by two fingerprint men and a police photographer. "I told you I should have taken a room up here, Lash," he added petulantly. "I've lost twenty pounds this week."

I shook Berlinger's hand, then ordered Daniels to take Frank and the Broctons back to the drawing room and stay there with them.

"Say, Lash, who's that babe in black downstairs who let us in?" Berlinger asked as he peeled off his hat and coat.

"That's Miss Forbes, a friend of mine. Why?"

"Well, if she ever needs a physical examination, I won't charge her a cent." His foot accidentally struck one of Lew's arms. "O.K., bub," he snapped, looking down at the corpse. "Keep your shirt on."

I didn't hang around to watch the boys earn their salaries. I had bigger fish to fry. I slipped quietly out of the room, crossed the landing, and entered a bedroom that was almost a duplicate of Lew's, except that it contained only one bed. At first I thought it was a guest room. Then I spotted a framed photograph of Frank and some dame—his Barbara, no doubt—and knew I was just where I wanted to be.

On tiptoes I crossed over to a closet door and opened it. There were five suits hanging on a rack, but a hasty examination of all ten cuffs garnered me nothing except a handful of lint. Purple sand was about as scarce in those cuffs as chorus boys would be in a blood bank.

I had no better luck in Jessica and Philip's bedroom. The cuffs of Philip's three suits produced no purple sand.

As I stepped out of the Broctons' bedroom I saw Daniels coming up the stairs.

"What's wrong now?" I inquired.

"Neely wants you on the phone, Lieutenant."

I scurried down the stairs, strode to the little marbletopped table, and picked up the phone. "Hello, Dan," I said.

"Say, Chris," he rapid-fired into my ear. "Strenz wants you to call him later at his home and give him the whole setup from A to Z, particularly Lew Partridge's motives for committing the crimes. Nothing's been tipped to the papers yet, because Strenz plans to give the press the whole story at his office in the morning. But he can't open up until you supply all the missing pieces."

Glancing over my shoulder to assure myself that the sliding doors of the drawing room were closed, I said to Neely in a quiet voice, "If you're standing up, Dan, you'd better sit down. I've got a little shock for you. Lew Partridge didn't commit suicide. He was murdered. And here's something else, Dan. I think I know for sure now who the killer is."

CHAPTER TWENTY-FOUR

It was two o'clock in the morning before Regan, Penny, and I cleared out of Highrock. Doc Berlinger, the fingerprint men, and the police photographer had departed around one o'clock, along with Daniels and the outside guards. But another thirty minutes had elapsed before Lew's body had been whisked off to the morgue.

"Let's go somewhere and dig into a steak," I suggested as the jalopy struggled out of the snow-blanketed driveway. "I'm hungry enough to eat a double portion of roast hippogriff."

Regan said, "Not me, feller. I'm pooped. Besides, I wanna get home before it starts snowing again. But I'll drop you and Penny off wherever you say."

Presently we stopped in front of the all-night chophouse that Penny and I had visited earlier in the week.

"Well, so long, chum," the Sergeant said, holding out his hand. "A tough squeal, Lash, but that's the way we like 'em. Lew sure gave us a run for our money."

"Lew didn't commit suicide, Regan," I said, opening the door of the car. "He was murdered. The killer was just too smart for us, I'm afraid. Instead of falling for our little trap tonight, he cooked up a nice red herring and spiced it with potassium cyanide." I stepped out of the car and helped Penny out. "Good night, Sergeant," I said sweetly. "Pleasant dreams."

"Oh, no you don't," Regan blustered, barging out of the jalopy and following us into the restaurant. "This is one time, Lash, where I've got you over a barrel."

But I insisted on ordering three steaks before I let the Sergeant sound off.

"Lew couldn'ta been murdered," he said as the waiter melted away from our booth. "I got three things to prove it. First, his door was locked from the inside. Second, the only fingerprints found on the bottle of poison and on the bottle of brandy were his. Third, he had Chadwick's dagger in his possession. And whose prints were on the dagger? Lew's."

"Hasn't it occurred to you, Regan, that the killer might have entered Lew's room and dropped the capsules into the brandy bottle while Lew was sitting downstairs in the dining room?"

"Sure it has. But answer this: If the killer doctored the brandy while Lew was downstairs, then how did the killer get into the room later on to place the dagger beside the corpse? And how did he wangle those fingerprints?"

I took time out to look at Penny. She'd placed a pitcher of water in front of her, tied a shoelace to a bread stick, and was fishing for two dead goldfish that were half submerged in the pitcher of water. She was so intent on what she was doing that I didn't disturb her. But I prayed something to the effect that the waiter wouldn't drop the steaks when it came time to serve us.

I gave my attention to the Sergeant again. "Our friend the killer is a smart cookie, Regan," I said. "Yet anybody could have pulled that dagger and fingerprint trick. For example, he could have slipped into Lew's room, dropped the poison into the brandy, and wiped the bottle clean of all fingerprints. Then, making sure there'd be no prints on the dagger and the bottle of poison, he could have placed them under the bedspread on Lew's bed."

"Wait, I don't get it. Why under the bedspread?"

"Put yourself in Lew's shoes. You come up to your room, lock the door, drag out your bottle of brandy, and sit down to drink it. But half a bottle later you don't feel so good. So you place the bottle on the night table and throw yourself on the bed. Immediately you feel something poking you in the back. It hurts. You stagger to your feet and make an effort to find out what the trouble is. You find it, all right—a bottle of poison and a hippogriff dagger under the bedspread. Naturally you pick them up. Somehow your brain now isn't functioning too well. Convulsions are coming on. You begin to weave on your feet. Then—wham!—you're in the death throes, and you drop the poison and the dagger and pitch headlong to the floor.

"I don't say the killer played the trick exactly that way. Maybe he didn't put the poison and the dagger under the bedspread at all. But there are at least a dozen variations to this trick, and all of them would have obtained the same result. I repeat, Regan, Lew didn't commit suicide. What's more, he had only one suit of clothes to his name, yet when I looked in the cuffs, there was no purple sand."

"But you didn't find any in Frank's or Philip's either," he argued. "I was right there when you looked."

"That's right. Later I even went into their bedrooms and had a look at their suits in the clothes closets. But there wasn't a grain of purple sand in any of the cuffs."

Regan scratched his head. "Honest, Lash, I don't know whether I'm coming or going. If Lew and Frank and Philip ain't the killer, who is?"

"Tell me something. How could the killer avoid having sand fall into his cuffs?"

"You mean he wasn't wearing pants when he strangled Chadwick?"

"Exactly. It's the only logical answer, Regan. The killer was wearing a dress."

It took Regan a long minute to get it. "Jessica, by God!" he exclaimed, his eyes glittering with excitement. "Little old Sourpuss herself."

The steaks arrived at that moment. Twenty minutes later our plates were as bare as Old Mother Hubbard's wayward daughter.

"The only thing we can do now, chum, is wait for the boys to crack Jessica's alibi," Regan declared as he pushed his plate away and leaned back comfortably with a cigarette between his lips. "That is, unless you've got another plan up your sleeve."

"Maybe I have," I said, kicking him under the table and jerking my head toward Penny. "Too bad you have to go, Regan. I could tell you about it."

"I'll take a rain check on it," he said, slipping out of the booth and into his wraps. Then, placing his hand on Penny's head, he said, "Quote: 'She dwelt among the untrodden ways beside the springs of Dove.' Unquote."

"Regan darling, that's wonderful!" Penny cried, clapping her hands. "Isn't that something from William Wordsworth?"

Regan's head drooped modestly. "Naw, it's just something from the public library. I hear my niece spouting it all the time. So long, kids." The next instant he was gone.

"Penny," I said, capturing both her hands in mine, "I've something important to ask you. Would—would you do me the honor of taking a blood test with me?"

"It all depends," she replied coyly. "Is there any insanity in your family?"

"We're all as mad as March hares. If I were to tell you how many skeletons we have in our closet, you'd—" A brainstorm broke in my head. "My God, Penny," I said in a stifled voice, leaping to my feet and beckoning the waiter, "get into your things, angel. We're going places."

"Jeepers, Chris!" Penny exclaimed as we tore out of the restaurant and into a cab. "I thought you were kidding about that insanity in the family. Oh, brother! They must have been pippins."

In less than fifteen minutes the cab pulled up in front of the Webster-Brocton Funeral Home. Save for a small night light burning in the rear, the place was in complete darkness. Quinn, no doubt, had locked up and gone home.

I had to produce my shield for the cabbie in order to borrow a screw driver and lug wrench. Before I departed to the rear of the funeral home I instructed Penny to remain in the cab. I even suggested that the cabbie park his hack on the other side of the street. With Penny at a safe distance, there'd be no chance of my getting a snowball behind the ear.

Seeing that the coast was clear for a minute, I ran down the ramp leading to the garage, then cut to the left and into the alleyway between the garage and the funeral home. It was pitchblack in the alley. However, by running my hand along the brick wall of the mortuary, I soon came in contact with the fire-exit door that Jessica, no doubt, had jimmied in the wee hours of Monday morning. Up until the discovery of Chadwick's head in Paula's casket, a two-man night guard had been kept on this alley. But now, of course, the place was unguarded.

I think it took me ten or fifteen minutes to jimmy the door. I had a helluva job trying to wedge the lug wrench between the new lock and the door jamb. By the time I finally succeeded in freeing the bolt, my face was as moist as a widow's kiss.

Pulling the door open, I stepped cautiously into the casket room and felt my way to the swinging door that opened into the embalming room. The door squeaked a bit as I pushed it open, and in the awful silence of the place it sounded like a dame standing over an air vent in the Steeplechase. I pressed my left elbow against my shoulder holster for reassurance.

Lighting a match, I found a three-button light switch in the wall. Thumb pressure on one of the buttons brought two wall lights to life—more than enough to light a path to my objective. My remark to Penny in the restaurant, that bit about the skeletons in the closet, had suddenly reminded me of the white cabinet I'd seen Monday morning in the embalming room. Maybe I was on a fool's errand. Still, if there were any suits hanging in that cabinet, I wanted to see them.

I peeled off my hat and overcoat, picked up my tools, and walked over to the cabinet. The door wasn't locked, thank goodness, so I put down the screw driver and the lug wrench, opened the door wide, and was disappointed to discover that there was only one suit of clothes hanging up, a black suit with an Army discharge button in the lapel. The rest of the stuff—a sweater, a white jacket, a pair of blue overalls—didn't interest me at all.

I opened the buttons on the coat, and the back of my hand hit something lumpy in the inside pocket. It was a spectacle case with a pair of tortoise-rimmed glasses in it. Then I went to work on the cuffs.

The trousers were folded over the wooden bar of the coat hanger, folded so neatly that it was ridiculously simple to examine the cuffs. What wasn't so simple was to refrain from throwing my head back and giving a lusty war whoop. God! I don't think I stopped trembling for at least two minutes. Moreover, the old skyrockets were going off in my head, swishing and zooming, then bursting in my brain until I could almost smell the acrid odor of burning hair.

There was purple sand in the cuffs! Beautiful, wonderful, magnificent grains of purple sand.

At last I'd stumbled on the killer. At long last I'd caught up with him. He'd outsmarted me every inch of the way, toyed with me, laughed at me.

But it's all over now, Frank, I thought, gloating at some of the grains of sand that I'd sprinkled into the palm of my hand. It's all over, Mr. Frank Webster, except turning on the juice.

Suddenly I tensed. For an instant I almost ceased to breathe. I could feel my face take on a mask of horror. I could feel the blood surge downward in panic. Somehow an innate sense told me that I was not alone in the room. Yet try as I would, I couldn't muster the strength to turn about. Every part of my body seemed to have turned to stone. That is, all except my right hand. Subconsciously it was stealing ever so slowly toward my holster.

"I wouldn't try that if I were you, Lieutenant," a voice drawled out behind me. "It might get you a slug through the back of your head."

Nothing was wrong with my hearing. I lowered my hand, turned, and came face to face with the killer—Frank Webster. In his gloved right hand was Philip's pearl-handled revolver, which he held with rocklike firmness, a menacing steadiness that left no doubt in my mind that if he let it spit, my head would be the recipient of the slug. But more frightening than the muzzle of the gun was the pair of smoke-gray eyes behind the tortoise-rimmed glasses: two unwavering muzzles that had death, my death, written all over them.

CHAPTER TWENTY-FIVE

"Turn around," he said in a voice that for all its lack of harshness made my flesh creep. "Go on, turn."

I swung about, every muscle rigid in anticipation of a bullet. Seconds ticked on. Still no blast; still no searing sting of a slug—only the sudden dull pressure of a gun muzzle in the small of my back. The next instant his left hand coiled downward under my suit coat and yanked the roscoe out of the holster.

"Now walk toward the casket room," he ordered tersely.

I stepped to the swinging door and opened it. Immediately I gave up my plan of sprinting through the casket room and escaping by way of the fire exit. The plan might have worked in the dark. But not now. Frank had switched on all the lights before entering the embalming room. He would, the bastard.

"Hold it," he said as I stood in the doorway. Then, switching off the two wall lights, he commanded me to back into the casket room. When he'd backed me between the two rows of caskets, he said, "All right, stop."

Flanked on both sides by three tiers of caskets, I realized with a sinking heart that my chances of making a dash to the fire exit were impossible. No, my only chance now of getting out alive was to leap at him and pray to Allah that somehow the slugs wouldn't find the target. But with six feet of space separating us, I didn't see how he could possibly miss. O.K., then. I'd have to depend upon words, gab, talk—lots of talk. I'd have to play upon his vanity. Anything to give Penny time to become restless and start looking for me. The noise she'd make stepping through the fire exit would give me the one long chance I was praying for: the momentary distraction that might startle the killer long enough to let me make a flying tackle.

Slipping my gun into his overcoat pocket, Frank eyed me quizzically. "Lash, I'm ashamed of myself," he said, lips twisting into a satirical grin. "I thought I'd done a pretty good job of befuddling you boys. Seems, though, I slipped badly. You know, I never thought of that confounded sand. In fact, I couldn't imagine what you were looking for when you searched the cuffs on our trousers tonight. Later, when I got into bed, I remembered the broken hourglass."

As calmly as I could I said, "Too bad you didn't get here ahead of me. That black suit you wore last Sunday has a lot of purple sand in the cuffs."

"Yes, I know. I was watching you."

"What are you going to do with me?" I asked, and I inched a little closer to him.

"Don't worry, I'll think of something." He glanced at the pearl-handled gun in his hand. "Who knows? Maybe I can make it look as though Philip rubbed you out." He chuckled softly. "I'd like that."

Again I moved a few inches closer. I said, "I'll say this much for you. You're head and shoulders above anybody I ever stacked up against. I know how you pulled that disappearing act in the taxi, and how you worked that business of making Chadwick's head appear at the study window. Yes, and I even know the answer to that locked study door. But there are some things I can't make head or tail of. For instance, why didn't you go to Cedar Palms Cemetery tonight?"

He smiled slightly. "It was so obviously a trap. In the first place, I knew Sergeant Regan was much too unintelligent to think up a bright idea like that all by himself. Secondly, even supposing he did think it up, I knew he was much too experienced a copper to blab it out in front of everybody."

Only five feet of space separated us now.

"On Wednesday night," I said, "I had the driver of the murder cab concealed in the study at Highrock. Yet he didn't recognize your voice. Did you know he was hiding in the cabinet?"

Up went one of his eyebrows. "No, I didn't. I must say, Lash, that was clever of you."

"Why didn't he recognize your voice?"

"Come, Lieutenant, you admitted yourself that I was head and shoulders above your usual customers. When I told the cab driver to take me to the Allison, I did everything possible to disguise my voice. For one thing, I placed a small wad of paper in my mouth. It's very effective."

I dug my toes into the carpet and tensed my legs for a tigerish leap. "How come you picked on the Allison?"

He grinned at me. The talk was beginning to get him, I think. I wasn't sure, but he didn't seem to be watching me too closely. Some of the tautness had gone out of his body. He stood languid-like, indolently at ease. Even the muzzle of the gun had drooped a trifle.

"It wasn't just something that flashed into my mind, Lash," he explained. "I knew there'd be a general alarm sent out, so the best way to stall the alarm was to send that cab driver on a fairly long trip. By the way, if you're wondering about those movies at the Allison, I caught the show on Thursday afternoon. Played hookey from work for three hours. I told Philip and Lew I'd had some engine trouble with the mortuary wagon."

Suddenly he lunged forward and struck me viciously across the left cheek with the revolver. The blow sent me crashing against one of the caskets on the right-hand middle tier. Slowly I straightened up. I didn't feel too good. This cagey bastard had been playing with me.

"Hereafter stand absolutely still," he cautioned me, and I noticed we were six feet apart again. "The next time I see you inching toward me I'll stop you—permanently." With that he eased into his languid pose. He even smiled a bit. But his eyes still gleamed with a hard, merciless intensity. "Lash, I'm curious about a few things," he said in a changed tone. "With the exception of the sand-in-the-cuff blunder, I can't for the life of me see where I made any mistakes. Yet I must have. Mind pointing them out?"

I'd no objection. Talk meant life, and while there was life there was hope. Penny was sure to come looking for me. Any minute now she'd barge into the casket room.

I said, "Your biggest mistake was your stabbing Helen with the sapphire dagger. You should have used the dagger you planted in Lew's room tonight."

Again he cocked an interested eyebrow. "Would it have made a difference?"

"No question about it. Those were birthstones in the eyes of the hippogriffs. Rubies for Paula, sapphires for Philip, amethysts for Helen. It was a bad mistake, feller. It convinced me that Chadwick was innocent."

"And what was that business of taking samples of our hair? You really had me worried."

In complete detail—I didn't leave out a syllable—I told him about the four strands of Chadwick's hair I'd found in Helen's hand. I even told him how Penny's dog had put me on the right track.

The smoke-gray eyes opened wide. "H'm. I've underestimated you, Lash. For a copper, you're almost intelligent. That message you found in the drawing room—did you concoct that yourself?"

"No, it was just a gag that Miss Forbes played on me." I was straining my ears. What the hell was keeping Penny? Had she fallen asleep in the cab? "Frank," I asked, and I really didn't expect an answer, "what was your motive for committing the crimes?"

The ensuing pause was so long that I wondered whether he'd heard me. He appeared deep in thought, so deep that I felt a crazy urge to attempt another inch-by-inch approach. It was the steady levelness of the gun, however, that deterred me.

When he finally spoke, I couldn't help detecting the note of bitterness in his voice. "Lash, you think you're face to face with a cold-blooded killer, a homicidal maniac, perhaps. Well, you're wrong. You happen to be face to face with a victim of circumstances. I had nothing against Martin. I liked the guy, admired him. But I had to kill him in self-defense."

I eyed him skeptically. "Is this on the level?"

"Every word. When Martin got fed up with being the family patsy, Paula and I began seeing a lot of each other. At first it was innocent enough, but then we—well, Barrett's boarded-up brownstone soon became our Sunday-afternoon meeting place. Unknown to Martin, Paula had two sets of keys made."

"It's beginning to add up," I said. "That baby Paula expected was yours, not Chadwick's. Right?"

"Yes. But from the moment Paula knew she was going to have a child, she refused to see me. For an entire month I didn't lay eyes on her. Then last Sunday, after Quinn relieved me, I went to the brownstone and called her on the phone. I called her several times, but she refused to come to Barrett's house. Finally I phoned and told her that if she didn't show up within an hour, I'd go to Martin's office the next day and tell him the whole rotten truth." He paused and wiped a film of sweat off his upper lip. "I don't know how Martin found out about Paula and me," he went on. "All I know is that he suddenly sprang into the living room where I was sitting and swung at me with one of his hippogriff daggers."

"Didn't Paula make any attempt to warn you that Chadwick was on his way to the brownstone? She could have called you on the phone."

"She told me she called twice. But I didn't answer the phone. I thought she was calling up to beg off from meeting me." Again he wiped his lip. "Martin meant to kill me, all right. He kept lashing at me like a madman. At last I knocked the dagger out of his hand, spun him around, and strangled him with his own scarf. It was when I spun him around that he knocked over the hourglass.

"Incidentally, Lash, I hope you didn't waste any time down there looking for fingerprints. It was extremely cold in the brownstone. I didn't remove my gloves."

A faint sound struck my ears as though someone had scuffed his shoe along the carpet. I held my breath, waiting for Frank to show some sign he'd heard the noise. He gave no indication.

"On arriving at Barrett's house, Paula was horrified to hear what had happened," he continued. "I assured her, though, that we had nothing to worry about; that I'd take care of everything. So I put on Martin's trench coat and fedora, pocketed the dagger, and took Paula out to the car at the curb. I did it quite openly. I figured if the police should ever get a lead to that neighborhood, witnesses would testify they'd seen Martin and his wife drive off in their car."

He looked at his wrist watch. Intuitively I felt he was getting a little impatient. He was eager to get done with the gabbing and get on with the business of rubbing me out. His next words proved it.

"And that's about all, Lash," he said grimly. "Paula, of course, was petrified with fright when I told her how I meant to dispose of Martin. She called me a fiend and a few other things. Finally she signed her own death warrant by telling me she was going to inform the police. I knew what that meant. A plea of self-defense would get me nowhere. They'd convict me on the old chestnut of a husband protecting his wife's honor.

"I didn't quite believe, though, that Paula was serious. However, when a red light stopped us, she leaped out of the car and ran up to the next block. I ran after her and saw her jump into a taxi. You're familiar, of course, with the rest of the story."

"On the contrary," I protested hurriedly. "When and where did you do the embalming and dismembering of Chadwick? And what about Philip? Did you stab him to build up more evidence against Chadwick? Or did Philip make up that story of the attack?"

A muscle twitched in his jaw. "You're stalling for time, Lash," he accused me quietly. "You're hoping desperately that some miracle's going to happen. Well, it won't, and I'll tell you why. When I came through the alley door and saw a light in the embalming room, I immediately suspected it was you in there. So to prevent any last-minute rescue I tied one end of a rope to the inside door handle, and looped the other around a nice heavy radiator. Oh, yes—I forgot. I also locked the door at the head of the stairs."

What little hope I had deserted me faster than a loose girdle deserts a sinking hip. Yet in the very midst of my despair, damned if I didn't hear that scuffling sound again. I stiffened as though a thousand volts of electricity were going through my body.

"Don't let that noise fool you, Lieutenant," Frank said with a chuckle. "It's only Blackie, our cat, sharpening his claws on the carpet." Without taking his eyes off me, he called, "Here, Black-ie. Here, Blackie."

From under the bottom tier of caskets on my right a black cat scampered into view and rubbed himself languorously against the undertaker's legs. I realized now that it was definitely cur-tains for me. Indeed, the black cat seemed to emphasize the fact. A black cat: portent of disaster, evil omen of impending death.

Frank's foot sent the animal yowling out of sight. "I'll give you five minutes more, Lash," he said, his eyes stealing a quick look at the wrist watch. "Which do you prefer—to spend them in silent prayer or to hear the lurid details of my descent into crime?"

In a weird croak I told him to make it the lurid details.

"Just as you say." He braced his back comfortably against one of the caskets. "Now where were we? Oh, yes. With the taxi on its way to the Allison, I drove Martin's car to Barrett's house. I won't bore you with the details of how I got him out of the house and into the car. Suffice it to say, I managed it easily. After all, handling stiffs is my business. If anyone saw us, which I doubt, on account of the darkness, I'm sure that person would have been convinced that I was merely helping a drunken friend of mine into my car."

He went on to explain that he curled Chadwick on the rear floor of the sedan, covered him with a lap robe, then drove up-town and parked the car a block away from the funeral home. From there he walked to Highrock. He arrived just a few minutes before Philip got the news of Paula's death.

"Haven't you wondered, Lash, how I got hold of the other two daggers?" he asked.

I said, "I can make a good guess. You found the daggers while all of us were looking for them Sunday night in Chadwick's apartment. When you walked out, you had them concealed on your person."

"Right." Another quick look at the wrist watch. "About half an hour after we arrived home I slipped out of Highrock and drove Martin's car into our garage at the funeral home. I moved the body into the embalming room, where I embalmed and dismembered it. Then I hid the parts in a couple of caskets. That is, all except the head, which I placed in my embalming kit." He smiled. "That head of Chadwick's, I figured, would come in handy later. In fact, I had occasion on Monday morning to use it with telling effect on Philip. Before I left here, however, I jimmied the fire exit and mussed up that casket over there on the dais. Then I drove off, parked the car on Broadway, and walked home."

"How did you manage on Monday morning to get down to Philip without somebody seeing you?"

He didn't answer immediately. After a time he said, "I came down to the casket room in the electric lift. I had Chadwick's head and one of his daggers with me. After I'd given Philip his little tap on the shoulder I ran into the embalming room, opened the rear door, then climbed into the lift in the embalming room and floated upstairs. Any questions?"

Sweat was running down my face, and my heart was pulverizing my ribs. "How did you know Helen had gone to the drawing room?" I asked. "How did you know she'd gone there to hide Chadwick's medallion?"

The question seemed to unnerve him somewhat. I saw an expression of pain flit across his face, and for a moment his cool, expressionless composure was gone.

He said huskily, "If you remember, I went to see Quinn that night. On returning home and opening the front door, I saw Helen through the glass in the vestibule door. She had Martin's medallion in her hand, and when I saw her run under the stairs, I suspected she was on her way to hide the medallion in the study.

"But when the lights went out, and I heard that terrible scream, I knew then she must have discovered Martin's head in the casket. In fact, she was trying to pull it out of the casket when I got to her."

"How come you had the dagger with you?"

"I didn't. After I pulled that trick of letting you see Martin at the window, I waited at the head of the stairs for you to run out of the study so I could offer my help. Then, when you and Daniels dashed out of the house, I ran downstairs and hid Martin's head and the two daggers in the casket."

"So while you held Helen by the throat with one hand, you fished in the casket for the daggers, dragged out one of them, and let her have it."

"Yes. And needless to say, I'd taken the precaution of putting on my undertaker's gloves while running to the study." Smiling a bit, he added, "Unfortunately for you, Lash, I happened to use the dagger with the sapphires."

I said, "Then later you must have removed the other dagger."

He nodded his head. "I took it out of the casket just before the funeral and concealed it upstairs in my room. Tonight, of course, I used the dagger to build up Lew as the killer. Poor Lew. You know, Lash, fate sort of pushed me into killing Martin and Paula and Helen. But Lew's death was really the only premeditated murder of the lot. I had to protect myself, put myself in the clear. I knew from the little trap you tried to spring tonight that the police were fully aware of what had happened to Martin, and that one of us at Highrock must be the killer. So after we'd gone upstairs to our rooms tonight and left Lew in the dining room, I tiptoed up to the lab, swiped Jessica's potassium cyanide, then entered Lew's room, and dropped eight capsules into his bottle of brandy."

"Just where in his room did you put the dagger and the bottle of poison so that Lew would be sure to get his fingerprints on them? Under the bedspread?"

"Tsk! Tsk! Tsk! You must have been peeking, Lieutenant. It so happens that's exactly—" He paused, glancing at his wrist watch.

When he looked at me again, I knew instinctively that the question-and-answer session had come to an end; that from this moment on my life depended upon how fast I could leap before his finger pressed the trigger.

"I've been very generous, Lash," he said through rigid lips. "My watch shows you've had an extra three minutes."

We stood facing each other silently now. No breath, no motion, only two pairs of eyes locked in mortal combat.

Then almost apologetically he said, "Well, this is it, Lieutenant. One—" He paused dramatically.

My insides shaking, I gauged the distance between us. He'd have at least four slugs into me by the time my shoulder hit his legs.

"Two," droned the death knell.

My thoughts were racing furiously. In the movies it's so damn simple. The bullets always fly harmlessly over the guy's head. But this was life; this was the real thing. Leap! Leap! my brain shouted. Don't! Don't! yelled the blocks of concrete I was wearing for shoes.

Then it happened. Two black arms snaked out of one of the caskets, wrapped themselves fiercely around Frank's neck, and yanked with a desperation that sent the killer's head tilting upward and backward for a moment. But as Frank rocked back on his heels his finger squeezed the trigger, and the space between the two rows of caskets was suddenly filled with deafening sound and the spurt of blinding yellow flame. Somewhere behind me I heard the splintering crash of a bullet.

What happened after that I've no idea. All I can remember is that I sprang forward, grabbed that gun hand with my left mitt, and brought my right fist up from the floor with a force behind it strong enough to split a two-inch plank. I heard a crack, a groan. Then something fell upon the floor with a heavy crash and slumped against my legs. Dazed, I glanced down. Frank Webster was out cold at my feet, and clutched in my left hand was the pearl-handled revolver.

"Chris, darling! Quick, put the handcuffs on him!" I heard a sultry voice exclaim.

I looked up at the top tier of caskets on the right-hand side. On her knees, and leaning over the edge of one of the caskets with a strained and serious expression on her face, was my adorable Penny.

"My God, Penny, how did you get up there?" I cried.

"The handcuffs, Chris!" she broke in excitedly, jabbing her finger downward. "Get the handcuffs on him."

I rolled Frank over on his face, handcuffed his hands behind him, and removed my roscoe from his pocket. Then I reached up and pulled a pert little face down to my lips. Even kissing her through a veil was wonderful.

"You saved my life, angel," I said with a tremor in my voice. "And if it's the last thing I ever do, the Racing Commission's going to hear about it. Come on, Penny, give. How did you get up there?"

Resting her chin prettily on the edge of the casket, she looked down at me with limpid eyes.

"I didn't want to sit in the cab, Chris," she explained. "So after you left I waited a couple of minutes and then walked into the alley and got to that fire door just in time to see you enter that other room." She hesitated as though she were embarrassed. Anyway, her eyelids fluttered, and a spot of color tinged her cheeks. "Oh, damn, I wanted to scare you, Chris, that's all. I wanted to make believe I was a ghost. I was going to pop out of a casket and say, 'Boo!' But I'd scarcely climbed up here when suddenly all the lights went on and I saw Frank Webster prowling around with a gun in his hand. Jeepers, Chris, I was scared to death. I tried to shout a warning but nothing came out of my mouth." She leaned over the edge of the casket and peered down at the unconscious killer. "Will—will he go to the electric chair, Chris?"

"Uh-huh. As my pop used to say, Penny, they dish it out standing up, but they cook sitting down." I reached up and pulled her pert face down to my lips again. Her arms went around my neck, and her lips pressed mine lingeringly. "I'll say it again angel," I whispered. "How's about taking that blood test with me?"

Penny sighed ecstatically. "You know what, Chris darling?" she inquired dreamily. "I bet I'm the only girl in the world who was ever proposed to in a coffin."

COACHWHIP PUBLICATIONS
CoachwhipBooks.com

THE SARA ELIZABETH MASON MYSTERIES

MURDER RENTS A ROOM

THE CRIMSON FEATHER

COACHWHIP PUBLICATIONS
CoachwhipBooks.com

THE
SARA ELIZABETH
MASON
MYSTERIES

THE HOUSE THAT HATE BUILT

THE WHIP

COACHWHIP PUBLICATIONS
COACHWHIPBOOKS.COM

THE QUINNY HITE
MYSTERIES

CHINESE RED · HERE LIES THE BODY

RICHARD BURKE

COACHWHIP PUBLICATIONS

CoachwhipBooks.com

THE QUINNY HITE
MYSTERIES

THE FOURTH STAR · SINISTER STREET

RICHARD BURKE

THE
RUMBLE
MURDERS

Henry Ware Eliot, Jr.

COACHWHIP PUBLICATIONS
COACHWHIPBOOKS.COM

KILL 'EM
WITH
KINDNESS

By
FRED DICKENSON

COACHWHIP PUBLICATIONS
CoachwhipBooks.com

A JUDGE MASSIE MYSTERY

THE CORPSE IS INDIGNANT

DOUGLAS STAPLETON
and **HELEN A. CAREY**

COACHWHIP PUBLICATIONS
CoachwhipBooks.com

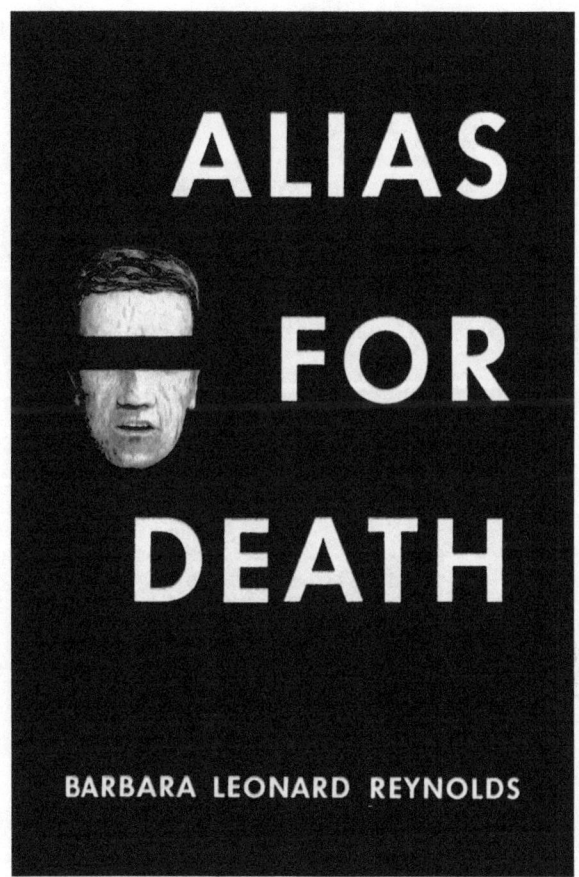

ALIAS FOR DEATH

BARBARA LEONARD REYNOLDS

COACHWHIP PUBLICATIONS
CoachwhipBooks.com

NARROW
GAUGE TO
MURDER

Carolyn Thomas

COACHWHIP PUBLICATIONS

CoachwhipBooks.com

www.ingramcontent.com/pod-product-compliance
Lightning Source LLC
Chambersburg PA
CBHW020949260626
47169CB00006B/1890